BELGRADE NOIR

EDITED BY
MILORAD IVANOVIĆ

D1568768

BROOKLYN, NEW YORK

This collection comprises works of fiction. All names, characters, places, and incidents are the product of the authors' imaginations or used in a fictitious manner.

Published by Akashic Books
©2020 Akashic Books

Series concept by Tim McLoughlin and Johnny Temple
Belgrade map by Sohrab Habibion

ISBN: 978-1-61775-749-5
Library of Congress Control Number: 2020935817

Akashic Books
Brooklyn, New York
Twitter: @AkashicBooks
Facebook: AkashicBooks
E-mail: info@akashicbooks.com
Website: www.akashicbooks.com

Acknowledgments

This book would not exist without my friend Tamara Jorgovanović. It was she who gave me the idea to contact Akashic Books. After several years and numerous e-mails, Johnny Temple and Johanna Ingalls finally agreed—and I am very grateful for their support and courage to enter this unknown territory. I owe a special gratitude to Professor Tatjana Aleksić, Eric Eaton, and Rachael Daum for their painstaking efforts to help me polish this collection of stories. I am dedicating this book to my parents, sister, niece, and my friends, who have always been by my side.

ALSO IN THE AKASHIC NOIR SERIES

FORTHCOMING

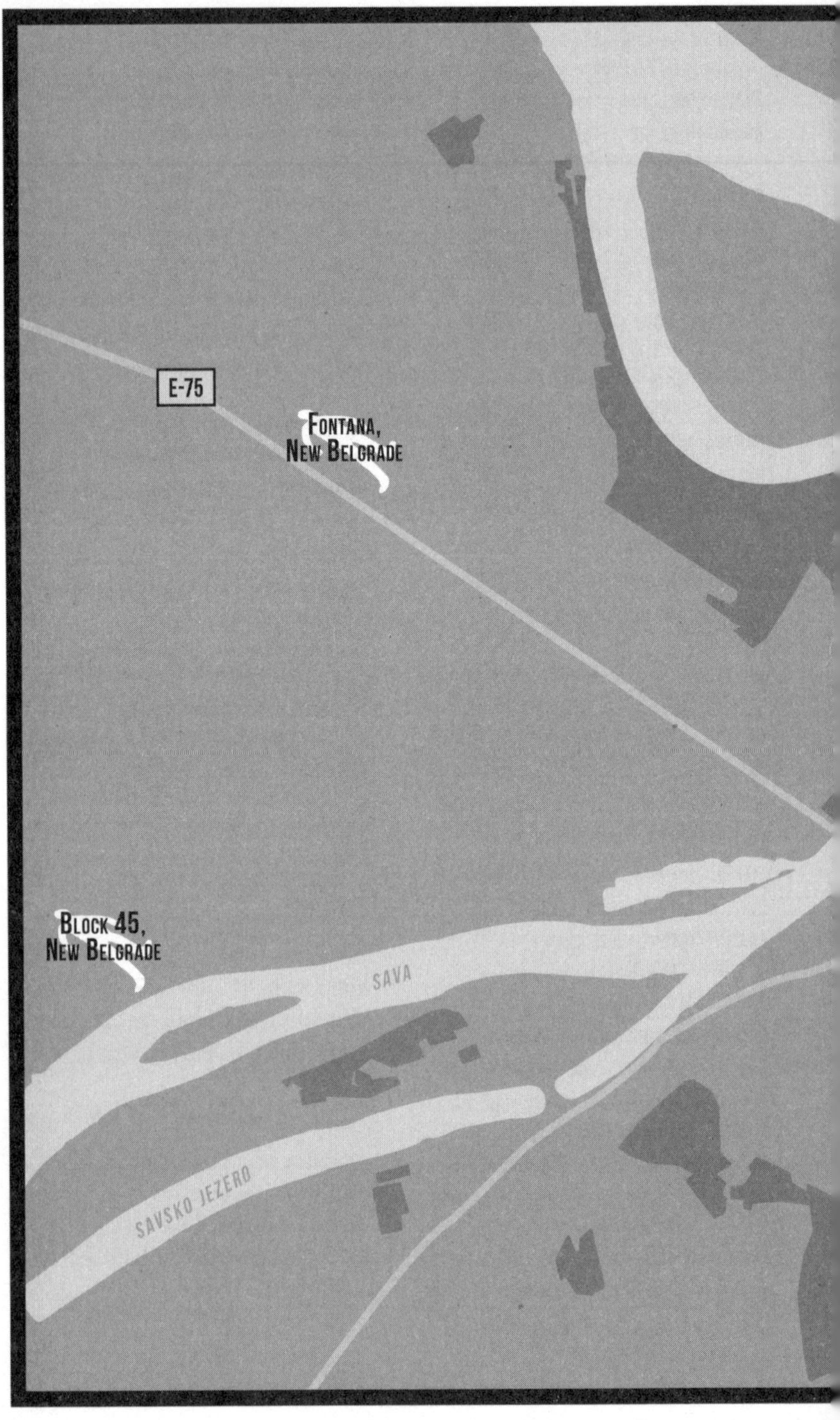

E-75
Fontana,
New Belgrade
Block 45,
New Belgrade
Sava
Savsko Jezero

BELGRADE

DANUBE

Dorćol

Knez Mihailova
Street

Maršala
Birjuzova
Street

Republic
Square

E-70

Palilula

Pioneer Park

The Manjež

King Aleksandar
Boulevard

Vračar

Topčiderska
Zvezda

Lekino Brdo

Učiteljsko
Naselje

TABLE OF CONTENTS

PART III: ONCE UPON A TIME

PART IV: KISS ME DEADLY

INTRODUCTION
THE DARK SIDE OF THE WHITE CITY

I t was summer 1997, two years after the wars in Bosnia and Croatia, and two years before the war in Kosovo and NATO's bombardment of Belgrade. Serbia was under sanctions and life was difficult. I had been working as a journalist for two short months when my editor sent me to cover the suicide of a famous Serbian painter. The crime scene was terrifying—in front of the elevator lay the body of the artist covered in blood. In one hand, he held a plastic bag containing the bread and milk he had purchased just a few minutes before in a nearby supermarket, and in the other he gripped a pistol that was still pressed against his forehead. Neighbors told us that just a few moments before he had sat in a *kafana*, drinking *šljivovica*. As I continued documenting the scene, a brand-new red Mazda pulled up and parked in front of the building. Two neat, clean-shaven, dangerous-looking men in very expensive suits exited the car, approached the policemen conducting the investigation, and showed their Serbian secret service IDs.

"Keep doing your job, we're here on other business," they said. The police officers stepped aside, allowing the men to enter the building. A few minutes later the agents reemerged accompanied by one of, at the time, the biggest stars of turbo-folk music. Dressed in a luxurious coat, and caked in makeup, her high heels elegantly stepped through the blood pooled in front of the elevator. She paid no attention to the macabre scene accented by the fresh dead body lying in front of her as she entered the red Mazda.

If you read the previous paragraph, and you fully comprehended it—recognized turbo-folk, reminisced about your favorite *kafana*, recalled the sort of sanctions Serbia lived under, and remembered why one European capital was bombed in 1999—then you will find it easy to understand the fourteen short noir stories in this anthology. If you did not, this will be a great opportunity to learn about and understand the city that Momo Kapor, one of the most famous Serbian authors, described as "a low-budget New York."

Short stories best describe the time in which they are set. John Selden, an English lawyer and scholar, said, "[T]ake a straw and throw it up into the air, you shall see by that which way the wind is, which you shall not do by casting up a stone. More solid things do not show the complexion of the times so well as ballads and libels." The historical facts of a time period fail to properly encapsulate the human experience when compared to the fictional works of the same era.

Swiss-French architect and urban planner Le Corbusier said, "Belgrade is the ugliest city in the world in the most beautiful place in the world." Belgraders would likely object. His ugliest city in the most beautiful place, throughout history, was usually the most beautiful city in the most terrifying part of the world, as Serbian writer Milorad Pavić often noted.

Belgrade, meaning "White City," is located in Southeast Europe at the confluence of the Sava and Danube rivers, at the crossroads of different civilizations. Belgrade was conquered by Celts, Romans, Slavs, the Ottoman Empire, and Austro-Hungarians. Since its construction, the city has been battled over in 115 wars, razed forty-four times, and changed its name fourteen times. Just in the last hundred years, Belgrade has been the capital of four states: the Kingdom of Yugoslavia, the Socialist

Federal Republic of Yugoslavia under the leadership of Marshal Tito, the Federal Republic of Yugoslavia, and finally the Republic of Serbia, which was reborn as a result of the disintegration of the previous state in a series of bloody ethnic wars.

Ivo Andrić, the only Yugoslav Nobel laureate, once noted that this grand city seems to always be torn and split, as if it never exists but is perpetually being created, built upon, and recovered. While Belgrade was destroyed in both world wars, the city ultimately emerged as a winner, on the side of the Allies.

Four authors in this collection set their stories in that Belgrade—the Belgrade we are proud of, a city of heroism, an ally in the fight for justice and freedom. In these stories, key characters travel through time and different decades of Belgrade's history, as the authors show the world that our glorious past cannot be ruined by the dark cloud hanging over the city during the nineties and its bloody conflicts. It should be no surprise that *vampire* is the only Serbian word in the English language.

The wars during the breakup of Yugoslavia are a leitmotif in four stories. In them, the authors bravely speak about bloodshed, and no stone goes unturned.

During this period, Serbia was completely isolated from the rest of the planet. And as isolated turtles on the Galapagos Islands evolved differently from their fellow turtles on the mainland, the culture in Serbia developed in ways that didn't exist anywhere else. The mobs were killing each other, dead bodies were buried in concrete, eventually becoming embedded in the foundations of buildings and bridges. Still, there were no random killings and the streets of the Serbian capital were among the safest in Europe. It should be no surprise that Belgrade is known as a city of absurdity.

Citizens found pleasure in "embargo cakes"—delicacies

made from only flour, water, sugar, and any fruit you could scrounge up—and listened to turbo-folk, a synthetic mesh of techno and folk.

But this book is about a lot more than war. Alfred Hitchcock once said that certain creepy parts of Belgrade unnerved him and would be ideal settings for thrillers. Thieves, traitors, spies, corrupt doctors, psychiatric patients, former policemen, mafia clans—they all appear in the pages of this book.

Even in the worst periods of its history, Belgrade was always a multicultural, multireligious, and multinational city. This anthology illustrates that. Alongside our Serbian authors, there are stories written by Croatian, Bosnian, British, and Finnish writers. The same is true for our great team of translators, which includes Americans, Serbians, Bosnians, and an Albanian.

Herbert Vivian, a British journalist, author, and newspaper proprietor who visited Belgrade in the late nineteenth century, wrote that more often than not when a traveler visits a famous place expecting a lot, he or she leaves disappointed. "This happens with Athens, Rhine, St. Peter's Church in Rome. But then again, I went to Belgrade not expecting anything—the decorations, the sights, not even the joy or anything interesting—and now I am a victim of its seductive charm, and I have to leave it with utmost pain. This is a new feeling: to fall in love with a city."

Right now, you likely believe there are a number of cities throughout the world that would make better settings for good noir stories. But I am quite certain that after reading this book, you will find yourself seduced by the dark charm of the White City.

Milorad Ivanović
Belgrade, Serbia
September 2020

PART I

WHILE THE CITY SLEEPS

UNDERNEATH IT ALL RUNS THE RIVER OF SADNESS

BY OTO OLTVANJI

Block 45, New Belgrade

"If I win, you'll help me spy on the neighbor on the fourth floor," Kozma said. Not waiting for my answer, he moved his bishop.

Not the bishop, I thought.

We sat at a concrete table in the children's park squeezed in among three four-story buildings. If nothing else, in the blocks you were protected from the wind. When you get old, the wind becomes your greatest enemy.

Kozma and I lived in Block 45, the last one in the row beside the riverbank. After us there was only the end of Belgrade, but it could easily have been the end of the world. At night, the darkness on the other side was that deep.

Before us stretched Block 44, which was kind of logical, but it was preceded by number 70, while on the other side of the wide avenue sprawled blocks 63, 62, and 61. Someone had had a lot of fun with numbering them.

All of it was part of New Belgrade, over 200,000 souls in the country's largest dormitory. That's what they used to call it anyway, but now big business had found its way here too. Car dealerships, shopping malls, private hospitals, a lot of eradicated green areas. Our little park was among the few resisting rampant urbanization.

Blocks and their history was my hobby, because retirees

need to have one. Well, they don't *have* to, but if they don't, they quickly go mad. It started with me wanting to know who'd built the uneven ceiling in my apartment. Every morning, I would try to imagine heroes of the socialist labor of the sixties draining the surrounding swamps, as part of the Yugoslav postwar reconstruction. I had trouble imagining it.

Just as I had trouble coming up with a defense against Kozma's bishop. Checkmate in two moves. When I looked up, Kozma was smiling at me.

I sighed and toppled my king. "I didn't agree to anything."

"But you will, won't you?" He raised his eyebrows. "Now you have to."

I didn't have to do anything, and he knew it. At our age, everything happens voluntarily. That's why I loved this oasis of ours, where we hid from the world, too-frequent elections, pension cuts, and uncollected garbage. That's why I loved this block, this park, this table. Our table.

"Didn't I tell you not to come here anymore?" shouted the girl with restless eyes as she hurried across the park.

Kozma and I rolled our eyes. Not everyone agreed it was our table.

They called her Gigi, nobody knew why. Nicknames don't always have rational explanations. She was between fifteen and eighteen—it was hard to say. Somewhere along the way I'd lost my sense of youth. Didn't matter, she was far too young to be shouting at the elderly.

All the girls she dragged along with her wore torn jeans and baseball hats. They all carried phones and beer cans in their hands even though it was only two p.m. (since they were probably underage, the time of day was, in fact, a moot point). One of them rolled a spray can between her fingers

Gigi stepped up onto our table, kicked over our chess pieces, and climbed down on the other side as if walking across a pedestrian bridge. "Mom and Dad think I'm in a gang, the school thinks I'm in a gang, the police think I'm in a gang." She was virtually growling at Kozma. "All because of you."

She swung her arm but only tucked a strand of hair behind her ear. Kozma twitched and closed his eyes anyway.

I stood up. "Now that's enough."

"Shut up, Grandpa. You'll get yours too. Being tall won't save you."

I remained standing and the moment passed. The aggression fizzled out of her. She seemed to realize it too.

"I'm watching you," she said, backing away. "If I see you after dark, you'll be sorry."

We watched them go. The last one gave us the finger as they disappeared toward the river. I turned to Kozma, who squatted down to collect the pieces.

"Almost getting beat up by little girls doesn't bother you?" I asked, while he stood up and started arranging the pieces. "Are you dragging me into one of your failed projects again?"

"So, you want to do it?" he asked quietly.

I sighed. "What have you come up with now?"

"It's not like with the girls, Ranko, I swear. This one's the real deal. I think he's killing women. New ones come to him twice a week, but no one ever sees them leave. They come in, they don't come out. I'm worried. Why are you looking at me like that? Here, you can be white this time."

In his former life, Kozma was a policeman. During his career he sat in an office, a pencil pusher. Maybe that was the problem: too much paperwork, too few actual cases.

So his retirement hobby was quite different than mine. He wanted to solve a case for once in his life, to see how it felt. That desire was stronger than any realistic possibility of him actually succeeding, and it was certainly against the law. Officially he did not represent any authority in any capacity anymore.

And he had already made some blunders. Because he reported their daughter to the cops, Gigi's parents were even more unpleasant to us than she was, if that's possible. Kozma's former colleagues had to warn him on several occasions, and they even threatened me. They asked what I was doing the whole day instead of keeping him on a short leash.

But Kozma was my best friend and my first neighbor. You don't say no to either.

After our second chess game—Kozma won both—I reluctantly looked up when Kozma whispered, "Here he comes."

He pointed to a balcony on the fourth floor where a pale young man wearing John Lennon glasses stood. He scowled at the yard below, his gaze not reaching our park, flicked a cigarette butt into the air, and went back inside.

"What do you say?" Kozma asked.

"He doesn't look like trouble, if that's what you mean. Or crazy. If you're so sure, why don't you report him?"

"He could be innocent."

"Ah. You're not so sure then."

Kozma smiled. "But what if the police don't find anything? He'll become cautious, and then they'll never catch him."

"How do you even know women don't leave his apartment? They might just sleep over and leave later."

He made a circle around his eye with his thumb and index finger.

"You look through a spyhole? The whole night? *You're* crazy, not him." I shook my head. "What do you think he does with them if they don't come out?"

He started sawing his forearm with the side of his palm.

"And stuffs their arms and legs into suitcases? C'mon! How come no one sees him removing the suitcases?"

"From now on we'll be watching for that too. That's why I need you."

Glancing impatiently down at the board, I noticed Kozma's rare oversight. I had an open passage to his queen, and after that his king was for the taking too.

"So, you have a plan?" I asked, mostly to divert his attention, and moved my knight. He seemed not to notice the threat since he responded with a pawn. His queen was mine.

"A new one is coming tonight, first time this week." He looked at his wristwatch. "Speaking of which, we have to go. I'm taking the first shift."

He stood up and started packing away the pieces, and with them the triumph within my reach. I sadly watched him close the wooden box and put it under his arm. He marched off not bothering to check if I followed.

I did follow. What else could I do?

We went around the building to the front entrance. We both lived on the ground floor, my apartment next to his.

In front of the neighboring entrance, virtually another building merging with ours through a double wall, there was a black limousine waiting, blocking us and cars from both directions. A robust, gray-haired man in a long coat exited the vehicle and hurriedly entered the next building. The limousine waited for one of the other cars to move and only then backed out of the street. Our neighbor Mira was sitting on a bench across the street smoking a cigarette. I asked her what was going on.

"Some big shot," she whispered. "Goes to see the cardiologist on the fourth floor."

"I know him," Kozma said. "The loudmouth threatening everyone in Parliament."

I didn't really know what he was referring to because I didn't read the newspaper, but it was enough information for me. A cardiologist on the fourth floor of a building without an elevator was quite the joke. A patient was prepped for the exam before even reaching the doctor.

If you wanted to truly disappear and never be found, the blocks were the perfect spot. Hiding in plain sight, inside the concrete beehive. Our labyrinth was a constant nightmare for the so-called *real* Belgradians from across the river, spoiled by conventional names and arrangements of streets, and for the couriers delivering stuff to people who behaved as if they did not wish to be found.

And you could make others disappear. Who knew if anyone would ever notice. What if Kozma was actually onto something? This predator could have been operating right under our noses for years.

"What did you mean about taking the first shift?" I asked.

"Just like in the army, two hours. The women usually arrive around eight, so we still have a little time left."

Did I expect anyone to come tonight? Not really, but I was ready for Kozma's game. We entered his apartment, the layout of which was the mirror image of mine, if we ignored the additional seventy-five square feet his had, another mystery that was probably the result of the builder's negligence.

Kozma set up a folding chair in front of the door. I spotted numerous grease stains around the peephole, probably from his forehead. Next to the doorframe, a notebook was hanging on a string. I had one just like that, but in my kitchen. I used mine to write down every penny I spent, keeping track until my next pension payment arrived. I doubted Kozma had his for that purpose.

I asked him how long he'd been spying on the young man.

"Four girls," he said. If they came twice a week, it meant Kozma had been active for at least a fortnight. All that time I'd failed to notice he had a new project. What kind of a friend and neighbor was I? I wondered.

We sat mostly in silence until we heard the heavy front door open or the buzzing sound of the intercom, and then he'd spring to his feet, peer through the peephole, declaring, "Baby," or, "Dog." He would write it down in his notebook. During Kozma's shift, we welcomed two babies and three dogs back from their walks.

When the front door opened for the first time after eight, he got up again to take a look. I knew he saw something interesting because his back stiffened.

"It's her," he said.

"Let me see."

I had enough time to catch a quick look before she disappeared to the left toward the staircase. Deep slit skirt, strong calves, assured walk. Black hair hiding her face. I listened until the clatter of her heels died down, then I unlocked the door and stepped out.

"What are you doing?" Kozma hissed.

While I was sneaking out into the corridor, I felt his disapproval behind my back, but despite this he followed me. We stood by the handrail listening to her footsteps, counting floors. She stopped on the top floor and knocked on a door. Someone opened it without any greeting. The door slammed shut behind her.

Kozma dragged me by my collar back into his apartment. He peered at me intensely in the darkness of his hallway, as if expecting me to admit defeat, but the fact that some woman had shown up on the fourth floor did not necessarily mean anything. I said nothing.

"Now you're waiting for her to come out, or not come out," he said. "Wake me up at half past ten."

I fought the urge to go to the toilet frequently. Whenever I ran off to the bathroom, I left the door open so I could hear any sounds from the hallway and I hurried back as soon as I squeezed out those few precious drops.

During my shift, two students from the first floor arrived home from their night out. I watched a drunken neighbor from the second floor fail at unlocking the door and eventually took pity on him, buzzing him in. "Thank you!" he shouted into the air, to no one in particular, unaware as to who had let him in.

Then it got quiet in the building, with no one coming or going.

I listened to Kozma snore. I listened to planes flying over us, a noise I'd gotten used to. Part of the problem was that we got used to everything.

When no one went in or out for a long time, I started nosing around the apartment. On the kitchen wall I studied framed photographs of Kozma's family. He lived alone, just like me. It's probably why we got close so fast. But it was not by choice that he lived alone, as it was in my case. His wife and daughter were no longer with us, and his son acted as if he weren't—living in Canada and refusing to speak to his father. All the pictures looked yellowed as if from another, more ancient time. They probably were, especially for Kozma.

The black-haired woman did not come back down. At least not by eleven, when I woke Kozma, having let him sleep an extra half hour.

He looked at me quizzically and I shook my head. Getting up without a word, he moved over to the chair, while I lay down on the couch, covering myself with his blanket.

* * *

I was woken by daylight. I didn't immediately realize something was wrong, but I slowly became aware that I should have taken over well before sunrise.

Kozma shrugged. "I didn't have the heart to wake you. You were sleeping so soundly."

He was right. I hadn't slept that well in a long time.

"Nothing much happened anyway," he added. His eyes were so red I did not doubt he'd stayed awake the whole time.

We heard steps outside. "People going to the market," he explained, yawning, and struggled to stand up in time to see who it was. "It's him!" he whispered loudly, although no one could hear us.

"Is he carrying a suitcase?" I asked.

He shook his head, frowning. "If he's headed to the market, this may be the perfect time to get into his apartment. To see for ourselves what's going on up there."

"What do you mean, get into his apartment?"

"Well, I have the keys."

"What? Where did you get them?"

Kozma could not hide his conspiratorial smile. "It's a long story." He opened a locker in the hallway and took a bunch of keys off a hook. "Mira found his keys left in the lock of his mailbox one morning. She took them for safekeeping and tried to return them, but he was gone for the whole day. She told me all about it over coffee. I offered to return them for her because she had to go to her mother's. Eventually I did, but not before I made copies."

"I can't believe it. How long have you had them? Why didn't you go into his apartment sooner?"

"I needed a lookout." He dangled the keys under my nose. "Coming?"

I came because I had no other choice. Over seventy years old and this was the first time I was about to break into someone's home. But I didn't feel guilty, maybe just a bit excited.

I prayed that we wouldn't run into anyone, because we would have had a hard time explaining what two retirees from the ground floor were doing upstairs. Not even the roof would serve as an excuse since it was sealed off.

It was smooth sailing till the third floor when we heard a door open one level below. We flattened ourselves against the wall and waited for that someone to leave. When we arrived at the apartment door, instead of immediately putting the key in, Kozma knocked. He wanted to be sure no one was home. But if he was right, there would be no one alive in there anyway.

We both took deep breaths and entered. Inside, there was a long, naked corridor. The apartment did not look so much abandoned as not lived in. That's why the voices we heard from the next room caught us off guard.

Behind closed doors, two men were talking. I could pick out a few words, "turnout," "electoral roll," and "polling board." My knees buckled as I completely panicked. I ran straight for the door, colliding with Kozma who reached it first. He darted into the hallway as if launched from a circus cannon and tumbled down the stairs. I followed close behind him, as always.

On the stairwell between the fourth and third floors, he whooshed past a man who was climbing up, while I ran straight into the guy. I felt as if I'd hit a lamppost and fell at his feet. He grasped me by the shoulders roughly as he helped me up, and only when I lifted my head did I realize it was the neighbor whose apartment we'd just broken into. I couldn't see his eyes behind his glasses, only my own reflection. An empty garbage can was dangling from his left hand.

Kozma was long gone. I wrestled out of the neighbor's grip

and hurried down the stairs. He shouted after me, but I paid no attention. I didn't stop till I got into my own apartment, where I slammed the door and leaned against it. I was sure my pulse would never slow down. I was so out of breath I almost didn't hear the knocking.

Through the peephole I saw Kozma nervously glancing around the hallway. I quickly let him in.

"Are you insane?" I shouted. "He didn't go to the market! He went to throw out his trash!"

"We have a bigger problem now," Kozma replied. "Do you know what we forgot? To lock the door!"

I slept until late afternoon, tossing and turning, waking up even more tired. I was studying the ceiling, wondering how it could even be possible to be that uneven. Which construction company did it? Who approved it?

I dragged myself to the kitchen, stepping around a bunch of chess books which were not helping me much. I swallowed a handful of pills. Routine was routine, it didn't matter if I'd gotten up six hours later than usual.

Like Kozma, I too had a framed photo from another time, only I kept it in an old suitcase under my bed. I would take it out every morning, wipe off any dust, and wonder how she'd look today, if she were alive, before carefully putting the picture back in the suitcase.

I opened a chess book to delay going outside. I read a section about the Slav defense, when the opponent declines to respond to the sacrificing of a pawn in a Queen's Gambit. The purpose was to narrow down the opponent's maneuvering space in the middle of the board. Too bad I probably wouldn't have a chance to use it.

Eventually, I came out with unbridled trepidation. The

thing I was afraid of most was that Kozma was right about our neighbor, that he would jump me in the hallway, push me back into my apartment, and torture me for hours.

Outside, the sky was grayish, but it was still too light for me. Smog, humidity, and concrete often raised the temperature by several degrees. Kozma was sitting at our table in the park when I arrived, staring into his lap, failing to notice me. Soon I realized why.

UNDER 70 ONLY was spray-painted in black across the table. Dog owners and young parents were frowning at us as if we were the ones who wrote it.

I don't know what made me look around, but it seemed logical that they'd stick around to see our reaction. I spotted the girls sitting on a bench just outside the park fence, in two rows, on the seat and backrest, just like soccer players posing for a picture.

Gigi grabbed her chest as if in pain from an imaginary heart attack and keeled over the back. When she got up, she and her friends laughed at us. They had every right to. They'd scored a strong point on their home turf.

I wanted to go, but I couldn't leave Kozma behind, so I sat down.

"What are we going to do now?" Kozma said.

"You're asking *me*? It's easy for you, he probably didn't even see you. It's always me who ends up bearing the brunt of your nonsense."

Gigi and the girls lit cigarettes as one, losing interest in us. Triumph sometimes has that effect on people. Without a real challenge, it becomes boring. Our challenge was on the fourth floor, but his balcony was empty.

"Nothing's going on," Kozma said. "I've been watching the whole time."

"You're not giving up, are you?"

"The conversation we heard in the apartment? Why would anyone talk like that? When I think about it, he may have left the radio on in order to warn off accidental snoops or burglars, because when you hear the radio through the door, you assume someone's home."

"Where did you get that idea?"

"Well, sometimes I do it myself."

"And does it work?"

"I don't know, but no one has ever broken in."

We watched the balcony until it got dark. After that we squinted at it.

I don't know what made me drop my gaze four stories to my ground-floor terrace, but when I did, I spied a movement through the windows. At first I thought I'd imagined it. Then it happened again. A shadow moved over from the kitchen to the living room. From *my* kitchen to *my* living room.

I turned to Kozma. "Did you see that?"

He gave a wide-eyed nod.

"You know I just shit my pants," I said.

"Me too."

I got up, but Kozma grabbed me by the wrist. "If you go through the yard, he will see you. Let's go in through the front."

My head was humming, the vein in my neck throbbing. When she saw us leaving, Gigi started rolling her clenched fists under her eyes as if crying. I let Kozma take my hand and lead me around the building. Smoking on the bench across the road, Mira looked at us as if we were old loonies. She was probably right.

The door to my apartment was slightly ajar, but there was no one inside. I found my garbage can emptied out in the middle of the living room. Everything else seemed intact.

"He's screwing with us," I said. "Now he's broken into my apartment. But where did he get the keys? The lock doesn't seem broken." I shook my head, overwhelmed by a feeling of anger that replaced fear. "You know what this means, don't you?"

"War," Kozma said.

Kozma turned me into a kibitzer, voyeur, spy. I waited in my hallway until after seven, when he knocked on my door three times. It was a signal that he saw the neighbor leave, this time hopefully farther than our dumpsters.

While we climbed to his floor, I didn't care about running into anyone. When Kozma unlocked the door, I heard the voices again, one male and one female, and recognized the words "sonata" and "philharmonic." I instinctively wanted to turn away, but Kozma smiled and walked into the room, calling me over. He pointed to a radio sitting on the windowsill.

We had no trouble searching the apartment because not only did it not contain any women—or suitcases or saws—but it was nearly empty. In the middle of the living room there was a double bed with clean sheets; a large mirror hung on the wall across from it.

The view from the window so high above my own was totally different. In the park, I made out a shadow of someone who looked like one of Gigi's girls looking up, as if watching this particular apartment. Over the roofs you could see the river, black and swollen.

"Something here isn't right," Kozma said absently.

The room next to the living room was locked. None of the keys matched, but this didn't stop my friend. He went on searching until he found a door in the kitchen. We looked at each other. It should not have been there on the apartment's outer wall.

This door was unlocked. We carefully peeked inside, mustered up the courage to enter, and stepped into a completely different apartment. It was covered in bathroom tiles, like a hospital. We passed a reception desk and in one small room found a bed and ultrasound and EKG equipment.

"The cardiologist from the next building over," I said.

"They drilled a hole through the double wall and made a passage. I wouldn't be surprised if I've fallen into Wonderland."

"I think we did fall into Wonderland."

When we returned to the neighbor's apartment, Kozma went on knocking on walls and wooden screens. Knock knock knock. *Thump*. In the living room he found a hidden closet. Two panels, floor to ceiling, hard oak boards, painted white just like the walls. It was not simple but we eventually found an indentation where we could fit our fingers in and slide the panel open. In one compartment there were stacks of cardboard boxes. It looked like the boxes had once contained an assortment of A/V equipment, but now appeared mostly empty. In the other, we found a wardrobe full of women's clothing, from doctors' coats and leather corsets to wigs of all colors. On the closet floor there was a similarly wide selection of footwear, from high heels to flats.

"What's going on here?" Kozma asked.

Instead of a reply, someone opened the front door on the other side of the apartment. In the empty space it sounded like a gunshot.

"Hello?" a woman's voice said.

Kozma started flapping his hands as if trying to fly. "This hasn't happened before!" he croaked. "They never come two days in a row!"

I interrupted him by pushing him inside the closet with the boxes, barely squeezing myself in. Pulling the panel after me,

I left a narrow crack to watch through. Kozma leaned over me hoping to see something too. We probably looked like a twisted totem pole, two sorry old men peering from their hidey-hole. I wasn't sure we were completely hidden from the outside.

A tall blonde in a business suit entered the room. I'd say I had never seen her before but for two minor details: her skirt slit and those strong calves. She peeked into the kitchen, snapped her bubble gum, and took off her hair in a single practiced motion. Underneath, she had short black hair. Now I was certain she was the woman from the night before.

She opened the other wing of the closet and threw her wig inside, then pulled out a leather corset. She took everything off, white jacket and skirt, black bra and panties. I managed to count three tattoos: a scorpion on her shoulder, a crescent moon on her stomach, and a whip on her thigh. She squeezed herself into the corset, her waist becoming so small I wondered how she could breathe. The two of us did not breathe, did not swallow, did not dare look away.

When she went to the bathroom and we heard her turn on the tap, I whispered to Kozma, "This is where all your women disappeared. Into this closet."

"I can't believe it," he whispered back. "She's the same one. But that doesn't explain—"

I shushed him. The front door opened again.

"I'm in here. Will be out in a sec," the woman called from the bathroom.

We heard someone turn off the radio and then our neighbor entered with a paper bag in his hand. He took out a hamburger and bit into it. He had his mouth full when the woman entered the living room.

"Sorry," he said between bites. "I'm sick of just snacks." He wiped himself off and they kissed on the mouth.

"How come we're working tonight?" he asked.

"He begged me for an extra day."

The neighbor nodded. "I'm going to get ready." He unlocked the next room with a little key from his pocket and closed the door behind him before we could see anything more.

The woman started rummaging through the closet, taking out more clothes. She draped herself with something and put some kind of cap on her head.

A sound system crackled. Over invisible loudspeakers we heard the neighbor's voice: "You look stunning, as always."

She leaned forward and pointed her bottom toward the mirror.

We heard him chuckle. "He rang the bell in the other apartment. Go get him. You know he doesn't like to wait."

When she went to the kitchen, the apartment remained oddly silent. Kozma started digging through the boxes behind us and pulled one out. The label on the box showed that it had once contained a video camera. I sat down on the closet floor and Kozma slid down next to me.

"We'll never get out of this one," I whispered.

"Let's wait a bit, then go for the door," he replied.

"You're not scared?"

"No."

"How come?"

"Everything I dreaded in life has already happened to me."

I shook my head. "I don't know how you survived."

"Life goes on," he said. "It's just that afterward . . . Well, there's always sadness underneath everything. Like a river." He smiled.

His answer didn't surprise me. He probably didn't know I would take his river of sadness over mine anytime, though he might've suspected it. Maybe that's why he put up with me in the first place.

Peering through the crack, I watched the woman enter the room. This time I clearly saw that she was wearing a green army jacket, while on her head there was an army cap with a red five-pointed star. She was followed by a gray-haired man in a long coat.

"The loudmouth," whispered Kozma.

It was the politician we'd seen the day before, a patient in the clinic connected to this apartment. He managed to drop his pants down to his ankles before she pushed him onto the bed. He tried to get up, but she wouldn't let him. She pulled out three different-sized lashes from under the bed and tried them all out in the air. He screamed after each swing although she did not touch him.

"More," he said, panting. "I need more. You're crossing all my boundaries."

The woman swung once again, this time hitting him. He moaned.

Kozma and I looked at each other in the dark. We sat back down and listened to the lashings and shouts for some time. Despite worrying about my bladder, I eventually dozed off.

I came to sensing a light on my face, and when I opened my eyes, I saw Kozma's eyes were shut too. The politician stood in the open door of the closet, his face purple and his body red all over. He only had on leather underpants with spikes.

"Didn't I tell you I heard snoring?" he said to the woman.

When Kozma and I fell out of the closet, the woman was standing in the middle of the room slapping the lash against her palm.

"Who are these people?" the politician shouted.

"Nobody," the neighbor said from behind him. "Annoying old nobodies."

The neighbor had come out of the next room with a small black gun in his hand. It seemed to me it was pointed more at me than Kozma.

"And who the hell are you?" the politician said.

I gestured toward the mirror hanging on the wall opposite the bed. "You think you're just having some perverted fun, but they have you on tape. They'll squeeze you dry before the elections, for money or something else."

"Don't listen to them," the neighbor said.

"Stop waving that under my nose or I'll shove it up your ass," the politician said, but then he frowned at the mirror.

"All right," the neighbor said. "Listen to them, then. You don't want us talking to your electorate. We recorded everything you two did. Just remember."

The politician turned to the woman. "Pandora!"

"Do what you're told," she said, holding his gaze.

"I'll tell the authorities!"

Pandora snapped her gum. "Give me the gun," she said to the neighbor.

The naked apartment suddenly became too crowded. The dominatrix playing a kinky partisan, the politician caught with his pants down, the psycho whose eyes I still couldn't see.

And us, two jinxes. I thought they'd kill each other off, and that Kozma and I would just have to sit back and wait it all out.

No such luck.

The politician burst into tears. He cried his heart out while collecting his clothes from the bed. Wiping his face, he asked, "What do I have to do?"

"First, get rid of these two," the neighbor said. "Then we'll talk."

"I have my man downstairs," the politician mumbled. "All my men are former police or military."

"Good for you," the neighbor said, then turned to Kozma and me. "Why are you two spying on us?"

While I was wondering if we should tell him anything, Kozma's eyes moved to the woman.

The neighbor caught it. "Ah, I see. She thought if she disguised herself she'd be inconspicuous. I begged to differ. But she also likes it."

Pandora blew him a kiss.

"You would have gotten away with it, if it weren't for him," I said, pointing at Kozma, who seemed at once ashamed and proud. "By the way, how did you get into my apartment?"

"I have your keys. Not only yours, the whole building's. I have cameras in each apartment." The neighbor laughed when he saw the expression on my face. "C'mon now, everybody out. I'm tired of you." He turned to the politician. "You too."

While we all obediently marched to the door, Pandora entered the room with a camera and started packing what looked like a bunch of video cassettes. I assumed they weren't, because technology did not wait for old farts like me. It was probably something you could store a lot of video recordings on, though.

At the door, the politician started to say something, but the neighbor cut him off. "We will get back to you. We have to tidy up here first." He wiped the handle of the gun with his handkerchief, dropped the weapon into the politician's hands, and slammed the door in our faces.

The three of us were left standing in the hall. The politician glanced at the gun in his hand, put his coat on, and waved for us to go.

"They'll probably go out through the clinic," Kozma said. "You could still wait them out in the next building."

"Shut up," the politician said. "The things we did to avoid my wife and the press, all for nothing. There will always be spies."

"You're just the one who got fooled," I said over my shoulder.

He whacked my ear with the butt of the gun. I moved forward, massaging the sore spot.

The dark limousine was waiting for us in front of the building. The politician motioned for us to get into the back, while he took the passenger seat. The driver looked at once confused and like someone who regularly witnesses these kinds of events. "To the summerhouse, chief?" he asked.

The politician nodded. "Up the riverbank."

We glided by the buildings on one side and the walkway on the other. I saw a girl stand up from a bench and start walking toward us. My ear was still ringing.

Kozma sighed. "Now we're done for. And I will never find out why you didn't marry her."

"What?" I said. Another girl was running toward us from the direction of the dumpsters on the right.

"I always wondered."

"You did?" I thought I saw someone standing in the middle of the road in the distance. "What can I tell you? I was afraid."

"Of what?"

"Arguments. Children. Family life. Everything."

"And you're not sorry?"

"Shut up!" the politician snapped, but he didn't sound very convincing. He suddenly noticed the figure standing in front of the car. As we approached, I recognized Gigi. Girls on our left and right started sprinting toward us.

"What are these crazy bitches doing?" the politician shouted. "Step on it!"

The driver floored it, but a girl on the left managed to get close enough to throw something at the car. A balloon filled with black liquid splashed across the windshield, blocking us from seeing where we were going. The driver panicked and swerved. We crashed into something solid, and the driver and politician were immediately engulfed in airbags. While they were trying to disentangle themselves, the door on Kozma's side opened. Gigi peered inside.

"Are you all right?" she asked.

Kozma had a cut above his eye. My shins throbbed from hitting the front seat. We both nodded as she helped us out.

Once outside, we watched the politician and his gun fall out of the car, which was bent around a pole. Gigi's girls played soccer with his weapon while he tried to stand up, his coat failing to conceal his spiked leather underpants. The girls had more balloons with thick black liquid inside them, but they chose to shower the man with flashes from their camera phones instead.

Gigi smiled at the sight, then turned to us. "They're not allowed to bother you," she said. "Only we are."

Two days later, I woke up in the afternoon. I didn't think sleeping so late would become a habit, but it felt good. My ear and my shins were still pulsing. I'd gotten off easy, I knew.

I continued some of my old habits. I swallowed a handful of pills and read chess books.

I gave up my hobby, though, of trying to figure out the meaning of my asymmetrical ceiling. I stopped studying the history of the place I lived in, and just lived.

I started by going out to buy a newspaper. I couldn't remember the last time I'd done so, but they'd printed some interesting photographs of our friend the politician. Maybe it was like that for him too, the river of sadness running underneath it all, but at least now he had something to be genuinely sad about.

On my way back, I found Kozma in front of the building talking to his former colleagues. They had come to unofficially interrogate him, but this time they did not shout or threaten. The criminal ring that acted as a BDSM cell was broken. Celebrities and people who had something to lose had been coming to the cardiologist and entering the next apartment, thinking they were free to do what they pleased. When the blackmailing started, they'd had no one to turn to for help. The only thing missing from the whole story was the ringleaders. When Kozma's former colleagues said goodbye, he and I set off to the park.

"Nothing?" I asked.

He shook his head.

They hadn't found the neighbor or Pandora. With so many people in New Belgrade, they could easily move to another building and no one would know. I wouldn't be surprised if they'd done just that. I knew they'd been hurt by the publishing of the politician's pictures. I only hoped they hurt like hell.

I didn't believe the neighbor about duplicate keys, but then again, how had he unlocked my apartment without breaking in? Instead of ceilings, I was now occasionally studying corners in search of hidden cameras. They tell me today's technology in that field is cheap, available, and efficient. I found nothing.

"Here they come," Gigi said, smiling, when we got to the park.

She sat down with me, put a tablet in front of us, and pulled up a virtual chess game. Choosing the white pieces, she played her first move.

Beside us Kozma set up the folding chair he'd started carrying to the park, and lay down in the sun. He said he would take a break from the game for a while.

"That thing with me being in a gang, that was funny," Gigi said.

"Hilarious," I said.

We agreed that the winner had to win two games. I was telling her about the Slav defense, but I somehow got the feeling she already knew all about it.

AN AD IN *VEČERNJE NOVOSTI*

BY KATI HIEKKAPELTO

Fontana, New Belgrade

Translated from Finnish by Aleksi Koponen

I t's all Mom's fault. I'm lying in a big double bed with a tall, squiggly iron headboard. That's the only furniture in the entire apartment. Nothing in the living room or in the kitchen. Windows without curtains. The sky outside looks the same as back home in the village, the fluffy gray clouds float by, heavy with rain, water pours down the windowpane. Everything's quiet and I feel like I'm about to cry.

The bed's covered in satin sheets with a bit of a sheen. Or they had a sheen, but not anymore. Mom chose them from the ones in her chest, saying she'd only used them a couple of times. First time away from home and in a new place, won't hurt to have something that smells of home, she'd said. It will help you sleep.

I can't move. If I try to lift my head, the fog comes down with a terrible pain that rips and burns everywhere. I can't feel my hands but I can see them above me, dripping with blood. They're cuffed to the iron headboard and my mouth is stuffed with some type of leather gag. It's difficult to breathe. Every part of me is broken. Mom's fine sheets are rumpled, doused and dappled in brown and red blood and feces and other bodily fluids.

It's the morning after my wedding and my wife's gone, having left me tied to the bed. She told me as she was leaving that
she was never coming back. She said it with an evil laugh. I
know Mom would save me, but she can't because she doesn't
know where I am. I can't call her with a gagged mouth and tied
hands, and besides, I don't have a phone. Mom wouldn't let me
have a mobile phone. She told me I'd get brain cancer from any
radiation near my head.

This was all Mom's idea. It wasn't me who wanted to get
married. I was happy with my quiet life in our village. She became obsessed with marrying me off. Yesterday was the same,
she was fussing outside the courthouse where we got married,
having packed three bags full of food so that I'd last until the
morning. She told my wife that I've always liked to eat. And
made us swear that as soon as we were awake we'd return home
so that she could make us a proper breakfast. She saw I was
nervous and said I'd be all right, nothing would change, except
now I had a wife and she'd live with us. Only one night away
from home and we'd see each other in the morning as usual.
Oh dear, did she get that wrong? I haven't had a single bite to
eat. My wife started torturing me as soon as we got here. It's
likely that before starving I'll bleed to death or my wounds will
get so infected that I'll die of blood poisoning. There's no one
who knows where I am and I doubt anyone will come until my
corpse starts to smell. It's not my wife's home and the marriage
ceremony was just an act. That's what the woman said before
she left.

I've slept next to Mom every night until now. She wouldn't let
me go on class trips or to church camps even though we did
go to church regularly. When I turned eighteen I asked her for
a room of my own but she just laughed and pooh-poohed me,

reminding me how scared I am of thunder. She said that some-body had to make sure I didn't masturbate, pour my seed into the ground. She made such an awful face that I didn't mention my own room again. I was scared she might really get angry. And, of course, I knew she was only thinking of what was best for me. She'd always told me I was very sensitive, not like other people, that I need to be protected from the evils of this world, from temptation and sinful thoughts. How did she not see this coming? The first night away from home and this happens.

I've had a nice life with not too many worries. Mom's looked after things. I wasn't keen on leaving the village or home, things have been peachy. I've had enough to eat and clean clothes. *That's everything a man needs*, Mom told me. Once one Fri-day I did want to go into the city to go barhopping but Mom wouldn't give me money for the bus, so that took care of that. I wouldn't have known when to press the button. Would've got-ten lost. So I stayed home to watch television as usual and it wasn't too bad. We kept a tally of how many questions each one of us got right. Mom said it's far easier to stay at home and she was right. She never went into the city. *There's nothing there for people like us*, she told me.

When I turned forty a couple of years ago, Mom changed her mind all of a sudden. She started nagging and braying and was always in a foul mood, especially when she was cooking or washing my socks or underwear or sweeping the front. *Just find a wife*, she'd say. *Get married. Good to have a daughter-in-law. Find one.* And so she went on. I did answer back once. *Where am I going to find her?* I said. *You don't even let me go to the shop on my own, someone might lure me into the* kafana *to drink and smoke.* It was brave of me to say that. Usually, I just listen to her in silence, because she does lose her temper and that's what happened this time too. She boxed my ears and started weeping, telling me I was blaming her for my own uselessness, an old woman who's given me everything. And how could she look after me if she got worse? *I'll be seventy soon!* she shouted, as if I didn't know. *And you need a wife! One who does your washing, your shopping, keeps a tidy house, and feeds you. Young, strong, and modest.*

I realized she was right, I could see she was old and ground down by her rheumatism. She was thinking of what's best for me, but it did make me anxious. A wife. *What am I supposed to do with a wife?* I asked her. *I wouldn't know what to do.* All sorts of slightly shameful thoughts started swarming in my head. *Phooey*, she said, and told me she'd give me advice. *I'll look after you and won't let her treat you badly. It'll go without a hitch. Just find the right one*, she said, looking worried.

Some years passed with her asking around, putting out feelers, telling people that her son was looking for a wife. *He's a good man*, she said, *who doesn't drink or fight or run around.* But there was no one really suitable for us. The ones she had in mind had left the village a long time ago. The remaining few weren't good enough for her. They went out in the city, their faces thick with makeup, looking for someone richer and smarter. And I don't know how to dance. *They wouldn't understand*, she said with huffy contempt. *Whores, the lot of them, thinking they'll get ahead and don't realize that if someone'd have them, they would've snapped them up a long time ago. Past their sell-by date, sour and off*, she complained. I didn't like her speaking ill of others even though she didn't really say nice things about anyone. There was one, a divorced lady who returned to our area, who Mom was interested in. I faintly remembered that she was one of the few who'd left me alone. I thought that I could build a marriage on that basis, but it all fell apart. Apparently, she was already going out with somebody, about to be engaged. Mom was furious. *The bitch is lying!* she shouted with her eyes ablaze. *How could no one have seen anything in the village? Somebody would have known because there are no secrets here.* That evening she calmed down and told me she wouldn't have wanted a divorced woman for her dear son, that something must be wrong with the bitch since the previous husband up and left. There was nothing to add. I was happy that we couldn't find anyone.

Then one day everything changed. It was one of those hot days where the air moves slowly, the cornfields breathe heavily, and the sun's your enemy. I'd stayed in all day. Mom had gone to the shop and I was waiting for her to come back with sweet treats. I was sitting in the kitchen listening to the radio, without a care in the world. As soon as Mom came back I knew something had happened. Her hands were shaking as she spooned coffee into the *džezva* and she had a big smile across her sweaty face. *I've got a great idea*, she said, putting a cup on the plate.

Mom had heard the shopkeeper gossiping with Jovanka next door, telling her about going to her cousin's wedding in the city that weekend. I kept munching on my *šampite* and said nothing even though I was getting slightly worried. *Guess how this cousin found her husband*, Mom said to me, her face glowing and red. I couldn't guess, I had no idea how to find a husband. I knew something was up. *The woman replied to a personal ad in the paper*, Mom said, nearly shouting. *The man, her future husband, put an ad in the paper looking for a wife, and she read it and felt in her heart that this was the one. And now they're getting married! Just think about it.* Pastry crumbs were flying from her lips as she excitedly told me the story. *We'll do the same*, she said. *My dear boy, we'll run an ad. I'll write it so you don't have to worry about mistakes. Think! All the women of Serbia are going to read it. Your wife won't be someone from our tiny little circles who could end up being a distant relative, yuck. The whole of Serbia will see our ad and there'll be someone who realizes right away that this is her man, the only one for her. This is how we handle it. This is how people do things now.*

She wrote the ad and I didn't object. I couldn't, even though I had a bad feeling from the start. I should've paid heed to that feeling. Maybe she would've listened to me if I'd protested enough. I could've stopped eating. That would've shown her how serious I was. But I couldn't. And I thought to myself, *Mom is wiser and more experienced and knows what's best for me.* Plus, I don't like to starve myself.

The ad ran in the July 15 issue of *Večernje Novosti*.

Women of Serbia! I am looking for a wife for my 42-year-old son. Only hard-working, honest women with serious intentions. "Country Mouse." (D094109)

And that's how we found a wife. She was from Belgrade, short and compact, like her name, Una. She called us two weeks after we'd posted the ad. I knew Mom was already worried after no one called even though she tried to hide it and pretended to be cheery and hopeful. *We'll find you a fine wife, my dear boy*, she said every night as she tucked me in. *There'll be a call tomorrow, I just know it.* A week later I felt secretly relieved. That's when I was sure I wouldn't find a wife, neither a fine nor a bad one, and was happy. I didn't want one. I wanted to be left alone with Mom. And then one night Una called. It was after my bedtime. Mom was watching a crime show she wouldn't let me watch. I heard the phone ring and Mom getting up from her chair.

They spoke on the phone for half an hour. I couldn't properly hear what Mom was saying but I realized something was going on. After the call, she was full of energy. She rushed into the bedroom, switched on the light, and told me with a shaky voice that it was my wife who called and that she'd be here tomorrow. She wasn't even angry that she'd missed some of the crime show. She started cleaning the house in the middle of the night, like a crazy woman. She rummaged around so that it was impossible for me to sleep. After she calmed down and laid down next to me, she proudly declared that it was now time for me to have my own room. For me and my wife, that is. *You'll move into the sewing room, we'll make a nice nest for you,* she said. I started worrying and wanted to cry. I didn't want my own room anymore, and I definitely didn't want to sleep with a stranger in a stupid nest, and besides, where would we put Mom's sewing? She told me to be quiet. She told me we'd just rearrange things, a bed by each wall and the sewing machine between them, where the window is. *That's not my own room then, is it?* I was about to say, but I didn't have the nerve. *You can always sleep in my bed if you feel like it,* she said before she finally fell asleep. I didn't sleep at all that night.

Una arrived the following morning. Mom opened the door as we'd planned and I peered through the curtains in the kitchen. I tried to be careful not to brush the curtains. Mom had told me to wait in the kitchen and only come into the living room when she called for me. Sweet suffering Jesus, Una was pretty. She and Mom talked for a long while on the steps and at times she'd glance at the kitchen window as if she knew I was there. She swayed around very slowly, and her long dark hair swayed too. I'd never seen anything like her. Her clothes were special, not at all what other people wore. Her shiny dress was skintight, like someone had doused her in oil. Her eyes and lips were painted black. No one in the village looked like that, not even in the magazines I sometimes secretly skimmed in the shop. As I saw her swaying on our doorstep, I started to think it wouldn't be too bad to have a wife of my own. My little mickeybob, which is what Mom called it when she was washing me, started to swell inside my pants and I became short of breath. I had to rub myself through my pants when they went into the living room and continued talking. I did feel a bit ashamed and dirty. Mom would've thrown a fit if she'd seen me like that, but I couldn't show up in front of my fashionable wife with bulging pants. She would've thought I was a fool and Mom had warned me time and time again that I shouldn't look like a clown. *Hair combed, no staring with an open mouth, no picking your nose, and whatever you do, don't fart, is that clear?* she'd shouted at me repeatedly that morning. Best to keep my mouth shut and let Mom do the talking. I said I'd try my best.

After Mom and Una had chatted for a while, Mom came into the kitchen and put the *džezva* on. She told me in a low voice that after the coffee was ready I could join them and that it seemed promising, she was really interested in me. Mom was not pleased that Una was forty. She wanted me to marry somebody much younger. *But then again*, she said, *best not to quibble when you've got a good one.* An older woman could be better than a young thing, might have seen the world and wouldn't be after something impossible, would understand how the world works. *Well then*, she said as she was putting down the sugars next to the cups and biscuits, *now it's time to meet our Una.*

Una said nothing to me and I was pleased because I was so scared my stomach was doing somersaults. She kept staring at me with her black-painted cat's eyes, and my cheeks started to flush. She looked at my crotch and I saw a flick of her wet, red tongue. Thank Jesus I'd sorted out my mickeybob, I thought, and remembered to shut my mouth. I felt sweat starting to run down my brow but I didn't have the gall to wipe it off because my hands were shaking something awful. Sweet Jesus, they were already planning for a wedding and life after that. *Yes, yes*, Una nodded, and promised to do Mom's washing too, and of course let the poor guy go sleep with his mother if ever there was a thunderstorm. It was okay with her that Mom would be in charge of cooking, no one else would understand what my appetite was like, but Una would help her with the chopping and peeling and slicing when needed. And wash the dishes. Una didn't seem to mind that I wasn't very talkative, she said she liked quiet men who weren't always blabbing. No, she didn't seem to mind that Mom would live in the room next to ours and would occassionally use it to sew in. Yes, she'd pull her weight when it came to living expenses like electricity and gas and water and could even pay Mom some rent. That's when Mom started to smile very broadly and asked Una if she wanted more coffee.

The earliest possible date was set for the wedding. Papers wouldn't take longer than two weeks and the ceremony would take place in Belgrade with official witnesses. Mom and Una agreed that there was no need to organize any sort of celebration, much less invite guests.

What a find, Mom said when Una excused herself. Una didn't sit back down but told us that for her it was all settled. Her lifelong dream was about to come true, and all she needed to do was go back to the city to sell her apartment and organize a few other things. Then she'd return for the wedding. She only had one condition: she wanted to spend the wedding night in her old apartment in the city. She wanted to have one last fond memory of the place where she'd thought she'd die an old maid. Mom didn't agree freely. *I don't know*, she said. *The poor boy hasn't even seen Belgrade during the day. He won't be able to sleep there. Would be best to come back right after the wedding.*

That's when I opened my mouth. I don't know what possessed me to make that mistake, I was so taken by Una's clothes and hair and cat's eyes and tongue. *Please, Mom, let me do it this once*, I said. *Since we've found such a good wife at last*. Mom stayed quiet for a long time and I could nearly see the steam coming out of her ears as she was thinking. Una did the correct thing with Mom. She didn't start pleading or reassuring. She just waited patiently, calmly looking out of the window. It took a long time until Mom finally agreed, this once. Una started laughing and sounded so happy that I couldn't help but laugh too. I had to clap my hands and jump up and down a couple of times, I felt so good. *Fine then*, said Una. She promised to take good care of me and to bring me back the following morning when she would also move in. She said that she'd drive Mom to the shop or even into the city if Mom wanted. No more schlepping heavy bags. That sealed the deal for Mom.

As I said, we were married yesterday. Mom took the bus home from the courthouse and Una and I came to her apartment. I thought about how my life had changed completely, and so suddenly. The day before I'd never even been to the city and now I'd spent a whole day there with my wife. My head was swimming from all the cars and crowds and noise and the closeness of Una. Outside the courthouse, she took my hand and kissed me so hard that my lip bled a bit. *Don't worry*, she said, *I'll take you home tomorrow. I love you*. It must be real love, this, I thought—I'd never felt anything as lovely even though my lip was awfully sore. I wanted to tell her I loved her too but I didn't have the nerve.

This apartment must be far from where we got married because we drove for a long time—at one point we even changed cars. I was nervous because I'd never been alone with a woman except for my mother, but she didn't count, and hadn't been in a car that often. But then on the side of a wall, I saw a large painting of two men whom I recognized from the news, probably presidents, and somehow they made me feel safe. I thought nothing bad could happen if those two were watching. We drove around until it got dark and started raining. The city lit up with a thousand lights. I saw tall houses pass outside the window, one after another, one street after another, the windshield wipers made screeching noises and puddles reflected the streetlights. Finally, we stopped in front of this building and took the clanking elevator to the sixth floor. There was no name written on her mailbox and I wanted to ask what her full name was, but I still didn't have the courage to speak.

When we were inside the apartment my anxiety took over. My little mickeybob was dead stiff and achy in my pants. I did know what you're supposed to do on your wedding night, and that's what made me so nervous. Maybe I wouldn't know how and she'd lose interest in me. I started making the bed with Mom's sheets to give me something else to think about. Una stood in the doorway of the bedroom. She was wearing a black sheer lace dress and tight red boots. She was so devastatingly beautiful I could barely put the pillowcases on the pillows—I was so distracted. My wife!

After I finished making the bed, she told me in a low voice that it was time for us to start, that for years she'd dreamed of this moment. She told me to lie down on the bed and clicked my hands into the cuffs and then to the headboard. Then she took out an ugly rubber mask from under the bed, I'd seen them in old war films, as well as a long, thick whip and knives wrapped in soft velvet. She licked her lips with her red tongue, smiling and breathing heavily. She told me again that she loved me, then she put on the mask and began.

HOW TO PICKLE A
HEAD OF CABBAGE

BY VESNA GOLDSWORTHY

Knez Mihailova Street

The temperature had been hovering around freezing for days, dipping below for a few hours at a time, just long enough to turn relentless rain into milky, snotty sleet. Even at midday, it was so dark you might believe that Belgrade was somewhere above the North Pole, and not in so-called Southeastern Europe. People bolted out of doorways and scurried along under the eaves like wet mice. It was the sort of weather that would drive an Islamic holy man to slivovitz. The few fools who bothered to open their umbrellas found them instantly turned inside out, like black flowers, unfurling only to be broken by the icy gusts of *košava*, the worst of Serbia's meteorological horrors. There are many more destructive winds around the world, but none that can match its malignant squall.

I spent my spare time smoking, feeling even more claustrophobic than usual, and daydreaming about Olga's demise. All that black ice, a town full of slippery slopes, and who could guess where her osteoporosis might take the two of us? A broken rib, a pierced lung, acute pneumonia, then goodbye world: mission accomplished. Or, days of changing smelly adult nappies and wiping her shriveled little ass while she smiled quasi-apologetically and I thought of a plan B.

This particular contract was taking its time. Three years into it and dear old Oggy was beginning to seem indestructible, while I edged toward two packs a day, hypertension, and permanent irritability. Every sound she made infuriated me—even something as quiet as the shuffling of cards, an activity she indulged in for at least four hours a day—yet I had to pretend I enjoyed her company. That was the deal. My line of work, looking after old crones in exchange for an eventual right to their property, consisted of a species of tantric prostitution for hors d'oeuvres, and death and housing for dessert. In this impoverished city where the distressed elderly had only their homes to offer, lots of people dabbled in the business. Very few were my equals.

Olga owned an apartment in Belgrade's epicenter, three floors above Knez Mihailova Street, on a block situated more or less diagonally across the road from the Serbian Academy of Sciences and Arts. Her building was pretty enough on the outside, with a faux-Habsburg yellow facade and chubby cherubs holding garlands of flowers above each window, oozing Central European ideas of grandeur. Inside, it was a honeycomb of crumbling passages and Dostoevskian courtyards inhabited by geriatrics who had known each other since they were toddlers, long before the Ottoman conquest of the Balkans. I am exaggerating, but not by much. You have to see the funny side when you are dealing with Dracula's little sisters.

The Knez had once been the best street in Belgrade, but it had lost much of its sheen when it was pedestrianized in the 1980s. Yokels started circling, munching popcorn and eyeing up contraband for sale in improvised cardboard stalls. No one had the money for the expensive shops whose pastel racks of cashmere and silk glared emptily over the wet sidewalks.

What passes for today's Serbian elite had abandoned the Knez soon after the death of socialism. The nouveaux riches want their properties detached and surrounded by bulletproof walls, and their drinking dens accessible only by armored vehicles. Nonetheless, there were still suckers moving in from the suburbs, or retiring to Belgrade after decades abroad, in numbers sufficient to keep property prices around here high enough to merit my three years with Oggy Schmoggy. A peach of an apartment, you could say, a fine salon with all the original features intact: I am speaking about quality workmanship which predates the shoddy half a century of the Yugoslav workers' paradise. But no feature could justify a fourth year with the wretched babushka. I was beginning to feel restless.

During that third autumn on the Knez, I spent more and more time in bed, watched over by myriad photographs of the old hen's family. Olga represented the narrowest point of a vast familial hourglass opening back in the mists of nineteenth-century Serbia as it emerged as an independent kingdom and then widening again in the global diaspora of the current century as those who could abandoned our Marxist paradise for opportunities abroad. Her World War I general father was executed by the Communists more or less as they entered Belgrade in 1944. Her mother lingered on in widow's weeds for another forty years. That's where the crow got her genes from.

Her twin sister escaped the country with the first Western diplomat she managed to meet and seduce: the fourth secretary of the Swiss embassy. There was something in that undistinguished catch that made me relate to the sis. When I smoked—and I had to blow the smoke through an open window, forty times a day, košava or not, or I'd never hear the end of Olga's nagging—I used the sister's photograph, in its silver frame, as a makeshift ashtray. I meditated on the winds of fate. The twin looked almost indistinguishable from Olga, but there was a slutty touch around the curled upper lip which made all the difference. You could see that the mouth was bloodred even in black and white.

Meanwhile, my Olga never married because no man would have been good enough for her and her mommy. So there were no direct descendants, or I would not be here, but the twin was fertile enough to compensate for Oggy's celibacy. There were grandnephews and grandnieces in numbers sufficient to populate a dozen picture frames. The sis and the Swiss had hatched a vast opportunistic brood which proliferated across the globe as though bent on some Darwinian world domination: half-Serbs, followed by quarter-Serbs, followed by eighth-Serbs, et cetera. They smiled at me from Boston, Cologne, Perth, and Vancouver. They loved Olga sufficiently to mail photographs as tokens of hope that they might inherit the property, but not enough to visit or really care. They wouldn't know what hit them until they read the will, silly fools.

And the will, signed by my dear little Olgica and witnessed by two of her neighbors and her cheapskate lawyer, Stanojlo Stanojlović, stipulated that her dwelling, with all its contents, down to the last silver frame, would one day soon—and I do mean soon in spite of everything—belong to the girl from the provinces. Me.

I know. I am less provincial than any of the brats on the walls. I am Belgrade born and bred, which is more than anyone could say about Olga's wider family, in their second- and third-best Western cities. But in the business of offering care in exchange for lodgings, one has to pretend that one is from some godforsaken Serbian hovel five hours on a slow train from the bright lights, or the gig ceases to make sense. I've done it before: thirty-six years old, and on my third property. An annual income to beat Boston salaries if you work out the hourly rate as spread over three years—but never four, let alone five.

And it's not as though I am short of job offers in a town chock-full of fossils with émigré children. Instead of doubting my nursing skills, whenever I mentioned my past "ladies," old biddies took me to be a woman of experience, an angel of mercy: so much so that I could pick and choose my real estate. They did not care about property. They were old enough to know that they couldn't take a square meter of it with them. So long as there was company willing to don a pair of rubber gloves when necessary, they chose not to worry that the angel might speed them along on their way to hell. Belgrade is a trusting sort of town, in spite of everything that has befallen it this side of the fourteenth century.

"Katya!" Olga shouted. "Katyusha! Would you be so kind as to . . . ?"

I pretended not to hear. It was four a.m. and the hag could not know that I was awake. Gusts of the *košava* rattled the windowpanes with a force gathered from as far east as fuck knows, in squeals almost as high-pitched as Olga's. Knez Mihailova sits on the brow of the highest hill between here and Russia, at the rim of a vast Pannonian plane. We're talking about a hundred meters above sea level, but you'd have to hit the Ural Mountains before you found anything to rival the Knez in terms of altitude.

As the shutters shuddered and the curtains billowed in spite of the double glazing, I carried on pretending not to hear Olga's clucking: a couple more minutes, just for fun. I opened the window a centimeter, shook the ash off the photo, and flicked the butt sideways, in the direction of the university building where I would teach a class, beginners' Russian, later that afternoon.

That was my other occupation, my cover if you will: an adjunct lecturer, with a decade's worth of waiting for a permanent teaching post, working four hours a week at a rate barely sufficient to buy a pack of cigarettes. Most people around here held two or three jobs, and often in combinations much odder than mine. A medievalist whose desk I kept borrowing for my office hours drove a taxi at night, while his tax-inspector wife moonlighted as a babysitter. My academic speciality was Fyodor Mikhailovich Dostoevsky: there was no money in FMD, not enough for a pack of cigarettes. Even Russian language was a tough sell, now that English killed all others like a giant rhododendron sapping the life of any plant that comes near it.

"Katya, Katinka ..." Olga called me by a selection of Russian diminutives in implicit affinity with my academic interests. A vicious Serbian nationalist in most respects, she also fancied herself Russian and saw no contradiction in that. Her father had studied in St Petersburg long before the revolution, and he brought her Russian mother back to the Serbian sticks, along with his diploma from the military academy.

"Would you be so kind as to give me a hand here, KA-TA-RI-NO-CHKA ... ?" she yelled from the kitchen. I finally got out of bed and shuffled over in my nightshirt as slowly as I could.

She was wiping her greasy claws on her pinafore, having already deboned a large chicken. The skeleton was sitting on the sideboard waiting for me to wield a meat cleaver. She believed that bones had to be broken in order to add a je ne sais quoi to the broth. She thought chicken soup a cure for all known ailments, possibly including all those I had ever had in mind for her. And she liked to cook at dawn on the lower nighttime electricity rate. We had performed this act before.

I tied an apron over my nightshirt. It was a birthday present from Olga, which had the English words *Take That* written on it. She'd purchased it from one of the contraband pop-ups in the street below. Have I mentioned that she was a cheapskate?

"Thank you, Kitty," she cooed as she watched me drop bits

of carcass into the large cauldron of boiling water. Carrots and parsnips floated in the liquid like amputated fingers. Kitty—not quite a Russian diminutive, but a Tolstoyan one nonetheless—that's what she called me when she was trying to use her dusty charm on me. She was too transparent to be efficiently manipulative, but it never stopped her trying.

She switched the lights off as soon as there was a faint promise of gray dawn outside. In the Serbian Academy building across the street, one or two windows were still—or already—lit: an early cleaning job or a sleepless geriatric trying to save the nation. I am not sure which is deadlier in its dotage, the male or the female of the Serbian species.

I took my apron off and shuffled back to bed. Olga turned the burner down, put the lid on the pot, left the soup to simmer, and followed me into my room. Annoyingly, she proceeded to lift the blanket and squeeze in next to me, fully clothed and without asking my permission. We had been here before too, in bed together, and not in any improper, sick way, but just her wanting to talk. I never knew which was worse, her cleaving to me like a barnacle, or hovering above me by my bedside, with her bony little bat shoulders and her straggly hair all messed up, while she rabbited on and I pretended to be half asleep. The woman had no notion of privacy, insofar as the concept even existed in the Serbian language. Privacy was for those who had something to be ashamed of, and she was shameless.

"And then the gate opened and on the other side was my father in full dress uniform, holding his ceremonial sword right up in front of his face . . . What do you think that means, Katinka?" She tended to describe her dreams so intricately that it was possible to fade out for three or four minutes and still catch her drift. The sword, in all its gem-encrusted glory, was worth a pretty packet. She kept it tucked away under her bed. I am not sure if she was hoping to protect her inheritance or her virginity from nocturnal intruders by hiding it there.

"Money?" I tried feebly.

She was not pleased. One-word dream interpretations were blatant shortchanging. My analysis should have been at least as detailed as her account. Was I not a literary critic of sorts? And the linking of her dearest daddy with something as vulgar as money was inappropriate, the very opposite of noblesse oblige. She kicked me in the shin with her dry hag-hoof.

"Do be a dear and fetch that *Sanovnik* from my bedroom, Kitty darling."

She possessed a six-hundred-page dream dictionary precisely for occasions such as this, and she studied it every morning, while the images were still fresh in her failing mind, with all the fervor of the most dedicated yeshiva student. Variants of father dreams alone, I knew already, had a dozen pages to themselves. Swords, four pages. All of it fortune-telling, not Freud. This could take several hours. The shorter her future became, the more she wanted to know about it in advance.

And she was equally interested in *my* dreams. I never remembered any but I occasionally indulged her by inventing one. Making a wreath of marigolds, for example: I came up with that only last week. I have no idea where the marigolds came from, but I was pleased to catch a glimmer of greed in her little eyes when she found, in her dream book, that these flowers portended a large fortune. She seemed almost jealous that she had not dreamed of marigolds first.

"Unless," she went on, "unless the flowers were wilted, in which case, Katyusha, your dream means exactly the opposite. You will lose a fortune. Except," she giggled with childish pleasure and jabbed me in the chest with a bony finger, "you have nothing to lose, do you?"

I left her searching for dead fathers and silver swords and got out of bed to sort out her medication. Olga consumed her medicine by the kilogram and religiously, the way vegans munch their granola. She had a pillbox from Switzerland consisting of sixty-three chambers: nine largish compartments for each of the seven days of the week, their names inscribed in three languages. The damn thing was bigger and, once loaded, heavier than the stone tablets Moses received from God on Mount Sinai. Some of the medication was Serbian and cheap, some Western and expensive. The list of her health conditions was long—what can you expect at ninety-two?

One of my regular weekly duties was to place the pills in their proper sections and ensure that they were taken at appropriate times. I always had to find a good moment to complete the task of sorting, an occasion when Olga would be distracted and preferably elsewhere in the apartment. What she got from me were placebos, if that indeed is the proper word. Placebo means something pleasing in Latin, I believe, and I hoped my pills would have the opposite effect.

I had long collaborated with a chemist in Mirijevo, one of those suburban hells which cluster around Belgrade like cold sores and in which a house built with official permits was rarer than a lottery jackpot. The man was a sort of illegal legal drug dealer, whose business, based in the garage of his concrete suburban house, was flourishing amid medical shortages. He was happy to sell off the genuine stuff, particularly the Western kind, so long as it came in its original boxes. If she knew what I was doing, Olga would have admired my entrepreneurial spirit. She was all for waste not, want not.

The replacement capsules I doled out contained harmless substances. I was too good at my job to risk imprisonment for poisoning. I made her take camomile extract, essence of chry-

santhemum, yeast, bicarbonate of soda, natural cake dyes—
whatever looked right, happened to be approaching its best-before
date, and was available at the Chinese supermarket amid the
tower blocks of New Belgrade.

I had assumed this regime would have killed her by now,
this non-taking of crucial medicines for chronic conditions, as
it had finished off my previous two ladies—each within a couple of years, give or take a few months and a few extra nudges
from me. Olga, however, seemed healthier than when I moved
in. More than that, she appeared to flourish.

"You have a magic touch, Kitty," she cooed as I returned
with her morning pills: a fig-based laxative, a couple of beetroot
compounds, and a milk-thistle lozenge. She opened her mouth
and extended her bird tongue toward my left hand which held
the capsules, and then to my right which proffered a glass of
water. A gust of the *košava* rattled the window.

"That silver sword, Katya, it's no good, I found. No good
at all," she said. "Double betrayal. Someone is plotting
against me. I am thinking of missing my mah-jong party this
evening."

"You shouldn't read too much into your dreams," I said.

She shouldn't have, perhaps, but she did, and then I started
reading into them too. The more impatient I became to see her
off, the more meaning I found in the messages Olga received
from the other side.

I began planning a weekend away after the old fowl had
told me about a dream in which she and I were engaged in
pickling cabbage on her balcony—an activity her social standing and her low salt diet made most unlikely in real life. And
anyway, we were hardly going to keep a barrel for just the two
of us, adding to the briny smell which pervades Belgrade's in-

ner courtyards in the six months of the year between the last grapes and the first strawberries.

The *Sanovnik* suggested that Olga's sword dream meant losing one's head, and in ways which seemed less and less metaphorical with every interpretative permutation she read out loud. She chose to ignore the warnings: she wanted sauerkraut and she wanted it homemade, not store-bought. Appetite so often seems to be the last form of lust to survive.

Strangely enough, given its ubiquity in Serbia, there was no mention of pickling cabbage in the dream book. A flicker of an idea lit my neural pathways.

"I know what we'll do," I said. "My parents! They produce the silkiest, palest pickled cabbage in Serbia. I will take a weekend off and bring a few heads back with me. I haven't visited my people since, what, April? As for having days off, I've forgotten what that even means."

Oggy shrugged. She never thought of what I did for her as work. On the contrary, she was such a peerless narcissist that she sometimes came close to suggesting that I should pay *her* for her company. But she liked the idea of free cabbage: organic, grown in fine Serbian soil, pickled by the witless peasants who had engendered me.

My reference to April was a lie. I hadn't visited my parents in fifteen years and had no plans to do so anytime soon. They were a couple of misery guts who did not deserve to be visited and they lived nowhere near a cabbage patch—if they were still alive, that is. Their stinginess was epic: it made Olga's nighttime activities in the kitchen seem extravagant by comparison.

Thereafter, I encouraged her to imagine the magnificent lunches we would prepare with our home-brined leaves: goose on sauerkraut, sauerkraut with dumplings, every variant of choucroute known to woman, and, above all, our Serbian *sarma*, those majestic cabbage rolls. Normally short of conversational topics, Olga and I spent hours discussing the exact proportions of rice, mince, and smoked meat we might fold into the leaves as soon as I got hold of a properly brined head of cabbage.

When I first offered to bring the cabbages from home, I had no plans other than taking a short break from Olga's claustrophobia-inducing company. If I let this continue, I realized, I'd be with her in a decade's time, an old crone myself, still dropping harmless lemon-balm supplements or whatever into her pillbox. And she would be getting more and more youthful until there was not a whisker of difference between us. Apart from those few hours I spent teaching, she and I were so welded to each other that I was beginning to find her unfailing mean-spiritedness a touch simpatico, in a way that made me understand the Stockholm syndrome.

I found myself complaining about her oppressive good health to my chemist in Mirijevo. I cited her robustness as a reason for divesting myself of her medication while secretly wondering if my strategy was not in fact counterproductive. The pills Olga was meant to take might have been more harmful than my substitutes.

"I've decided to leave her on her own for a couple of days next weekend, Živorad," I said. "Let her taste life without me. Let her see how much I do for her each and every day."

Živorad shoved his hand into the front of his tracksuit bottoms and scratched himself pensively.

"I see your point, Kaća, but you should not leave an old woman all alone overnight. Belgrade is full of opportunistic scum, keeping tabs on people like her, always ready to rob or burgle. Those old folks are like fruit ripe for the picking. They mistrust the banks. They have mattresses stuffed with money, don't they, Jovo?"

He turned to his Montenegrin assistant who was sitting quietly in the corner, sucking a cigarette propped in the gap left behind by a missing molar, and packing what looked like multicolored aspirins imprinted with smiley faces into plastic pouches. Živorad's business was clearly diversifying.

Jovo emitted a croaky laugh. "You should give the lady one of these just before you leave." He laughed some more, then snorted through his broken nose.

"She does sleep on one of those mattresses," I said. "Full of Swiss francs. But I'm not worried about her safety. She has a gem-encrusted saber under the mattress. There would be slaughter if anyone tried to enter the property while I was away."

Jovo and Živorad winked at me in unison. I did not at first think they believed a word I was saying, yet halfway through my little speech I saw a glint in Jovo's bloodshot eyes.

I felt guilty about all that laughter after I left Mirijevo. And I almost shed a tear a day or two later, as I wheeled my small suitcase along the Knez. I turned back to see Olga in the kitchen window, still waving at me, rocking what appeared to be an imaginary baby in her bony arms, but what must have been an ethereal, golden head of cabbage.

I wasn't going very far. I owned a small apartment some fifteen minutes' walk away, just below the Kalemegdan citadel which stood between the Knez and the Danube, and so close to the zoo gardens that you could hear lions roar if you kept your windows open on a summer's night. I had bought the place from the proceeds of my previous property sale. Indeed, I had been planning to retire when Olga appeared on the scene, scared of the big nine-oh alone and practically begging me to take her on. Just one more lady, she said. She had seen a glowing report from my long-deceased first employer.

"Katya, my dearest child, I hope you will consider me," she pleaded at the end of the interview as though I was about to hire her and not the other way around. "I am sure we will get along very well, and you will want for nothing. And I am very easy to get along with," she added, with an absence of self-awareness that was beyond spectacular. The memory of our first meeting is almost touching.

I managed to shed more than a few tears in Olga's apartment when we gathered there to hear her will. It was the morning after the forty-day memorial service in the family crypt at the New Cemetery, Belgrade's oldest burial ground. The Orthodox believe this to be the day when the soul of the departed finally leaves the earth, but Olga's presence among us was still palpable.

The assembled company included Stanojlo Stanojlović, eleven of the twelve grandnephews and -nieces, a total of three nephews and one niece, and a couple of Olga's fellow crones who had served as witnesses when the final version of the will was signed two years previously and who were also, as it happens, the first to find Olga dead. Stanojlo was wearing his best, grotesquely ill-cut brown suit with his best green tie. The young were in denim, the old in black.

The crones got the crochet collection. The nephews and niece got the sword, split four ways. The youngest generation got nothing. Do I need to say who got the apartment?

The way Olga had met her maker was as dark and violent as the weather that autumn. Two elderly women had found her spread-eagled on the terrazzo floor of her vast hallway just an hour before I returned to the apartment. She was still lying there when I stepped in, looking small and deflated in her quilted dressing gown, like a chalk outline on the site of her own murder. Her head was turned to one side, a semblance of a wry smile on her lips and a meat cleaver in the back of her skull, the same cleaver I had often used to dismember those chicken skeletons at dawn.

The two elderly women had known that I was away and they hoped to entice Olga to attend the evening prayer at the old cathedral down the road. She had failed to open the door on either Saturday night or Sunday morning, and she wasn't answering her phone. They became convinced that she had suffered a fatal stroke and were about to call the police to force open the door when they tried it again and found it unlocked, and Olga just a few feet beyond it.

"Like that," one of them said, nodding toward the corpse as though Olga had rammed the cleaver into the back of her own head and arranged the dressing gown to reveal her skeletal knees when she fell.

"And she had not seen a priest in years," the other added, sobbing. "Her mother would have been appalled."

They had called the police, and they knew enough from watching endless whodunnits on television not to touch anything at the crime scene. For there was no doubt that it was indeed a crime. One of Olga's checked house slippers sat accusingly next to her hip, like a failed weapon of defense. I was holding a plastic bag containing three smelly heads of cabbage in my left hand, and the pull-out handle of my suitcase in my right, not quite knowing what to say or do. The poor thing looked awful with that cleaver in her head. I did want her dead, I admit, but this was a touch too dramatic.

The policeman seemed nonplussed. He had unbuttoned his thick blue winter coat and just stood there, speaking into a walkie-talkie and waiting for reinforcements. It was an emergency, obviously, but not that much of an emergency any longer.

"Bloody Montenegrins," he said. "I bet you it's them."

One of the old crones crossed herself. She looked as though she might faint. The scene before us represented every Belgrade old lady's nightmare. Cases like it were reported in the popular press all the time, or so it seemed. Serbian hacks loved milking the drama. The country may be going to the dogs, but that story is not nearly as vivid as a nonagenarian meeting a violent end, however timely that end might be.

There was always a brutal man, or a whole gang of them, keeping an eye on your movements, and then, the moment they knew you to be alone . . . *whack*. It was a meat cleaver in this case but it could equally well have been a Black & Decker drill. They threatened and prodded you until you told them where the money was. Most of their victims talked sooner rather than later, but Olga was a general's daughter, made of sterner stuff. Dear old Oggy, in cold blood, lying on the cold floor, murdered, robbed, and God knows what else.

Finally, as if coming out of a delayed shock, I let out a little shriek and dropped the bag. The policeman turned toward me as though he hadn't noticed me before. The cabbages fell out and bobbed along the floor wetly until one of them rested between Olga's dead feet, as though she had just given birth to it. Like something in one of her dreams, I thought.

You may complain about the Serbian police as much as you like, but they can be scarily, even brutally efficient when they want to be. And a little bit of criminal thoughtlessness goes a long way in these parts. They caught up with Jovo barely a week after they found Olga's body, on the Serbian–Montenegrin border. He was on his way to Podgorica with that sword and with two buckets of top-grade Colombian powder in the trunk of his Benz. He was either unbelievably blatant or unbelievably stupid, the hacks reported, leaving no one in any doubt that the latter was more likely.

There is nothing as cute as a handsome, well-spoken Montenegrin man in a finely tailored suit, with an expensive watch on his wrist. Jovo was not one of those. I can't say that I felt guilty about the fool.

Živorad will have to find a new assistant, but I won't be going to Mirijevo again. I have other plans, businesswise. A woman knows when to stop tempting fate.

Anyway, here we are. The paperwork is a nightmare, as it always is with property in central Belgrade. The lease changes hands with every war and revolution, and there is no shortage of either, so you never know what lurks in the land register. I'm not worried. I've been here before and I have a lawyer much better than Stanojlo. I stand in my kitchen and I watch the lights at the Serbian Academy go out.

UNDERMARKET

BY MIRJANA ĐURĐEVIĆ

Vračar

Translated by Genta Nishku

H ari drags herself through the market like a beaten cat. From each stall, the lively colors of the Indian summer scream at her—hills of red peppers, small cucumbers, purple eggplants, all sorts of greens, big and small, with names she doesn't even know, *fifty shades of screaming green* and orange pumpkins. All that's missing is something blue.

It should be a magical sight. But it all just makes her want to vomit. She trips on a box and stumbles. Grapes. Aha, here's that blue, or, rather, more of a plum. She clutches the edge of the stall with both hands, catching her breath, pretending she's just looking.

"Are you okay?"

"Everything's fine," Hari mutters, turning her head. Standing next to her in the stall is a gray, withered old woman, her gaze worried and hard. With a straw hat on her head, a too-wide summer dress—ha, wait, *bablje leto*, what in America they call Indian summer, we call "old woman's summer" in Serbia. *God, the things that come to my mind.* Or maybe she is not an old woman at all?

"Want some water?" comes a faint voice from across the stall. A young peasant, dressed in the latest fashions from the

Chinese markets, extends a half-filled plastic bottle with a cal-
loused hand.

"Go ahead, I'm not sick."

Hari barely shakes her head no and stares at the peasant,
who appears to be in her early thirties. Missing a front tooth,
she gives her a half smile. Cynically, or is she tripping?! And—
wait—she's wearing a wig—a cheap synthetic nest, the color
of hazelnut—in this heat?! The wig has shifted to one side. A
woman with no hair, not even *one* visible strand.

"Wait, I have a full one," the straw hat digs through her
canvas bag, her harsh voice matching her gaze.

The straw hat underneath which there is no hair, nor a wig?
Am I hallucinating or has the illness spread to my head? Hari now
shakes her head no to both women, as well as to herself, but
does not let go of the stall edge.

"We know each other," the straw hat says, like she's making
a statement, not asking a question.

Hari throws her another look. A real ghost.

"I don't think so. I remember faces. Excuse me, I need to
go. And thanks."

"You'll be fine. I'll walk you out," declares the straw hat.
Turning to the peasant she adds, "Mara, I'll see you tonight."

That authoritative tone! *There'll be no escorting, sister, fuck off.*
Hari gathers enough strength to turn and walk faster, at least
up to the market gate.

But at the gate of the hundred-year-old house on Petrogradska Street, a new wave of weakness comes over her. She is
unable to insert the key into the lock. And there is no one to
call. The owner of the house, Laki, her best friend and partner
in their failed business, has taken his wife to the mountains
for two months. They're saving their marriage. They left Hari
to take care of the house. For Hari it is conveninent. With her

chemo treatment coming up, she can easily walk from Laki's house to the hospital in ten minutes, instead of having to drive from New Belgrade across crowded bridges. She'll also avoid the stress of having to find parking around the medical complex. Frazzled after her surgery, she did not object too much when Laki pointed all of this out.

She finally manages to get the key to work, locking the gate behind her. Once in the garden, she tears off the colorful bandanna from her head, wiping away the sweat from her bare scalp, convinced she'd imagined what just happened.

Harijeta, Hari to her friends, fifty-plus, former chief inspector with the Serbian police in the homicide and sexual crimes division, former chief of security in a large department store in Chicago, former returnee to Belgrade. Soon she will be the former co-owner of the private detective agency Lucky Charm, which she started with her friend Laki, this she has firmly decided. Soon she will also be a former oncology patient, at least so she hopes. She needs to make it through her last round of chemotherapy, which is hitting her especially hard. Damn chemo brain . . . Everything is in a fog. But this, too, will pass. Provided that she does not die in someone else's home, in this elite part of town.

Weekend. Two days without a needle. Harijeta keeps her eyes closed, reclining on the antediluvian lounge chair, in the shade of the old cherry tree, and pretends to relax. That is what they told her—she needs to rest. They also told her, though, that she must eat. Did someone say food?

The bell at the gate is ringing. Harijeta looks at the time on her phone. Quarter to ten, Saturday. She'll play dead.

Like hell she will!

"Juhuuuuu! It's me! Open up!" Nađa. Laki's wife Lila's

friend since childhood. Who will not be satisfied with the pretense that Hari is dead, but will march into the yard even if she has to jump over the fence. Every Saturday, at exactly quarter to ten, the voice is heard: "Juhuuuuu! It's me!" and there is Nađa with her cart, crammed with the entire damn market, and with small Tupperware containers of cooked food in her bag.

Reluctantly, Harijeta gets out of the lounge chair and opens the gate.

"Why do you even lock it? My whole life, this yard has been open," babbles Nađa when she passes Harijeta as if she doesn't exist, walking right into the house, then into the kitchen, where she opens the fridge and unpacks the containers.

"You will eat all of this later, do you understand? You have to eat! And now, go put something on your head. I'm taking you to the Story Café. Well, you don't have to wear anything, you're great just like this too. When someone has a nice skull—"

"They can even go through chemotherapy without fear of ruining their beauty," Harijeta interrupts. "I am not going anywhere."

"You're going. I need you. For tonight's theme."

The café is some twenty meters from the house, on the corner of Petrogradska and Topolska streets. It's a prewar, one-story, witchy-looking house, surrounded and covered by vines, with a wonderful garden.

Every Saturday at ten in the morning, Lila meets her two friends from elementary school at the Story Café. When they're all together, they are a real trio. They cling to the idea that they are all committed intellectuals—Lila is a lawyer, one friend is a doctor, the other a journalist. Naturally, Nađa is the journalist. And every Saturday when they meet, they tackle a different sociopolitical topic. And some commitment it is! A meeting of the minds, at least according to Nađa and Lila.

Laki had told her all of this. He also has a best friend, Hari.

But the two of them guzzle beer and don't give a fuck about politics. At least that's what they did when Hari was healthy. How happy she would be to have a beer now, but she fears the nausea that she feels with every bite or sip of anything other than water. Hari is afraid! Fearless Hari has been terrified for months.

Shit! Squeezing behind Nađa, the first thing Hari notices near the table under the purple wisteria flowers is a straw hat balancing on a bare neck and thin shoulders. *That straw hat.* She cannot turn around and leave now.

"Let me introduce you. This is Vera, our doctor."

Two bald women look at each other and shake hands somewhat reluctantly.

"We know each other," announces the straw hat.

"From the day before yesterday," Hari retorts as she sits down.

Vera's face is expressionless.

Nađa is impatient. "Harijeta is a guest. It would be great if she could join us on future Saturdays, of course, but today she is here on a mission."

Harijeta gives her a confused look.

"I told you I had a topic for our Saturday discussions." Nađa looks at them intensely. "You read about the events at the oncology clinic?"

If she expects some type of reaction from the two bald women, she is wrong.

Harijeta and Vera are silent. Disappointed, Nađa stares at both of them.

"I don't read the news. I've had other concerns lately, in case you haven't noticed." The last thing Harijeta wants to chat with these women about is the oncology clinic.

"You don't read the news either?" Nađa is persistent, calling on Vera now. She pulls out the cover of the *Vračarski Glasnik* from her bag. "'Corruption Club Unraveling!' 'Bribery Scheme Uncovered.'"

"I read that, but if you're looking for an insider, I can tell you that nothing much happens in the chemotherapy department."

"You didn't hear what the nurses were talking about when—"

Vera shook her head.

"But here we have an *ideal* situation. I looked into it—all the corruption cases the newspapers mention happened at the exact same time the murders were recorded." Nađa takes out another cover. "'Fourth Doctor from Oncology Murdered. Police Closing in on Murderers.'"

Closing in, my ass. The old Hari would have jumped on that piece of news. This new one, with chemo brain and a desire to forget, hardly even remembers her doctor Milošević.

"It's suspicious that no one connects these two things. And you and Vera had your surgeries just then," Nađa blabs on.

We were there? Hari examines Vera's gray, tortured face. Didn't she say that we knew each other, the other day at the market? And again now. Vera purses her lips and shoots a glance at Nađa. Those eyes . . . Harijeta's brain feverishly scans images from her memory, images she is vigorously trying to delete, with varying degrees of success. No, they still don't know each other.

"We were there together, so what?" Vera comments dryly.

"I wouldn't say so," Hari counters.

"Well, it turns out that here we have at our disposal a true detective, and two eyewitnesses, so to speak. So we can solve the murders. Imagine how it would be—"

"You don't have anyone at your disposal," Hari cuts her off, and readies herself to leave the garden.

"And there were no eyewitnesses," replies Vera, showing no intention of leaving.

"Come on! What's with you today? With all our talents combined, and the help of a professional, we have the opportunity to find the serial killer of these corrupt doctors! And to finally do something that matters, something this rotten state is never able to accomplish."

Hari leans over the table. "Nađa, let me explain something to you. As a professional. And then I'm off. Look—never, ever, has one individual solved a crime in real life. Or a group, even if they were idle merry wives of Vračar. That only happens in crime novels. Go and write one, it's your job to write, whatever it is you write about. And let the police do *their* job. And let me do my own work, getting cured, if that's possible. All right now, goodbye, I'll see you if you ever drop by the New Belgrade blocks with regard to some new topics . . ."

She gets up, sets a crumpled banknote on the table, and hurries out of the Story Café, and out of *their* story too.

She succeeds in eating something green and tasteless—let's say some broccoli puree—and doesn't throw it up. She succeeds in taking a shower without looking at the open red wound around half of her left breast. She succeeds in getting into bed—who cares if it's noon? The one thing she doesn't succeed in is napping. Or she almost does. But a tap on the glass of the open windowpane startles her. And frightens her. From the bed she sees only a bent index finger tapping.

"What now?!" says the former Harijeta, who jumps from the couch and marches up to the window, carrying a heavy crystal ashtray in her hands that she grabbed from the bedside. The intruder is wearing a straw hat that reaches the sills of the ground floor's high windows.

"Why did Nađa send you?"

"She didn't." Vera raises her head to Harijeta. The hat dangles backward precariously, she holds it so it won't fall off. "Open up. We can also talk outside, if you don't want me inside the house."

Against her wishes, Hari leaves the old yellow house.

"Wait a second." She stiffens and turns around. "How did you get inside the garden at all? I locked the gate. I'm sure of it."

"I came in from the back." Vera motions to the back entrance of the house. Next to it, for as long as Hari has known this yard, some rusty metal sheets have been propped up against the tall wooden fence. Finally, the purpose of that trash becomes clear to her, since there were three boards missing from the fence behind her. Just enough to let a child, or this skeleton of a woman, squeeze through.

Stunned, she peers into the neighboring yard, right into the foundation pit of the construction site on Topolska Street. Where, until recently, there had been a very beautiful old house, maybe even older than Lila's, certainly more decrepit. Now, a white four-story monster will rise up, let's say the nouveau Vračar baroque style, with an underground garage for SUVs . . .

"Hey, you out of your mind? You could have been crushed there, fallen into the hole, had cement poured on you. They would never find you inside that hole. Why didn't you ring the bell like a normal human being?" Feeling tired, Hari settles on the lounge chair and points Vera to a wobbly bamboo chair, possibly older than both of them combined. "So, what do you want from me?" she asks, already annoyed, but with no desire to move again.

"I need your professional help," Vera declares, then goes quiet, taking off her hat.

Huh, I suppose I really do have a beautiful skull, thinks Hari.

An urge comes over her to get her phone and take a selfie, because Vera—

They look at each other.

"Lucky Charm is closed. My last client was the first killed in the series of oncology clinic murders. He was sitting in the exact same chair you are now sitting in when he told me that I had cancer. There you go, you can have fun at the Story and then go chase after the murderers."

No reaction comes from Vera at first. Then: "Doctor Milošević? I know."

The reaction from Harijeta is visible, her eyes popping out of her head. "How do you know?"

Vera takes a moment to think. "I saw him come in here. I was walking down the street, from the market. And I read the news. A few days after I saw him, the news was that he was gone. What did he want from you? Money?"

"That's a trick of the trade," Hari snaps, intending to stop this insane conversation. "And I don't believe that Nađa didn't send you here to get some dirt."

"She didn't. I told you, I need help."

"C'mon, woman, how can I help you? I can't even get up from this chair. If I could, I'd throw you over the fence right now. And how can you, when you're so—" She was about to say *cadaverous*. "How do you even have the strength to run about, move metal sheets, sneak around, and harass—"

"I'm sorry. I have to." Vera's facial expression doesn't change even when she apologizes. "Mara has disappeared. I'm begging you to help me find her. It's urgent."

"Who the fuck is Mara?"

"The peasant from the market, from the other day. I have to find her."

"Then get yourself to the market and find her." Harijeta has really had enough. For the umpteenth time this morning.

"She's not there. The day before yesterday I insisted that she move in with me. She didn't show up. She wasn't at the market yesterday, nor today. Her phone is out of service."

"Insisted? To move in with you? What right do you have—"

"What *right* do I have?" Vera barks. Then she goes silent, thinking for a few seconds, and continues, "Okay, I'll explain it to you."

"Just be quick, I need to lie down soon."

"I've been buying fruit from Mara for five or six years. We got to chatting, almost became friends. I was already alone at home at that time . . . And so we made an agreement that on Mondays, when the market is closed, she would stay in Belgrade and clean my house."

"Wait, you were already alone? You divorced?" Hari is unaware that she's entering the standard routine. Interrupting the client with more questions.

"No, I never married. I don't have children. My father left us when I was a child. My sister died. Mother before her. Before Mother, my aunt. The four of us lived together ever since I can remember. And they left, one by one. Breast cancer. Now me, it's genetic. I won't be long now . . . That's not important, but Mara . . ."

Harijeta is speechless. And her scar burns, it burns terribly. *It's the nerves*, she thinks to herself, staring at Vera. *Genetics?* There was this woman who was in the same room with her during pre-op, deeply sedated and babbling about genetics, murders. There was chaos in the hospital that morning, the body of Dr. Milošević had been discovered, already decomposed . . . But she can't remember anything clearly!

"Mara's family ordered her to leave Belgrade, they needed her to work in the village. Then she appeared at my door, with a lump in her breast the size of a child's fist . . . just around the same time you and I were running into each other in the hallways of the oncology clinic, waiting for surgery."

"I don't remember you," is all Hari can say.

"And it's better that way. But I remember you, it was hard not to notice your red mane. Sorry, you'll grow a new one. Anyway, I wrote her first referral to a specialist, and somehow I expedited her surgery."

"You bribed someone? Someone from the newspaper?"

"No. It doesn't work like that with doctors—bribes are taken from patients, rarely from colleagues. Doctors are a mob." She goes silent and then corrects herself: "*We* are a mob."

"I figured that out on my own even without your help, a long time ago. What you're saying doesn't absolve you from—"

"I didn't come for forgiveness, I came to look for Mara. She's had her surgery. She has a chance, chemo started on time, but those criminals—"

"You doctors?" Hari brazenly interrupts again.

"No, her people, from the village, they solved the problem of her chemo by sending her to the market, to sell grapes. Between treatments. No wasted time. That's why I insisted that she move in with me—I see you're frowning at my interference. As if I care. She's only halfway done, but soon she'll feel sick. She needs to rest, she needs to eat, and not be like you." Vera waves her off, as if Hari is a lost cause.

"And you think *you'll* look after her? Look at yourself, woman, you're like a twig."

"And do you know where the sellers from the market sleep? I'm not talking about wholesale merchants, but peasants, the ones who lure half the city to Kalenić Market. *Authentic*, I heard one nouveau riche cow say in passing, how she only buys from *authentic* peasants. Do you know where all the boxes and carts of vegetables and fruit that can't remain in the stalls disappear in the evening? They move to Vračar basements, along with the sellers. Have you ever walked around here at twilight? Or at six in the morning?"

"Frankly, no. Or I don't remember. Neither did I look around. Sometimes Laki and I drink beer at Kalenić . . . Is it okay to drink beer, doctor?"

"You can, if you're able to. Mara. She sleeps in a basement with her grapes. Half of the old buildings around the market stay standing by renting basements to peasants. That's how they supplement their budget. Maintaining these houses has become too expensive. People sell them and leave Vračar. Lila might do that too, someday. Who knows what they could build in this spot then? A spa. A casino. A villa for some criminal, a villa even older and more beautiful than the one they demolished."

"If you thought we'd go around nearby villages and look for her, forget it. I can't drive." *And you even less so, you phantom,* Hari thinks to herself.

"No. I wanted us to look for her together down below. In the basements. To be honest, I'm afraid to set out alone, maybe something has happened to her, she got sick or—"

"Which one of them is her basement?" Hari makes an effort to get up and look for her bandanna. She'll take the skeleton to the fucking basement and be done with her.

"I don't know. They all hide their burrows from each other, because somebody will come and pay more, for a bigger basement, closer to the market."

Fuck, Kalenić under Kalenić seems to be the business center of Belgrade, Hari thinks while dragging herself off the lounge chair. "So what's the problem? Afraid you'll see a corpse, *doctor*?"

"No. I've seen plenty of them. But I don't know my away around in the dark. And I don't know how to get past the door buzzers. I'd have to lie so they'll let me into the buildings. You probably know some tricks."

"True, I got a degree in ceiling and basement navigation, and a doctorate in buzzer deceit. Idiot . . ." Hari is now up, unlocking the door. "C'mon. We're going, and after that you are getting out of my life."

The two bald women, one with a straw hat, thin like a ghost, and the other with the colorful bandanna on her head, in jeans that were always too baggy, visit eighteen Vračar basements around Kalenić Market in total, posing as mail couriers, godmothers who came for a birthday and forgot their glasses, pizza delivery . . .

Hari hasn't done this before, but her imagination flies when she's in action. They couldn't get into some basements because their doors were locked. In others they found nobody alive, or dead, luckily.

Their flashlights reveal hills of potatoes, crates with apples, large plastic bags containing carrots purchased in some supermarket—which are obviously repackaged and sold as homegrown—two inflatable mattresses, an occasional pillow, one camping bed, a decommissioned couch, pears, imported cauliflower left to wither and appear organic, a mirror next to a basement window, blankets—some folded up but more often thrown over a makeshift bed—sneakers, plastic canisters with water . . . and no grapes anywhere, or any trace of Mara.

Vera stops by the fence of the gray one-story house where she lives, the one with a peeling facade, and pets the two cats stretching on the wall. She opens the metal gate with a creak and enters the yard. A few crates of grapes lie by the open basement door. Mara comes out, looks at her, and cracks a toothless grin. Definitely cynical.

"Where have you been, doctor? You scared me shitless! Are you done? I was afraid. All I could think was, *She's stronger than you, maybe she even knows karate . . .*"

"Nothing is done," Vera answers tiredly, and sits on the steps by the back door. "The spots you picked were stupid. And we ran into at least five people who knew me. You can't plan a murder willy-nilly. There's nothing I can do for her, she was at the wrong place at the wrong time. My fault, I shouldn't have told her that I killed all those corrupt doctors, scum profiting from others' suffering. But we were sedated, waiting for surgery, you remember how it is. For a second I had my doubts, I wasn't sure if she'd heard me, if she really understood. But the way she looks at me. And how she refuses to admit that we know each other. And some things she says . . . Besides, she gave me a better idea. But this time you have to pull your weight too."

"That won't be so hard for me. Now you're father and mother to me, may they both drop dead! I only have you. If they lock you up, I'll end up six feet under too."

"Stop your blabbering. You'll live, I promised."

Mara goes to the basement with two crates of grapes in her arms. Vera digs into the canvas bag. She takes out a bottle of chloroform, a cloth, an old metal medical box with syringes in it. At last she finds her cell phone.

"Hello, Nađa." She is silent for a long time. Nađa is monologizing. "Can you check when the construction is scheduled to start at the house on Topolska Street? They'd know in the municipality, because of the traffic. So let's organize a protest. Peaceful, of course. This is Vračar, after all, we're not savages, we'll let them work, but we'll stand in the street with banners. They'll respond better to that, it's more publicity . . ."

PART II

THE DARK CORNER

A DIFFERENT PERSON

BY VLADAN MATIJEVIĆ

King Aleksandar Boulevard

Translated by Sibelan Forrester

Peppy, I've decided to kill someone. I decided in one instant and then didn't think any more about it.

A river of people was flowing around me, King Aleksandar Boulevard, the *bulevar*, was breathing deeply. The sun-roasted cars were racing around, beggars asking for money. Street vendors were offering sunglasses, umbrellas, underwear, socks, shoelaces, insoles, cosmetics, children's toys, medications that hadn't yet expired, to passersby. They sold their goods from improvised stands made of cardboard boxes and pieces of clothesline.

I was standing, just like every morning, close to the Ðeram market and shouting from a wobbly footstool: *"Vlast ima kapacitet!"* ("The authorities have a tremendous capacity!")

Hardly anyone looked at me, the rumble was constant, but I didn't give up. Kombucha was playing Clapton on his guitar, I had to outshout him too.

"The authorities have a tremendous capacity! The authorities have a tremendous capacity!"

I didn't give up my political protest. People in this city don't care about anything but politics and the crime report; if you want them to pay attention to you, you have to stay within the framework. The daily newspapers have turned into mouthpieces of the regime, no one reads them, people have more faith in *me*. And I have faith in the people. I eavesdrop on other people's conversations.

Yesterday by Lipov Lad *kafana* a patient fell out of an ambulance and died instantly, last night on Maxim Gorky Street a man bashed a woman's head with a beer stein . . .

Every so often in Belgrade a husband kills his spouse. The women have never looked better, every second one could be a runway model, but they get no benefit from their beauty. I say that some devil has entered into people, but no one gives a damn. Inspector Vasović gives me a barely perceptible nod. He goes to the market every morning, but when he's not in his office he has no interest in what's happening in the city.

I met an interesting young woman. The way she walked reminded me of Žana, my first love. She was going down the *bulevar* to the Vuk Monument and suddenly came to a stop in front of me. She addressed me as *druže*, "comrade." She was tiny, with red hair and a ring through one nostril. She gave off an air of cleanliness.

"Comrade, will you sign my petition against trashy culture, *schund?*" she asked. Two pimpled teenaged boys stood behind her.

"Against *schund?*" I asked.

She nodded.

"I will," I said, and started to get down from my stool.

She held me by my upper arm with both hands, she was afraid that I might fall and perish before I could fulfill my promise. I'm sure she didn't think I meant to run away from her, it was obvious that I wasn't hesitating. Who, Peppy, could miss out on an opportunity to settle accounts with *rubbish?*

As I took the papers and pen I noticed that there were

already many pages filled with signatures. The campaign they had started had accumulated plenty of supporters. In addition to my signature, the girl wanted my personal ID card number. I pulled out my military service booklet, to this very day I have no other documents, and I copied the number from the first page. A photo of our little volunteer, um, paramilitary brigade was sticking out of the booklet, I pulled it out for a moment and looked at it. The girl didn't like that, she made a face. *Perhaps I could kill her* went through my head.

The two hunched, pimply kids neither moved nor spoke. I thought they might be mute. I asked the girl what her name was, she said Ira. I decided she had gotten her nickname from the Irish Republican Army, and I liked that. Kombucha had moved on to playing Bob Dylan.

Belgrade, Peppy, has become a monster. Mothers here name their sons after famous criminals, politicians have run out of neglected relatives, so they put their house pets in government positions. Now our leaders moo, baa, bark, and meow at us from their official armchairs.

Anyone who's dissatisfied with the condition of society can complain, the counter's open every weekday from ten a.m. to four p.m. However, there's always a long line, plus the computer has crashed, and you can't get anything done without the computer. They say they've called the IT man, but he won't show up, he hasn't been paid for the last time he fixed things.

Thus, no one will be surprised when I carry out a murder. It's a firm decision, Peppy. But who should I kill? At first glance, it seems easy to choose a victim. In Belgrade, no matter who you look at it seems that you wouldn't be wrong to kill them. However, that isn't so. Many of them aren't worth the time or energy . . .

Yesterday, the Danube tossed up the lifeless body of an opposition party leader, last night a television magnate overdosed in the Intercontinental Hotel . . .

A couple of police are walking in my direction: a young woman and a tall, bare-chinned young man. Pairs of handcuffs jingling against their butts, the weight of their pistols pulling down their belts.

"The authorities have a tremendous capacity!" I shout as loudly as possible. They don't even look at me.

I can't say anything wrong, the police never pay any attention to me, nobody mistreats me. People are tolerant of me. Both when I was shouting "Let's clean up Serbia!" and when I stood at the intersection by the Lilly drugstore and directed the traffic, no one did anything to stop me. No one wants to get into an argument with me, Peppy. Probably because I'm crazy.

My health's pretty good, I can't complain. Sometimes I mix up the past and the present, but that's not terrible.

Peppy, nothing's terrible here, people quickly get used to everything. No one minds that they pour water in the gasoline, that they mix air into the natural gas, that they send your electric power at a low voltage. Babies don't mind that their milk's diluted, sick people don't mind that their injections are diluted, drunks don't mind that their *rakija* is diluted. Pedestrians don't protest that the streets are dug up, that cars are parked on the sidewalks, they jump and fly like the Chinese warriors in the movie *House of the Flying Daggers*.

I asked Doctor Teodosić to prescribe me a higher dose, what I get isn't enough for me, but he won't. He thinks I might be selling my medication. Why would I sell my meds when I don't even have enough? Doctor Teodosić asks me how it is I haven't died yet—I ought to, if I'm taking everything he prescribes for me.

"Why would I die, doctor?" I act surprised. "A person quickly gets used to everything here."

There's always someone outside his office who'll make a fuss that I've cut in line, but I don't pay any attention to those losers. Maybe sometime I will, when I have a weapon on me. "The authorities have a tremendous capacity!"

If only Kombucha knew about all the pills I have, he'd shove me off my footstool, snatch my key, and hotfoot it to my apartment. Nothing would stop that guy, whose nickname comes from fermented mushrooms, from robbing me. As it is, whenever he lands on hard times he brings his books and sells them cheap. It's mostly philosophy, Kierkegaard and crap like that. Sometimes I buy one of his books—to be honest, philosophy relaxes me.

The woman whose husband hit her with a beer stein has passed away. The doctors fought for her life, but the hospital didn't have enough units of blood on hand.

Peppy, we never have enough of any of the blood types. Every day more people die a violent death here than are born. Death drives an electric lawnmower and clears out the streets of Belgrade, if you aren't a killer then you're a victim. Neutrality has lost its foothold, the laws are the same as on the battlefield. Perhaps that's why I've succumbed to the general atmosphere, the euphoria so to speak, and have firmly resolved to kill someone. I probably won't be punished for the crime, which gives me additional motivation to carry it out.

Peppy, the Belgrade police don't chase criminals anymore. The detectives and killers sit in *kafanas* at the same table and eat dinner together, criminals practice shooting at the police gun ranges. If by some miracle a person is arrested, and at the end of a marathon trial is convicted, they don't go to prison because there's no room. The prisons are packed: it's those who don't pay off their bank loans, who owe for parking tickets, who don't pay their cable bills, who are serving prison sentences. Farmers who didn't respond to the order to root out ragweed are serving sentences. There's no room for long-term prison sentences.

Last night on Vračar a well-known lawyer's Jeep was blown up; this morning a bank guard was killed in Čukarica . . .

In Senjak this morning they found the lifeless body of a sixteen-year-old girl, on Zvezdara some teenagers locked a homeless guy in a shaft and left him there to die without food or water . . .

I can hardly wait to kill someone myself, for the adrenaline to flow through my veins. I've been useless for so long, it's time for me to take my place in society and come back to life a bit. I just have to figure out what criteria the victim must fulfill; I've suddenly become conscious that I don't want to spill just anyone's blood.

A line of police cars rushes down the *bulevar*, the sirens wail. They're simulating a major kidnapping.

"*The authorities have a tremendous capacity!*" From time to time someone looks at me in an unfriendly way, they probably take my words as a provocation. Then I start shouting with all my strength, and I myself marvel at my throat's power. "While you were all sleeping, I guarded you!" After I shout that, one turns his head away and picks up his pace—an airplane wouldn't be able to catch up to him, he's so fast.

Do you remember, Peppy, how our own fighter planes accidentally bombed us, the volunteers, as soon as we crossed into Croatian territory? It happens, the commander explained to us later. The important thing was that we suffered no casualties, only that fat guy with the crossed bullet belts lost some of his hearing from the explosion. But in any case, he died in the first skirmish after that. What would good hearing do for him in the grave?

I recognized her immediately, even though this time her hair was blond with some multicolored streaks. She still wore a ring in her nostril. She stopped near me and squatted so she could look over Kombucha's books. Her T-shirt pulled upward and on her back, just above her butt, she had a big tattoo, a five-pointed star with a hammer and sickle in the center.

The pimply teenagers were standing behind Ira, they were her bodyguards. I called them Tom and Jerry, after the cartoon characters. I wondered whether I should consider killing one of them. But I quickly rejected that idea. I didn't want to separate them, and I considered it too much to kill both of them. It's not good to overdo things, nor to throw your weight around unnecessarily. One dead person is quite enough, it would satisfy my requirements. Besides that, I sensed that they didn't fulfill my requisite criteria for a victim.

Kombucha stopped playing his guitar and started chatting with Ira. I felt jealous, as if that tiny girl belonged to me. I could hardly restrain myself from interrupting them and acting ignorant. Ira was delighted when she saw a Kropotkin book and an issue of a literary journal devoted to Bakunin.

"Look, they've published his letters." She showed the journal to Jerry. She bought both the journal and the book.

Kombucha has been a drug addict for a long time and he needs a lot of money to feed his habit, so he visibly livened up after taking the money from her.

I asked her whether she had collected enough signatures

against trash culture. The smell of roasted meat came from a nearby fast-food kiosk, and the beggar Drago was drinking *rakija* from a bottle. She had, she told me, succeeded in collecting a thousand signatures, but she had a problem. She didn't know who to send the petition to.

"Is there any point giving *trash* a petition against itself?" she asked me. Clearly this was a rhetorical question. The problem always comes down to that. And I told her so.

Kombucha went back to playing guitar, an older man tossed a few coins into his case.

Last night at the main train station a man without documents was stabbed with knives, today on Knez Miloš Street a transvestite threatened to blow up a whole building . . .

Not for a single moment did I doubt the correctness of my decision, but I still didn't know who to kill. A young person or an old one? Woman or man? Someone I know or a stranger? A friend or . . .

Peppy, I don't have any enemies. I never did have any. In '91 and '92 I fired a gun because that was the current practice. Someone in a high place had declared the Croats my enemies, on the TV they talked day and night about their crimes against the meek Serbs. I killed them cold-bloodedly, although I had nothing against them personally. The commander told us that all the great nations had committed great crimes, that ours can't always be someone else's prey either. You believed that and rolled up your sleeves, they called you Peppy the Beast.

But I was different. In my heart, I kept on rooting for Hajduk, the Croatian soccer team from the beautiful city of Split. If I didn't hate anyone on the battlefield, then clearly I wouldn't hate anyone here either, in Belgrade. And I know a lot of people. And because I don't have a bad relationship with anyone it's hard for me to choose a victim. But I have to take someone's life, that's the trend, we can't live as if the world doesn't involve us.

Last night someone threw a Molotov cocktail at the house of a turbo-folk music star, two children were seriously burned . . .

Along with everything else, I haven't decided how to carry out the murder, either. Tenderly or sadistically? In my apartment, I have a Kalashnikov with seven full clips, a CZ 99 pistol with ten bullets, a bayonet with a long blade, and five hand grenades. The grenades are on my table in a crystal fruit bowl, the other weapons are locked in a wooden trunk. It won't be easy for me to choose the means either. I know that you, Peppy, would surely use cold steel.

That day the sun beamed hot, I was in a shirt and jacket, all sweaty. A tie was squeezing my neck. I can't be poorly dressed, what would that look like? I have to be different from the beggar Drago.

Red fireflies played before my eyes. If someone had asked me why I didn't go home, what I was hoping to find in that crowd, I wouldn't have known how to answer. But that person wouldn't be able to tell me what I should do by myself in a basement studio apartment. I think anyone who spent two hours in my apartment would understand why first thing in the morning I take my blue footstool and come to this place, out among the people.

I heard that they're going to repave the *bulevar* again. I have the impression, Peppy, that the spaces of beauty and freedom in Belgrade are quickly shrinking.

A man with a beard down to his waist was explaining to his hunchbacked friend that Faulkner was a Serbian writer, that only a Serb could understand *The Sound and the Fury*. An older woman in a blue blouse offered me a ten-dinar coin. I took the coin, but I didn't thank the woman. I don't have time for that, nor for explaining to her that I'm actually doing fine financially. I receive a monthly disability check and it's enough for me. Whatever I earn unexpectedly I always give to Oliver, the kid who washes the windshields of cars that stop at the traffic light by the Vuk Monument. Washing windshields is the best job this state can offer a person who isn't a party member. "*The authorities have a tremendous capacity!*"

Kombucha was running madly out of the market, knocking cabbages off stands, bumping into people who swore at him as he passed. His hands were empty, he had probably tried to steal something and hadn't succeeded. A farmer was running after him. It would be better for Kombucha to be chased by the Sicilian mafia, I don't believe that anyone can get away from a Serbian farmer, especially one who has the nerve to sell his produce in Belgrade.

Kombucha was hoping he could reach the *bulevar* and we would protect him. Everyone here who sells, begs, and picks pockets has some kind of cold steel: a knife, an awl, a hatchet . . . Even Miljana, the little woman who sells handicrafts, has a chunk of rock at her feet. Only Drago is weaponless, he stinks so badly that surely no one would touch him. I don't have anything on me either, but I look dangerous.

The two young police officers were patrolling the area. The proprietors spoke to them sweetly. As I had expected, the farmer caught up with Kombucha. He grabbed him by the hair and pulled him backward. Kombucha fell down, the enemy sat on his chest, put his hands around his neck, and started strangling him. At first, Kombucha resisted, then he went limp. The young policeman started walking quickly in their direction, but the policewoman pulled on his sleeve and they went off in the other direction. Afterward, the farmer went back to his stand. Kombucha lay there without moving, and it wasn't until half an hour later that he painfully got up and staggered toward us. His face had gone dark, unrecognizable, his neck was blue, with broken capillaries.

In Dedinje a terrier bit off a woman's hand, four elementary schoolchildren beat a math teacher to death with baseball bats ...

Did I imagine it, or did someone among the passersby mention Iron Butterfly? I concluded that the American rock band must be coming to Belgrade: lots of older musicians have gotten back together in order to tour here. I got the urge to go to a rock concert after not having gone to one in the past twenty-five years. *The authorities have a tremendous capacity!* I shouted with all my strength that the authorities had the capacity and snickered, satisfied. I knew what kind of person I should consider as a victim, the circle was narrow. The farmer who throttled Kombucha had helped me. I realized that I didn't want to kill *him*, but I'd be glad to bump off Kombucha.

Peppy, I want to feel grief after the murder. That emotion lasts longer than others. This society, along with every individual in it, lacks continuity. Therefore I'm going to kill someone who's dear to me. The first one I thought of was Ira. Then I thought the best thing would be to kill Oliver. I like him the most. Oliver is nice-looking, lively, and cheerful until a limousine with tinted windows stops next to him in the evening. Then he gets unhappy and reluctantly climbs inside.

Oliver is forced to prostitute himself because he's supporting his sick mother and two younger sisters. I'll definitely kill someone I like, someone whose death will make me suffer for a long time. The grief will help keep me from drowning completely. I don't believe in the torments of conscience, just the way you didn't believe.

Yesterday at a construction site in St. Sava Street, a supporting wall collapsed and buried three people; last night two men impersonating police officers handcuffed a salesclerk in a grocery store on Kosančićev Venac and emptied his cash register of all the money he'd made that day . . .

My day was complete—I saw Ira again. Her hair was the same color as last time. I asked her how I could get a ticket for the Iron Butterfly concert. She told me to ask Smiley. "He has everything, and if he doesn't have something he'll always find it."

I told her that I didn't know who Smiley was.

Ira couldn't believe it. "Everybody knows Smiley," she asserted, "he supplies all of Belgrade. This city would fall apart without him."

I had the impression that she appreciated how I wasn't like everyone else. I looked at her pleadingly and she promised she would get Smiley involved to find me a ticket for the concert by the group with the beautiful name, which she hadn't heard of until then. After that, she talked for a long time about that Smiley, with great respect, admiration, and love. I thought he must be her boyfriend. "Smiley is a power," she declared. "At the 1991 demonstrations against the government in Belgrade he wanted to charge the police cordons, he wanted to topple the Slobodan Milošević regime with his bare hands and stop the war."

I didn't respond, she probably wouldn't understand my sense of humor. You shouldn't joke with anyone these days, Peppy, every person here is a ticking bomb.

* * *

A man in a wheelchair approached me, the one who hands out leaflets all day by the Vuk Monument. His brother pushes him there every morning and leaves him, it's unbelievable how much they look alike, maybe they're twins. In the evening, his brother comes for him and takes him home. When he offered me a ticket to the concert, I realized that Ira's surprise at my not knowing Smiley was well-founded. I'd seen him every day, I was pretty sure he was supplying the addicts of the *bulevar* with drugs. When he was in withdrawal, Kombucha would be running to him every minute. I just hadn't known they called him Smiley, nor that he had participated in antiwar demonstrations. Which is really absurd. He had struggled against the war and wound up disabled, while I'd taken part in the war and had all my limbs. But in spite of his handicap, Smiley radiated serenity. I tried to figure out his age, but I couldn't. He looked youthful, but at the same time, something told me we were about the same age.

"How much do I owe you, sir?" I asked him. Calling him *sir* didn't really fit him, but I didn't want to be too familiar. He laughed and asked for almost nothing, probably the ticket had cost that much at the ticket office. I don't like it when a service fee is not included in the price, and then I have to think about how much to tip. I consider myself a miser, but this time I was generous. But Smiley returned the extra money, vehemently refusing to take a tip. I hate it when someone won't let me pay for a service, and then I wind up owing them. I noticed that Kombucha was acting as if he didn't know the man in the wheelchair.

"What's your interest in this business?" I asked Smiley.

"It's important for things to get done," he answered, and laughed again.

A girl was raped last night in the restroom at the Hotel Bristol, a well-known actress was beaten up in the National Theater . . .

* * *

Oliver holds a half-liter bottle in one hand, a squeegee in the other, a red bucket of water sits on the sidewalk. While the cars are racing by, he fills the bottle to the top. When the light turns red, he comes up to the first car and starts washing the windshield, ignoring the driver's disapproval. He washes slowly as if he has all the time in the world. Then he goes to the second car and does the same. When the light turns green, he goes back to the first car and takes the money from the driver. People behind the wheel get impatient, the whole line of vehicles sounds their horns. Oliver darts to the second car, the driver has already put out his hand with the cash. Oliver's face is cheerful and because of this he gets more from the drivers than they were planning to give him. Oliver's a great whore, he's ideal for the role of victim. I was sorry I didn't have a weapon with me, I would have executed him right then. Starting tomorrow I'll carry a pistol, I've decided to be ready at all times.

Last night a bank employee died after a ten-day hunger strike, today a young man died in a fight between fans of the Crvena Zvezda and Partizan soccer teams . . .

Last night a teenager from Mirijevo slashed her wrists, an old woman from Dorćol drank acetic acid . . .

Ira once again addressed me as *druže*, "comrade." I don't like that Communist lexicon, but I didn't object. She asked to see the picture from my military service booklet. She's a marvelous girl, I wanted to kill her right then. And I could have, I had the pistol tucked into my belt, I only needed to unbutton my jacket and pull it out. I don't know what stopped me from doing it. I would have grieved for Ira my whole life.

"You're a war veteran?" she asked me.

"How can we have veterans?" I answered with a question. "We lost the war. We can't have war veterans."

"What a crank you are," Ira said, which surprised me.

I held out the photograph. We all had long hair and beards, we looked like the bandits in Walter Hill's *Long Riders*. She said I'd been handsome when I was young. I didn't want to tell her that I wasn't in that photograph. I myself don't know why not, probably I was out on patrol that day. But despite my absence, the photograph is infinitely dear to me. It was taken in front of the cantina that Fat Ceca ran. Surely you remember, Peppy. Ceca had a heavy Mauser hanging at her hip, above the cash register it said, *No Credit to Anyone*. Nothing there was unclear. All around in the meadow lay soldiers, professionals, and mobilized reserves. They drank beer, wrote letters, cleaned their weapons. Some were removing lice. We were paramilitary volunteers, we didn't acknowledge anyone's command. At the same time, cross my heart, no one wanted to command our regiment either. The devil himself would have had a hard time paying our bills, and even harder getting our attention. Ira gave me back the photograph, deep in thought. I allowed her to walk away, I didn't shoot her.

Some graffiti appeared on the university library building: *ONLY WINNERS HAVE VETERANS. WE'RE THE SONS OF DEFEAT.*

I didn't like that at all. I didn't want to participate, nor to inspire anyone. True, Ira for her part had already read Bakunin, but her literature didn't rehabilitate me, nor did her defiant character. Clearly, the girl liked me. That was an additional reason for me to kill her. If I didn't do it in time, she'd stop admiring me, and that would be painful for both of us. I waited impatiently for her to appear.

On Mihajlo Pupin Street a father-in-law shot his pregnant daughter-in-law with his hunting rifle, there was a multicar accident on Gazela Bridge with fatalities and serious injuries . . .

Before me stood a Gypsy, terrifying in appearance. I was just his height standing on my footstool. "What do you want?" I asked him. He kept silent. Although his skull was close-shaven, he irresistibly resembled Chief Bromden from *One Flew Over the Cuckoo's Nest*. Another person suddenly spoke up. I lowered my eyes and in that enormous man's shadow I saw Smiley. Several frightened kids were standing to one side, I recognized Tom and Jerry among them.

Smiley was upset and confused, he kept repeating that Ira had been arrested. I concluded that he meant my young acquaintance, yet I couldn't grasp why Smiley was saying this to *me*, what *I* had to do with her arrest.

I looked back at Chief Bromden. He started muttering, I almost fell off my footstool. I managed to understand that the two of them expected me to intervene with Inspector Vasović. They knew, just like everyone on the *bulevar*, that I worked for the inspector, they'd noticed that every morning he gave me instructions and signals.

"So you have to go to his office right now," the leader ordered me belligerently. "Let the inspector see that Ira has someone to take care of her."

"Her parents have disowned her and surely won't help her," Smiley chimed in. He was pleading with me to help.

"Why did they arrest her?" I asked, just to say something.

"She was fighting with some soccer fans, she cut one on the arm," Chief Bromden answered.

I said that I wouldn't undertake anything. While I was saying it I saw astonishment on the chief's face and heard the angry cries of Ira's followers.

* * *

Žana left me in that cursed year, in '91, and I left *Filmski žurnal*. So I was writing film criticism, I was writing. I made peace with the fact that I was never going to make my live-action film and I went off to Slavonia—the bloodiest front in Croatia. I thought I would heal myself of my frustrations in battle, or at least die. Preventing the creation of an independent state of Croatia and protecting the Serbian minority, I admit, was not my goal. But in Slavonia there were cannons and howitzers. Great cannons, great howitzers. Dark-green trunks of ammunition. Snipers' bullets and newly composed faux-folk music worse than death. *Rakija* and beer, and everything they lead you to. Kettle, ladle, and mess tins. Dysentery. Pigs, rats, crows, worms . . . Land mines and the sanitation crew . . . And my acquaintance with you, dear Peppy.

That afternoon Ira came along with Smiley. They were both smiling. I concluded that Ira took drugs too. I was angry at her because she was friendly with a man like that, at the same time sorry, because I was disappointed in this girl. She was worthless; everything indicated that I would have to kill Oliver.

Smiley told me, along with some jokes, that yesterday Strongman had planned to give me a beating because I'd refused to mediate on Ira's behalf. I understood that Chief Bromden was named Strongman. Smiley had barely managed to calm him down, told him he knew me well and that I would certainly go see Inspector Vasović.

From the ensuing conversation, I grasped that Smiley really thought they had released Ira thanks to my intervention. Ira didn't deny it, and it looked as if she too thought I had gone to the police for her.

I was getting more and more nervous. Ira considered the whole episode with the soccer fans not worth discussing, which was the right thing to do. Then she told me I shouldn't feel responsible for her, that I had struggled in the way I knew how to and was able to, and that now it was her generation's turn. Ugh, how she got on my nerves! I decided that I would no longer talk to her, she definitively didn't deserve to be killed.

On Uzun Mirkova Street a married couple jumped from a sixth-floor window, a seven-year-old girl was kidnapped from her bedroom on Knez Mihailova Street . . .

Miljana is sitting on her folding chair and selling handicrafts. Drago is begging so he can buy *rakija*, Kombucha is playing Van Morrison. Employees of the university library have been erasing Ira's graffiti for a whole hour, supervised by their glowering director. I shout: "*Vlast je obezbedila ambijent!*" Today I'm shouting that the authorities have created a great ambience, and I admit with regret that I'm not capable of killing anyone. I've decided not to carry my pistol anymore. I don't need it. I'll make peace with my lazy fate, I'll continue vegetating. I'll leave the action to other people.

Citizens lynched an old man who had groped a girl on a public bus, robbers broke into an apartment on Banovo Brdo and tortured a whole family until they handed over their jewelry and their life savings . . .

Today Strongman came to see me and threatened me. He said that not a hair on Ira's head may be harmed. With his two fists resting one on the other, he mimed the wringing of a goose's neck.

I didn't go to the Iron Butterfly concert, I was wondering where Strongman could have gotten the idea that I wanted to kill Ira.

* * *

Dear Peppy, my hands are bloody, but I'm not satisfied. I keep feeling that the person I was trying to kill might still be alive. It seems likely that I'll have to go to the penitentiary.

By the florist's wall, at the place where Miljana always sits, there was a stone. I bent down, picked it up, and struck Smiley in the head with all my strength. He all but flipped over, along with his wheelchair. His head was completely covered in blood, but he didn't give up. His body flailed, I could hear wheezing from his throat.

The streetlights were on, cars were racing along the *bulevar*. Fortunately, the sidewalks were empty. It was a cold evening, you could sense autumn.

I hit him in the head several more times, but awkwardly. I wanted to pound him in the temple, but I missed, I nailed him in the forehead, the chin . . . His face turned into a bloody mess, his eye hung out of its socket, but his limbs continued twitching; I also heard that gruesome rattle. The drivers were minding their own business, they didn't look to the side, but even so I screened Smiley with my body. I had to finish him off as quickly as possible and clear out of this place. I struck him with all my strength, the blood spurted, pieces of bone flew. Smiley fell out of his seat and slid down on the sidewalk, with his back leaning against his wheelchair. Then the chair moved and he lay down on the sidewalk. His body kept on twitching. I kneeled beside his shoulder, took the stone in both hands, and hit him on the head twice. He didn't go still. I grabbed him around his chest and lifted him, his blood soaking through my clothes and touching my body. It was hot, it seemed that way to me. I put him back in his chair. His head was the wrong shape, he had a black hole in the crown of his skull.

Cars were racing past us, not one slowed down. At the trolley stop across the street several people had gathered. They were watching the tires go by or staring at their cell phones, deep in thought. They didn't notice anything out of the ordinary, and even if they had they wouldn't have wanted to get mixed up in things that had nothing to do with them. I held the rock under my jacket and went down a side street, less well lit than the *bulevar*. Smiley remained sitting and waiting there, dead, for his brother. Blood was flowing out of him and making a black puddle around his wheelchair.

It was inevitable that the night would end like this. Did he want something from me when he approached or did fate draw him to me?

Around ten p.m. he called his brother to come get him. Then he told me nonchalantly that his brother had been in the same unit with me. I looked at him in an unfriendly way, he had to notice that.

Peppy, you know we weren't in any kind of unit, the officers acted as if they hadn't even heard of our regiment, never mind seen it in the vicinity of the regular army.

I kept quiet, I didn't contradict him. Sometimes words aren't the right means, you have to express yourself in other ways. But Smiley didn't keep quiet, the devil wouldn't leave him in peace.

"They called you Peppy," he said. He wasn't asking, he didn't doubt, he concluded.

I saw in his eyes that he wouldn't believe me if I told him I was a different person.

BLACK WIDOW, WHITE RUSSIAN

BY MUHAREM BAZDULJ

Palilula

Translated by Jamie Clegg

S he was beautiful and instantly reminded me of Nastasya Filippovna from Dostoevsky's *The Idiot*. She had blond hair and dark eyes. She acted like she was thirty years old and, as it turned out, was exactly that. She looked a bit older than she was, in fact, but not in a bad way. She had a kind of alluring maturity, an aura that said that she hadn't been a kid for a while. Said her name was Nađa. I wondered what she was doing at my apartment door.

It was spring of 2014. I was forty-six years old, freshly divorced, and freshly unemployed. Fortunately, I still had an apartment. I'd recently read in some book how *apartments on the ground level exude a peculiar loneliness*. I'd bought the apartment on the ground floor, at the very end of Palmotićeva Street, across from the Institute for Mental Health—which taxi drivers referred to as the *loony bin*—more than twenty years earlier while the war in Bosnia was still going on and Serbia was still under sanctions. It was relatively cheap—that's how it was in those times—and apartments on the ground floor were always the cheapest. It was important for me to be in the center of the city, so living on the ground floor didn't bother me. I even enjoyed that feeling of *peculiar loneliness* I already carried with me. It wasn't so bad that the apartment came with it.

She said that Nikolina, a friend of hers, had given her my address. They'd met at some diplomatic reception, then saw each other a few days later at a café. She asked Nikolina if she knew anyone in Belgrade who could help her with an investigation. It had something to do with Bosnia, so Nikolina recommended me, since I'm from Bosnia, know half of Belgrade, have good connections, and am generally an okay guy.

In 1993, the same year I bought the apartment, Nađa's father was killed. That's what she told me as she came into the room and sat on the armchair I offered her. I sat directly across from her. She said that she was born in Rudo, a little town in Bosnia along the border with Serbia. The place is only known for the fact that the first brigade of Tito's partisan army was founded there on Stalin's birthday in 1941. That was the twenty-first of December. However, after Tito's break with Stalin in 1948, the date was subsequently changed to the twenty-second of December in our history books.

Nađa's father, as it turned out, was a Bosnian Muslim, while her mother was originally a White Russian. Her father was a senior official during the Communist era, a true Yugoslav. When the war started, he was certain that nothing bad would happen to him. Still, a Serbian paramilitary unit raided their house in Rudo and took Nađa's father. For years he was missing until they found his remains in a mass grave ten years after the war.

Not long after they took her father, Nađa and her mother escaped to Montenegro, where Nađa's uncle lived. Several months later, they left for Sweden. Nađa finished high school and college there, gained citizenship, and now worked at the Swedish embassy in Belgrade. She'd been here almost a year and a half and loved it—it felt good to return to her childhood culture. And then, a month ago, as she was jogging through Tašmajdan Park, she nearly froze with terror. On a bench, in the area of the park closest to St. Mark's Church, she had noticed an old man reading a newspaper. He looked familiar. Then she realized: it was the commander of the group that had taken her father.

When I asked if she was sure, she completely lost it. I said it was hard for me to believe that after twenty-two years she could clearly remember a face she'd only seen once. She looked at me contemptuously and said that in those twenty-two years there wasn't a single day or night that his face wasn't the first thing she thought of when she woke up in the morning, and the last thing she thought of before falling asleep.

I asked her if she knew anything about him—his name or something. She said she only knew that he wasn't from Rudo but from somewhere in Serbia. Some said he was from Priboj, and some said he was from Raška. They called him Vojvoda, which was an aristocratic title often used for Chetnik leaders. I told her to describe him, and she spoke slowly but without pausing, as if she had repeated these sentences to herself over and over: "He was wearing white sneakers, light-blue jeans, and a black T-shirt. He's balding a little in front, but barely—you could say he's got a high forehead. Big brown eyes. A large nose speckled with capillaries, like an alcoholic. Clean-shaven. Above his left eyebrow there's a deep scar in the shape of a rotated parenthesis. He's slim, doesn't have a belly. Medium height. On his right forearm there's a tattoo of a cross." Then she fell silent. I asked her if she remembered tattoos and scars from the time she first saw him, when they took her dad. "Of course I remember," she said. "I remember everything."

I looked at this young woman who every day remembered the trauma she'd experienced when she was only nine. They took her father and killed him around the same time I had returned from America. Actually, it was my second return. The first time I went to America was in 1987 when I got a scholarship to improve my English and finish high school there. I returned, served in the army, then enrolled in law school in Sarajevo. I went to America from a normal, healthy country, and in just two years—one of which I spent in America, the other in the army—the country started to fall apart and it seemed like there was no hope for it. In the spring of 1990 I went back to America, and this time I enrolled in a sociology program at Vassar College in Poughkeepsie, New York. Everything there was great, while everything in my homeland was already seriously going to shit.

And although both my mother and father are Serbs—respectable and wealthy people, the director of a bank and a lawyer—I didn't feel like a Serb until the beginning of the war. I had a Yugoslav passport, I served in the Yugoslav army, I stood for the Yugoslav anthem, and I felt proud of seeing Yugoslavia's flag fly when our athletes won medals.

Then the country started to fall apart and everyone did some fucked-up shit. Serbs made up the country's majority, so most likely did the most shit, but they were far from being the only ones. In America, however, and especially since the siege of Sarajevo began, a consensus was reached that Serbs were guilty for all of it, at least judging by newspapers and TV reports.

Nađa's father was definitely killed by Serbs. I asked her what she wanted from me. She said that she wanted to find and identify Vojvoda so she could send that information to the prosecutor's office in Sarajevo. Allegedly, there was an investigation that'd been open for a while but they didn't have enough information to indict anyone. Nađa took out a purple 500-euro bill that the local punks call a Gaddafi because the Libyan dictator supposedly had a weakness for them, and would hand them out to waiters and musicians when he was in a good mood. She asked if that would be enough. I nodded my head and asked if she wanted a receipt. She smiled for the first time since she entered my apartment.

"No need. You look like a trustworthy guy." She took out a business card and set it on top of the bill. "Here's my number and e-mail address. Call me when you find anything out, but don't mention any details except in person. When you call, I'll come over." Then she stood and slowly walked out.

How did she feel when she thought her father was still alive? I remember I was completely unhinged when the siege of Sarajevo began because I didn't know what was happening with my parents. But thanks to connections and money, they were able to reach Belgrade by the summer of 1992. It's not that as Serbs they had any major problems in Sarajevo until then, but there was suspicion and provocation. In any case, they were lucky to have escaped the city in time. Still, a lot of our relatives, like many of my schoolmates, stayed in Sarajevo.

In the fall of 1992, after two years of being an excellent student, I practically gave up on my schooling in America. I almost never went to lectures. I incessantly watched television and read newspapers, and at school I fought with colleagues who repeated stereotypes about "Balkan savages" without thinking. Ironically, I only confirmed those stereotypes with my aggression.

I drank a lot, and the American prices for alcoholic beverages took a chunk out of my student budget. In the spring of 1993, I realized there was no way I could pass my exams, nor did I feel particularly motivated to take them. When I called my family in Belgrade, it seemed like they were good: Dad was working again in some bank, though not as a manager, and

Mom had succeeded in getting a job in the office of one of Belgrade's best attorneys. I knew that they'd managed to get most of their savings out of Sarajevo. I decided to return to Belgrade—if it's possible to *return* to a city you've never lived in, only knew from a few short visits, and knew as the capital of your home country, Yugoslavia, which no longer exists.

And yes, my parents told me that I had fucked up by coming back, but on some level they were also happy. I guess that's why they gave me the cash for this apartment. They were living in a big apartment in New Belgrade that had enough rooms to make one mine, but they understood that at the age of twenty-five and after three years of living on another continent, I just couldn't share an apartment with them. They gave me enough pocket money to live off of. Out of love for them, I enrolled in law school in Belgrade, though I had even less motivation to study here than I did in America.

For the next five or six years, I mostly fucked around. I found a couple of buddies, witty and smart types who, because of the general breakdown of society, had given up on their ambitions, studies, and careers. We'd get together at my apartment, listen to music, drink, and smoke. If I was alone, I would read, watch films, and wander through the city. Near my apartment, on Kosovska Street, there was a movie archive where they showed classic old films two or three times a day. I loved black-and-white crime films with Humphrey Bogart and Robert Mitchum the most, but my absolute favorite was Jean-Pierre Melville's *Le Samouraï* with Alain Delon. I got a big poster of the film, framed and hammered it to a wall in the living room. I often strolled through that strange district of Palilula that leads from the city center toward distant suburbs. My favorite walk was from George Washington to Roosevelt Street. I'd go, say, past the Botanical Garden, then walk down November

29th Street, amble all the way to Pančevo Bridge, turn toward Bogoslovija, then walk down to New Cemetery, cut through Liberators of Belgrade Cemetery, pass through Professorial Colony, through all those beautiful houses where intellectuals and White Russians who escaped the October Revolution lived during the time of the Kingdom of Yugoslavia, then up through Dalmatinska and back home.

There were, of course, women. I mainly indulged in brief and rather meaningless relationships, mostly with younger female students. At some point my parents realized that I wasn't studying or doing anything, so they decided to try to discipline me by withholding money. It was sometime in the fall of 1998, a few months before the NATO bombing of Serbia began. I had just started working as a night guard. Some guy had a private pharmacy on March 27th Street near Palilula Market. Drug addicts had broken into the store a few times looking for narcotics and strong painkillers. He needed a guy on duty from midnight until eight in the morning. It was perfect for me: I usually read at night and slept in the morning anyway.

I bought a gun just to be safe, but no one actually tried to break in once they saw the light on and a guy inside. In February of 1999, I met Katarina there. She pounded on the door; she urgently needed Voltaren suppositories. Her son had a fever, and she couldn't get anything else to work. Even though I wasn't the pharmacist on duty and it wasn't in my job description to sell drugs, I gave her a box. Two nights later, she came to thank me. I invited her for a coffee, and so it began.

She was four years older than me, her son was in third grade, she was divorced. We married in November of 2000, right after Slobodan Milošević fell from power and things were returning to normalcy. I was thirty-two and went back to college. It just suddenly made sense. Katarina's husband had left her with a large apartment on Cvijićeva Street after the divorce. When we got married I moved in with her and rented my ground-floor apartment to students. Katarina was a dentist and earned good money, so she supported us financially while I, through some of my parents' connections, got a job as a lawyer in one of the few banks that were still state-owned. The pay was good, and the position was mostly protocol. I barely lasted five years there.

Katarina supported my idea to open a *kafana*. I found a perfect place near the pharmacy I'd worked at as a night guard. I'd sit in the *kafana*, sipping a White Russian cocktail, imitating the hero of the only film from the nineties that I loved the way I loved old black-and-white films: *The Big Lebowski*. The *kafana* did quite well for some time. I enjoyed being the owner, flirting with girls who came in, treating them to drinks and all that, but I tried not to engage in full-on adultery. But then I hired Anđela as a waitress. Anđela was twenty-five and I was forty-five, but the age difference didn't bother her. And stereotypically—in the middle of a midlife crisis—I was madly in love again, and this infatuation fucked up both my business and my marriage. Less than a year later, the *kafana* was bankrupt, Katarina had left me, and in the end I left Anđela too.

More than twenty years after I bought the apartment on the ground floor, and fifteen years after I started renting it out to students, I went back there. I didn't know what I would do with myself. I had some savings because I kept the money various tenants paid me over the years in an account that I mostly hadn't touched.

It was at that time that Nađa appeared at the door. After she left the apartment I looked at her business card. At the top was Sweden's coat of arms, below was her name, then farther down, *Embassy of the Kingdom of Sweden*, while her number and e-mail address were at the very bottom. I was considering where to start.

My friend Mirko was a journalist specializing in stories about war and war crimes; I could ask him if he knew who came from Serbia to run riot in Rudo and thereabouts. At one point while owning the *kafana*, one of my bartenders was from Priboj. His name was Petar. He was too young to remember the war, but Priboj is a small place, and he'd know who to see about a guy by the nickname of Vojvoda.

Mirko didn't answer the phone, so I called Petar. He still worked as a bartender, but now in some neighborhood near Bogoslovija. His shift had just started and the bar wasn't crowded, so if I had time, he suggested, it'd be best that I come over right away for a drink.

Like he'd said, the *kafana* was practically empty. Petar was listening to Leonard Cohen. I sat down at the bar and ordered a whiskey. I started in a roundabout way, saying I'd recently heard from a high school friend now living in Canada that he hangs out with some guy from Priboj supposedly called Vojvodić. Petar frowned and said he'd never heard of any Vojvodić from Priboj. I said maybe I remembered wrong, maybe that's not his last name, maybe they just call him Vojvoda. Petar burst into laughter: "Hey, now that's a different thing. There's a guy in Priboj who everyone calls Vojvoda, but fat chance he ever went to Canada." I started asking questions, but the answers disappointed me. It turned out he was some village idiot, a slow kind of guy who lived on charity. He was called Vojvoda because before the war, during the rise of nationalism, he used to sing Chetnik songs in the street.

That couldn't be the guy who had taken Nađa's father. I lit a cigarette, and as I put the lighter back in my pocket, I felt my phone vibrate. A message from Mirko. He'd been doing an interview outside the city in Novi Sad earlier and hadn't been able to answer. Now he was on his way to Belgrade and hadn't been able to grab a beer. *Great*, I texted back and sent him the address of where I was. As time passed, the *kafana* slowly filled. Petar had less time to chat, but when I realized he couldn't help me I wasn't really up for talking anyway. I waited for Mirko, turning to the door every time I heard someone walk in. They were the typical early evening *kafana* customers from the edge of the city. Like in one of those Springsteen songs, these were people who'd lost something that was the center of their lives: sometimes a woman, sometimes family, sometimes work, sometimes an apartment—sometimes all of it at once—and they were just looking to get through the day. They bet on soccer, bummed cigarettes, drank the cheapest *rakija* only to pass the time faster, until it was time to go to sleep, and after hundreds and thousands of these days and nights, it came time to die.

At first glance, Mirko looked like a regular at one of these joints: unshaven, balding, with an eternal cigarette in his hand. Disheveled clothes. He was, however, one of the most reputable journalists in Serbia. He had been a brilliant medical student at the time the war broke out. In the summer of 1992, during the break between his third and fourth years, and after he'd taken all of his exams, he was hired as a fixer for foreign journalists reporting from Bosnia. He never went back to school, or even to his old life. The horrors he witnessed urged him toward a search for truth through writing. He became a journalist, focusing on writing about the war, war crimes, criminal privatization, and transitional theft.

He was very skinny and could drink three, four liters of beer without seeming drunk. It wasn't clear to me how he could hold that much liquid in his body. He was on his third pint when I asked him about a guy named Vojvoda who ran around Rudo and that area.

"You know what," he said, "that's the thing about the war in Bosnia. It was so awful that there were some places where, for no reason whatsoever, thirty or forty people were killed, but your automatic reaction was to say that nothing notable happened there since in neighboring cities hundreds, even thousands, were killed. Same with Rudo: shit happened there, but much less compared to Foča or Višegrad. But I think I remember a few accounts of the guy you're thinking of. He ran a small unit that mainly targeted prominent rich people who sometimes managed to survive because of their connections with local police and military at the beginning of the war, in small towns where there wasn't any direct armed conflict. They would pay money for protection, and it would keep them safe for a few months. In addition to Rudo, I think he also showed up in Čajniče and Trebinje, all during the summer of 1992. By early fall he was gone. He was probably a careful guy, stole as much as he could, then went back to Serbia to milk it as long as possible. Yeah, he was definitely from Serbia, somewhere close to the border, like southeastern Bosnia or eastern Herzegovina, but I don't know how you singled out Priboj and Raška—it could've easily been some other place. I think he had one of those generic names like loads of other Serbs—our 'John Smith,' if you know what I mean."

When I asked him if it was possible that Vojvoda was in Belgrade these days, Mirko said of course it was possible; people from all over Serbia were moving to Belgrade en masse.

We parted ways around ten in the evening. I was completely plastered; he looked like he had been drinking tea the whole time. On the way out he said, "You know, if you want to find this guy, the best thing would be to check out Romanija, a hole-in-the-wall near the Pančevo Bridge run by Ranko—they call him 'Leopard.' He did five years in prison for crimes around

Rogatica. A lot of people who fought in that area hang around there. Someone there's gotta know him. But be careful, those guys are fucked up. And take money to buy them a few rounds of *rakija*. That's the easiest way to loosen them up."

On the way home, I went to KGB for one more drink. It was a *kafana* near my apartment named after the Russian secret service, an appropriate symbol of the Serbs' ambivalent attitude toward everything Russian and Communist. With that thought in mind, I ordered a White Russian. I was resolved to only have one. It wouldn't bode well for me to be hungover tomorrow.

My life would certainly be different if I'd been rational enough to stop drinking when I should have. And unfortunately, KGB is one of those *kafanas* that's open as long as there's a customer. So I stuck to the bar until four in the morning, drinking at least five cocktails too many.

It took me ten minutes to drag myself home, then I slept for ten hours. I woke up around half past two in the afternoon. A cocktail hangover is fucking rough, but when a man gets enough sleep everything's better. Anyway, it was unlikely that Romanija would even open before four or five in the evening, and it was highly unlikely that the types I was looking for would come in before nightfall.

I first went to the Stara Hercegovina restaurant to eat some veal soup, *pljeskavica* with *kajmak*, and *šopska* salad. That combination raises the dead. I had to be somewhat fresh: in order to gain the trust of the old drunkards there, I'd have to drink too.

At six thirty p.m. I was at Romanija. The *kafana* was in semidarkness because only one flickering bulb illuminated it. Inside were five tables, two of which were occupied. At each sat a guy in his sixties. On the tables were checkered tablecloths and ashtrays. I sat down and ordered *šljivovica*, a plum brandy.

The fat, middle-aged waitress looked grotesque in a mini-skirt. As she came toward me with a tray in her hands, one of the guys smacked her ass. She acted like she didn't even notice. Another guy stared into the darkness through the window. No one here seemed particularly communicative.

After drinking two brandies alone, it turned out my lighter wasn't working, so I went to beg a light off the guy who had unsuccessfully attempted to sexually harass a pudgy woman. I figured he was giving communication a wild shot. The whole time, the other guy stared off into the dark like a zombie.

This guy handed me his lighter without a word. When I lit the cigarette he motioned for me to join him at his table, again without a word. He waved at the waitress and said: "Give us two *rakijas* on his tab." I nodded my head. He asked me why I was in the bar. Said he'd never seen me before.

He had a strong Bosnian accent, which gave me an idea: I told him, "I'm Sarajevan; the war started while I was a student in America, I lived there a long time and recently came back. Some friends from high school told me about a graduation reunion, and I only then learned that my best childhood friend had been killed in the war. His name was Bogdan and he died as a Serbian soldier somewhere around Rudo, so I'm interested in knowing more about his death, since no one in our class is in contact with his family. You know how it is in Sarajevo: before the war we were all together—Serbs, Croats, Muslims, Jews, you know—and after the war, everything fell apart." I made up a bunch of lies from a kernel of truth, hoping it wouldn't sound like complete bullshit.

The guy started giving me shit. "Why didn't you come back from America to fight with your people?"

My problem with the war was that they were *all* my people; Nađa was surely more *my people* than this idiot or Vojvoda, but

I had no intention of saying that out loud. I was even okay with him giving me shit—at least then I knew he believed me.

My interlocutor motioned for the waitress to get us two more *rakijas*, then casually nudged the zombie: "Hey, were any of our guys in Rudo?"

The other guy was silent for a minute, like he didn't even register the question. Then, without even taking his eyes off the window facing into the dark, he replied: "Stevo was there, with some guy called Vojvoda."

At first, my guy couldn't remember who Stevo was. I talked nonsense about how I didn't know if Bogdan had a tombstone, how we'd like to put together some money to get him a cross—maybe even write up a story since we wanted to publish a booklet about our class for the reunion. After another round of *rakija*, the guy murmured that I obviously had money for drinks, since stonemasons and printers didn't work for cheap, so maybe I could jog his memory. I gave him fifty euros, and he immediately remembered that Stevo's last name was Perić, then asked the waitress for his number. We had another drink.

In the meantime, three other people came into the *kafana* and sat at an open table. They called the guy from my table to join them. As he stood up he said, "You have what you came for, so you should get out of here. If you call Stevo, tell him Ranko *the Leopard* gave you the number."

I was tipsy, but not enough to fall asleep easily, so I returned to KGB. I smiled a little to myself for not realizing that the guy who'd slapped the waitress's ass owned the joint. Him asking her for Stevo's number came back to me. It seemed like he was one of those old-fashioned types who didn't even own a cell phone. I decided to try something crazy. I took out my phone and wrote a message to Stevo: *Hey compadre, I'm sitting here with Ranko the Leopard. He gave me your number and says you know Vojvoda. I haven't seen him for thirty years, and we've known each other since we were kids. Give me his contact info if you can.*

I didn't even finish my first White Russian when his reply came: *I don't see him much anymore, but I know his wife owns a flower shop on Ilije Garašanina Street.*

My hands started to shake. It was nearby, and not just near me now, but near Tašmajdan Park where Nađa had seen him. I paid for the cocktail and headed for the street. I knew it was too late and there was only a slim chance of the shop being open, but I wanted to see where it was. The street wasn't too long and not very close to the cemetery, so I doubted there were many other florists.

Sure enough, there it was near the intersection with Takovska Street: a tiny, inconspicuous flower shop with *Owned by Đorđe Jovanović* written on the glass door. I stood there and laughed aloud. Ah, the patriarchy, I thought. This one wouldn't allow his wife to formally own the shop if his life depended on it.

Walking slowly to the apartment, I wrote a message to Mirko: *Could our "John Smith" be Đorđe Jovanović?*

He replied within a few seconds: *Fuck if I know. I could swear that was his name, but if you wrote Jovan Đorđević, I'd probably tell you the same thing.*

Normally I didn't make cocktails at home, but I had a bottle of whiskey handy. As I set a glass on the table in front of me, I saw Nađa's business card. Warmed by alcohol, I texted her: *There's been a little progress in the investigation. See you tomorrow?*

She responded in less than five minutes: *Are you in Palmotićeva? I'm nearby, and can come right away.*

Without even thinking I responded: *Come over.*

I lit a cigarette and for the first time started thinking about what I really wanted to say to her. I wouldn't tell her everything, not yet. I'd tell her I had a lead on a guy from Vojvoda's unit, and explain a bit about how I investigate, tell her a few stories.

The cigarette hadn't even burned out when I heard knocking on the door. I opened it. She was smiling, had obviously been out, and was a little drunk. She looked younger to me than the last time, in a short skirt and heels with a little too much makeup.

She came in and I offered her a drink. She nodded. I handed her a glass, she took a good long sip, and then she looked at me. "So, did you find him?"

I lit another cigarette. "Not yet, but I'm close." I told her what I'd been up to, leaving out a few details. I didn't tell her I already had the number of a guy in Vojvoda's unit, but that I was going to get it.

When I was done, she dropped her head. I thought she'd fallen asleep, that she was comatose from drinking, but then I noticed her shoulders shaking. She was crying. It wasn't like I couldn't really console her from a professional distance. I approached her, kneeled in front of her chair, and took her hand.

"Don't cry," I said.

She abruptly stood up, and I stood too. She hugged me and mumbled something I didn't understand, probably thanking me. I stroked her hair, felt on my cheek that her cheek was wet, and then suddenly, and a little surprisingly, that her lips and tongue were too. We kissed, and I realized that *this* was why I'd called her.

We stumbled to the door that divided the living room and bedroom, where we fell onto the bed. The rest is history.

When I woke up, it was still early morning, but she was already awake. She acted completely sober, as if she hadn't drunk anything the night before. She was lying at the end of the bed, flipping through a book. *It's easy being young*, I thought to myself. "Want coffee?" I asked.

"Sure," she said, so I got up to make coffee.

When I came back, she'd already gotten up. She wasn't fully dressed, just wrapped in the shirt she was wearing the night before.

She took a sip of coffee. "You know, last night I wasn't myself. My emotions got the best of me. Like everything came full circle. Like my dad rose up from the grave to tell me everything would be okay."

I put my index finger to her lips. "I understand everything," I said.

She stayed for another half hour. Told me to let her know if I learned anything new, and that she'd tell her mother nothing until it was certain. "You know," she said, "my mother hasn't really lived her life since that day. She's not herself anymore; she's not a person, not even a mother; she's just a widow, a widow dressed in black."

At the door, she asked me if I needed more money. I said what she'd given me was already too much.

When she left I went back to bed. I was tired and thrilled. I lay my head on the pillow that still smelled of her, and slept until two in the afternoon.

When I woke up, I went to Stara Hercegovina for lunch. I didn't exactly know what to do next. I needed additional proof of identity, as well as another witness, before calling my friends in the police department and prosecutor's office so they could arrest this guy. Now I was even less in the mood to reveal his identity to Nađa; it was more important to me to make sure he went to prison. If I just told her who he was, the rest would fall on her, and she was a foreign citizen who had no idea how the system in Serbia functioned. She'd already suffered enough.

After lunch, I went back home, then read about trials for war crimes on the Internet: the Hague, Belgrade, and Sarajevo.

I didn't dare dream too much about Nađa, but I wasn't afraid to fantasize about how grateful she'd be if Vojvoda was thrown in jail. I caught myself playing psychoanalyst, thinking that, because she lost her father so young, she certainly had a weakness for older men.

I sipped some whiskey, and around ten I was drunk enough to send her a message about how great the previous night had been. She didn't reply. I kept drinking, and around one I was intoxicated enough to go to sleep.

When the phone woke me in the morning, I hoped it was Nađa. It wasn't; it was Mirko. "Hey man, you know something I don't know?" he yelled into the receiver.

"Mirko, dude, I just woke up. I have no idea what you're talking about."

He laughed. "C'mon, take a shower and wake up. In half an hour it'll be all over the Internet. Early this morning at Tašmajdan Park near St. Mark's Church, someone shot Đorđe Jovanović. I asked around a bit. Turns out his old friends call him Vojvoda."

And before Mirko hung up, in a tiny fraction of a second, shorter than the one between the moment I felt that her cheek and then her lips were wet, I realized that although I'd said nothing to her, everything she'd needed was in my phone. I realized that I'd never hear from or see Nađa again. And I realized that I should stop drinking White Russians. Even without them, I'd think of her too often.

REGARDING THE FATHER

By Vladimir Arsenijević

Topčiderska Zvezda

Translated by Ena Selimović

Whenever one body exerts a force on a second body, the second body simultaneously exerts a force equal in magnitude and opposite in direction on the first body.

—Isaac Newton

"We goin'?" I say.

"Yeah, let's go," Zoe responds from the front passenger seat.

I listen to her quickened breathing in the dark. Then I put my seat belt on. I turn the key in the ignition. The car rumbles. The headlights switch on automatically. As the two powerful beams illuminate the tree-lined plane before us, the ancient trees seem stunned, as if caught in some wrongdoing.

Before we set out, I look at Zoe again. I raise a questioning eyebrow. That almost always makes her smile. But, apparently, not now.

Zoe doesn't return my look. She stares straight ahead. Her forehead is coated with droplets of sweat. Beneath her white shirt, her chest rises and falls visibly in the darkness.

"Okay," I sigh. I lower the handbrake, then move my foot off the brake pedal. I slowly press on the gas and release the clutch. "Then let's go," I say.

From a poorly lit side path, we drive onto a freshly paved road with a line of evenly spaced streetlights that border the northern end of Hyde Park on the slopes of Topčider.

It's late and cold. An easterly wind is whistling, and a sharp icy rain is falling diagonally. Except for the occasional superenthusiastic runner on the trail winding through the small woods, there is nobody around anywhere. Even the private security guards, tasked with protecting all those mansions in the vicinity (which have for decades alternated between various generations and members of the political, economic, and entertainment mainstream), are holed up in their poorly heated cabins.

In the hollow silence, we drive toward Topčiderska Zvezda. Even though it's only early November, the roundabout is all stacked up in tacky Christmas and New Year's decorations. It shines in front of us like a lone galaxy in the desolation of a dark and cold universe. The two life-size wire giraffes, which have stood in the very center for years, have now sunk entirely into darkness. There were once three, but then one was mowed down by a drunk driver. The remaining giraffes have stood there in solitude ever since. When thick vines cover them in the spring, they give the impression of being almost imposing. Now, though, in November, it is as if they are there by mistake, like lost characters in the wrong fable. While one of them, the smaller one, appears to be grazing calmly, the other has lifted her head on her long neck and with pricked ears scans the surroundings in unending concentration. *There's no relaxing*, they seem to be telling us as we enter the gravitational field of Topčiderska Zvezda. There's no relaxing; someone always has to be on alert in this fucked-up city.

We followed him for days. And we just loved it. Well, at first, anyway.

We didn't argue. We slept well. Even sex became more frequent and passionate than usual. Every morning, after a mutual orgasm, sitting over Zoe's ginger tea and my Turkish coffee, we made plans and delegated different tasks to one another. Then we methodically went about executing them. Zoe and I had finally been living a life worth living. A life that seemed to emerge directly from a very specific pulp subgenre that we both simply adored. We were self-proclaimed heroines of a real, bona fide lesbian noir detective story.

Childish? Fuck if we cared.

We followed him all day long, literally. Wherever he went, you could bet we were sniffing around after him. From this point in time, it seems like a real miracle to me, considering all our goddamn amateurism, that he didn't notice us. But he didn't, no. The fact that I'm now behind the wheel, that Zoe's in the passenger seat, and that the load's in the trunk—that, in other words, everything turned out just as we had planned—this is evidence that miracles do happen. Well, sometimes at least.

It was not too long before we felt like we knew his routine. Each morning around half past eight he would leave his mansion in the Dedinje neighborhood—that paradise for the nouveau riche fuckers and sons of bitches alike—sitting in the back of a shiny black car with tinted windows. The silent driver would take him to the headquarters of his construction company in New Belgrade. Other than for an occasional business meeting or lunch, the car would leave the company garage around seven in the evening and head back to Dedinje. But it didn't go toward Tolstoy Street. Instead, it would continue straight toward the Pink Television building where he would pick up his wife who had just wrapped up her daily TV show. Together, they would then go off shopping or to some kind of cheesy social event with politicians or whatever, or to some sort of reception. Or maybe to dinner. Then finally back home to Tolstoy Street. Occasionally drunk. And bickering or arguing more often than not.

Whatever the tabloids write about them, their lives appeared remarkably uneventful to us, their paths beaten and well worn out.

This discovery depressed Zoe and me quite a bit. To the point that we were ready to abandon everything. There didn't seem to be a single crack in the routine of our prey. But then one night, just as we got into a vicious argument in the car, parked not far from his mansion, he slipped past us, dressed from head to toe in fancy sports gear. That's how Zoe and I discovered, to the eternal shame of all lesbian detectives ever, that our prey runs three or four rounds around Hyde Park every Wednesday around midnight. And sometimes on Fridays too. And always with the tiny headphones of his MP3 player implanted deep in his ears.

We felt stupid beyond belief to have missed this for so long. But we quickly made a decision: we'd come up behind him while he stretched after running. And we would easily overpower him. Using the darkness and discretion offered by the Topčider woods, we'd knock him out and stuff him into the trunk. And then we'd drive to the darker recesses of Košutnjak Park to do away with him in peace and quiet.

My name is Maja, BTW. From a very young age, they filled my head with stories about how my name relates to spring. To the month of May, precisely. Maja, or Maia, they chirped, is the Roman goddess of fields and produce associated with nature's awakening and rebirth.

My mother was a mean-spirited woman who taught me

many false things. And so it took me awhile to independently uncover that the truth about Maia—like the truth about many other things—was totally different than what I'd been told. I was quite relieved when I learned that Maia was no hormone-driven psycho goddess who frolicked in a white gown on freshly bloomed fields weaving flower wreaths, but actually one of seven mountain nymphs—a dangerous bitch, if you will. Titan's daughter who fucked Zeus in the darkness of a cave and gave birth to Hermes, god of thieves, merchants, and orators.

As for Zoe, her name means "life" in Greek. That's what Hellenized Jews, translated from the Hebrew *havvah*, called the biblical Eve. It was only logical that someone entirely un-burdened from any history and free from it, like Eve, would appeal so strongly to Zoe, who wanted more than anything to free herself from the weight of her own past. To the extent that she changed her previous name to the one that, she felt, suited her much more. And thus became Zoe.

And now we can safely make a great leap over time and space to this very moment when the two of us, Zoe and I, the dynamic duo of lesbian-detective-avenger-murderesses, are driving in our little Japanese car through the Topčiderska Zvezda roundabout with a heavy load in the trunk.

They've taught you Newton's laws, I assume? They definitely have, you've just forgotten. You don't remember those kinds of things. What's it good for? you think. But you're wrong. Take Newton's second law, for instance. Or the law of force. Owing to the fact that the total mass of our car is now greater than usual, and by about two hundred pounds of male body weight which, bound with rope and tape, is jerking violently in the trunk right now, its rate of acceleration is slower than usual. Because of that, this dizzying movement around a quarter of the Topčiderska Zvezda roundabout is taking forever.

I'll use that time to tell you how Zoe and I met.

It was seven years ago, during an open mic poetry festival at an alt-cultural center in Belgrade where I performed among a crowd of comparable losers. At the time, presenting myself as a radical poet-performer still seemed exciting to me. I believed passionately in the transformative power of words. My idealism began to fade when I realized that those who fared best at the aforementioned festival were the notorious psychos. And maybe a talentless idiot or two.

That's why I consider it a real wonder that poetry, the thing I progressively lost faith in, eventually brought me something so vital. I mean Zoe, of course. What attracted me, in a word, were her eyes. Enormous and green, with a distinct hazel lining, they looked right at me from the audience during my last performance where I read that long poem dedicated to Pat Califia. When they tried to get me off the stage, I started to resist and cry out against the oppressive heteronormative patriarchy and the impotent militarism that bars a poet even from reading her poem to the end. Only Zoe jumped out of the audience to help me. We fought with the organizers and got wasted together later that night at some dive bar in lower Dorćol. We made out until the crack of dawn in a dark dead-end street that smelled like rotten trash. What can I say? I was beside myself with love and happiness.

What delights me most about Zoe? Basically: *everything*. Our love was and remains a real spectacle. Today, after this many years, I can openly declare that my love for her is eternal. All you women who aren't fortunate enough to get to know Zoe, you don't even realize what you're missing.

Zoe is a privilege. She is, admittedly, also a mystery. Although life with Zoe is not all sunshine and rainbows. Because the past stalks Zoe and breathes down her neck with its rough, putrid breath. Zoe does everything to shake it off, but it isn't easy.

I remember that I read somewhere, Faulkner I think, that the past is never dead. And that more often than not it isn't even the past. Well, that is one big, painful truth. In Zoe's case, at least. The past has inextricably enmeshed itself in her present. Demons grip her constantly and the tightening of their sharp claws inflicts unending pain on her.

Finally, after a lifetime or two, we exit the roundabout and turn into a cozy unlit boulevard. It bores through thick woods to the lower parts of Topčider and on toward the neighborhoods of Banovo Brdo and Košutnjak. In all that darkness and peace and quiet around us, a bout of forceful drumming coming from the trunk startles us both. I can feel Zoe freeze up next to me. The load then jerks even more forcefully than before and the car suddenly reels to the side. "*U pičku materinu.* Motherfucker," I murmur, searching for support in Zoe's gaze.

And Zoe? She just shakes from the feet up. Like a volcanic eruption. This also happens in accordance with some law of physics, though no Newton can be of any help here anymore. "Stop now, please," she says through clenched teeth. "Here, stop here."

Zumreta.

That unusual name was, for a long time, the only tangible information Zoe had about her past and her origins. She learned of it at the age of sixteen, from her foster parents. Zumreta was, apparently, the name of her mother. She also learned that she was born somewhere in Bosnia during the war, in 1993. They couldn't tell her much more than that. But even that was enough to tear her apart. Truth crumbled noisily before her eyes. When it settled, she discovered that not much remained.

Nothing but scattered fragments. Unsubstantiated, unreliable, impermanent stories.

Some years later, however, her fragmented knowledge was largely validated and significantly supplemented, during the trial popularly known as "The Case of the Women at the Korzo Motel."

A good part of the testimonies of two female witnesses under protection codes BP-76 and RN-72 focused on a certain girl that both witnesses had shared a cell with in a female prison in the Republika Srpska territory. She was called Zumreta.

The mere mention of that name was enough to attract Zoe's complete attention. She almost fainted when she learned that Zumreta had already been very well into her pregnancy when she was brought there. A certain unnamed Republika Srpska army soldier or corporal or officer had pulled her sometime earlier out of the notorious Korzo Motel and had held her captive in an apartment for several months. But when she became pregnant, he simply disposed of her and left her to rot in the prison.

According to the testimonies of the two witnesses, Zumreta gave birth prematurely, maybe a month after arriving at the prison. She had a beautiful girl. But three or four days later (at this point, the statements diverge somewhat), the child was viciously seized from the cell. Two days after that, Zumreta was also taken away. And she was never seen again.

Only much later would the witnesses get wind of two opposing versions of her ending: that she threw herself, as one claimed, or that she was on the contrary thrown, as claimed by another, through a window during one of the nightly "interrogations."

It took quite some time before another significant piece of information came up about Zoe's mother. Half a decade later, precisely. Two years ago almost to this very day, a confessional article entitled "Cries from Korzo Motel" appeared in a popular national weekly, signed by the well-known and quite infamous journalist M.N. She was then quickly fading in the oncology department at the Clinical Center in Belgrade. So this text can be seen as her attempt to redeem a life filled with political subservience, an extreme betrayal of the profession, and all sorts of other improprieties. This unusual and unexpected testimony on the systematic rape and sexual slavery of Bosniak women during the war in Bosnia and Herzegovina complemented and shed light on what the public had only heard about from the women at the Korzo Motel.

The text was published, almost simultaneously, by several regional media outlets. It also circulated for quite a while on social media networks and was lauded, disputed, and ignored in equal measure. But since the journalist M.N., "due to a serious illness," was first totally unavailable and then passed away quickly thereafter, the circumstances around the text's publication added the necessary dose of mystery to the whole thing and it stayed in the public eye for quite a long time.

We read the text together, Zoe and I. Words fail me every time I try to describe the look on her face when we spotted the name on the page: *Zumreta*. Followed this time by a surname: *Alispahić*. According to M.N., the story of that particular young girl—Zumreta Alispahić—begins in the early summer of 1992, when the armed local Serbs began to wreak terror on Bosniak locals in her village. One night they broke into the Alispahić home and, after a brief altercation with Zumreta's father, shot both of her parents right in front of her. *Everything moves fast*, the journalist contended. *Much faster than one thinks. People are sacks of blood, flesh, and bones, you attack them with a bullet, knife, or bayonet and they fall apart, dissolving into nothing, like deflated balloons. Nothing. People are nothing and death is nothing.*

Zumreta Alispahić screamed for a long time. She trembled, huddled in a corner of the room. Much later, she was taken, along with eight other girls and women, to the Korzo Motel, that bullet-riddled building on the main road not far from the little town. A group of about thirty soldiers was already there. They greeted the women with impatient cries, wild chants, and a burst of uncontrollable, drunken laughter.

On that first night, ten men raped Zumreta Alispahić. At first, she resisted. So they hit her with their fists and thrashed her with their belts and kicked her with their boots until she could fight no more. Covered in blood, she lay motionless while the soldiers took turns.

Out of the nine women brought in the first group to the motel, three did not survive the night. The rape and torture, beatings, mutilations, and random killings continued into the days that followed. When they were not being raped, they were treated like slaves. After a while, each one of them was allocated to one of the soldiers who would occasionally reside there in the Korzo Motel. Except Zumreta Alispahić. She was, as they liked to point out, "at everyone's disposal."

At this point in the narrative the journalist herself makes an appearance. She also swiftly introduces a third character to the story, a certain Neđo, describing him in a few off-hand strokes as a tough, unwavering soldier assigned as her guide during her first visit to the Korzo Motel. He drove her there from Pale, that depressed little mountain town that became the political and military center for Bosnian Serbs during the war.

The journalist's fascination with Neđo is evident through-out the text but it doesn't affect her professional judgment. For instance, she does not fail to notice that he was nowhere near as shocked as she was with what they encountered inside the motel. And she couldn't but notice a gleam in his eye when he caught sight of a dirty, malnourished girl, with bruises, cuts, and burns all over her body.

The journalist spent a greater part of the day interviewing soldiers. But she was strictly forbidden from speaking to the women.

Neđo, on the other hand, was free to roam around. Later in the day he approached a frightened young girl and gave her a shriveled apple that he dug out from the pocket of his uniform. The journalist remembers watching the girl from the corner of her eye as she "grabbed the withered fruit and started devouring it ravenously, like a starving little animal."

When Neđo came to pick her up and led her toward the jeep, she was somehow not surprised to find the little emaciated creature by his side. Hobbled by confusion and fear, the girl was helped into the backseat. On the way back to Pale, M.N. tried talking to her over her seat. She asked for her name repeatedly, but the girl kept turning away and hiding her face.

"Her name is Zumreta," Neđo finally spoke for her.

"Zumreta," the journalist repeated, as if tasting the word, and then turned again to the little girl. "Really?"

"Yes," said Neđo. "Zumreta Alispahić."

The rest of the way, they drove in complete silence through the apocalyptic beauty of Bosnian landscapes razed by the war.

Even though that name—Zumreta Alispahić—stayed with M.N. forever, she confesses that at first she did not think much about the girl's personal fate. As far as she was concerned, Zumreta Alispahić was saved. Neđo had taken her with him, and that was that. "And so I forgot about her," she admits. "Simply because I believed she had more luck than the others."

She supposedly dedicated herself to the more pressing fate of all those women who still remained in the Korzo Motel and claims that she used all the influence she had on a few of the

Bosnian Serb authorities in Pale. "And," she wrote with glowing pride, "things actually started getting better."

The women presumably began receiving food more regularly. They were allowed to gather in the dining room. They were even provided with basic toiletries. Rapes were thinned out significantly. As was the harassment. And the beatings. Days passed without even one of them being killed. And most importantly, the steady stream of "contingents" or "packages" was completely suspended. Then the resettlement began. They carted them away one by one or in small groups. Although the journalist spent many days at the Korzo Motel, she couldn't figure out where they were taking them. The soldiers kept quiet, and the women knew nothing. Only much later would it become known that they were distributing some of them to the local fitness center and some to the construction site of an electrical power station. In both locations the individual and group rapes, torture, and killings continued with undiminished intensity. A number of women were also distributed to a former women's prison. The same one where Zumreta Alispahić would also arrive, although much later.

Several months passed after the journalist had last seen Neđo. But Pale is small and she spent a lot of her days there, so it was truly just a matter of time. When they literally bumped into each other on the street one day, Neđo took the opportunity to invite her over to "his" apartment. She happily agreed and they walked together to a neighborhood at the very edge of town.

Even though it really couldn't have been that long since she had last seen him, she couldn't help but notice certain changes in Neđo. That conceited prince with his long limbs and light step, who once seemed to float high above all the horrors of war, had gone through a striking transformation. *His head was no longer raised on his slender neck in that aristocratic way, but as if it had grown heavier and had become difficult to hold up, so much so that his beard constantly touched the top of his chest. The expression on his face had become suspicious, maybe even evil, his step significantly heavier, and his posture revealed an unending tension. He was quieter than before, but simultaneously more crude and short. But his eyes,* at this point the journalist's words were nearly rapturous, *dear God, those eyes! Intensely green and sad. Like the Neretva River he grew up near.*

Together they went to a one-bedroom apartment on the last floor of a standard three-story building. She was very surprised when Neđo pointedly rang the bell and when, a moment later, a girl opened the door. It took her a second or two to realize who she was. It was Zumreta Alispahić, of course, but more properly nourished and changed so much from that first encounter that M.N. could barely recognize her. Her eyes gleamed and her cheeks charmingly blushed whenever Neđo addressed her. She fulfilled every order at once and without any comment. She was his faithful, obedient slave. That was obvious from the beginning. The journalist, who had recently read a lengthy essay on Stockholm syndrome, had it all quickly figured out. *Or at least I thought that I had it all figured out,* she wrote.

As the evening wore on, Neđo, who tossed back brandy like there was no tomorrow, grew increasingly drunk. He babbled about anything and everything, but the journalist *could barely concentrate on his words.* Instead, she observed how his behavior toward Zumreta was gradually changing. *It was,* she wrote, *increasingly less commanding and increasingly more intimate.* At one point, slapping his knees with his open palm, he called her over to sit on his lap.

(Zumreta obeyed that command, like all the others.)

With affection, in which there was at once something of the father and something of the lover, Neđo enlaced his rough soldier's hands around her thin waist. He kissed her forehead, eyes, and lips, stroked her hair and cheeks.

(Zumreta, so small and slender, bent supplely into his large body.)

Only then did everything become clear, the journalist wrote. She felt dazed as she watched the two lovers, the victim and the perpetrator, exchanging hugs and kisses. *Maybe Stockholm syndrome works in both directions under certain circumstances?* But then disgust overwhelmed her and all she wanted to do was leave.

"Don't worry, I'll help you," she whispered to Zumreta in the kitchen as they waited for the coffee to boil.

In the living room, Neđo, already dead-drunk, was singing a sorrowful *sevdalinka* off key.

Zumreta smiled in response. She reminded M.N. of a stuffed bird. "Why?" she asked.

Zato što će te ubiti, budalo, thought M.N. "I'll save you!" she rasped.

"No one needs to save me from anything. Or save anyone, for that matter," Zumreta calmly replied. "Neđo loves me," she added, arranging the *džezva*, cups, sugar cubes, and Turkish delight onto a tray. And then she turned and looked straight into M.N.'s eyes. "I'm carrying his child."

"I'll save you," the journalist repeated, though this time less forcefully.

The next day M.N. fled, helter-skelter, from Bosnia and Herzegovina. She felt sick, was out of breath, and thought she was going to have a heart attack and die. But her breathing became much easier, she admits, as soon as she crossed the border into Serbia.

Although she never again returned to the war-ravaged Bosnia, she continued to produce, almost mechanically, article after article on *the heroic fight of the persecuted and suffering Serbs against the invasive hordes of Muslim militia.*

And then the war was over. And then the years went by. Maybe she was once somewhat scared of possible consequences, but this changed over time. She grew more relaxed and understood that no punishment awaited her around the corner. But she was riddled with a guilt that kept growing stronger. She would often remember the emptiness in the eyes, the blush on the cheeks, and the broad, happy smile of Zumreta Alispahić. Whenever she dreamed of her, and she dreamed of her often, she inevitably woke up in sweat and tears.

She would discover the rest of the short and unhappy fate of Zumreta Alispahić years later, however, from the court testimonies of the Case of the Women at the Korzo Motel. But sparse evidence collected at the court hearing was not enough for her. She acquired permission to interview the two survivors and thus gathered additional data. Here is what she was able to add to the story.

According to M.N., Neđo brought Zumreta, already far along in her pregnancy, to the women's prison in the early spring of 1993. She was placed in a cell with six other prisoners. She spent her days mostly sitting in the corner and looking out into emptiness. She didn't eat. She spoke little. The other women didn't believe she would, in the state she was in, be able to survive the pregnancy. But she did. She gave birth prematurely on the concrete floor of the cell. She screamed to the heavens and back. Her distraught fellow prisoners strove to help her and they called for help but no one showed up. She bled profusely. They stopped the bleeding with the clothes they had. She gave birth to the most beautiful girl they had ever seen. They all cried together in a big group hug. Zumreta smiled wearily. Two guards entered the cell the following day. They snatched the little sleeping child without a word and took it away. Later they came for Zumreta as well. They took her away too.

"And that's that," both witnesses said.

Indeed, that's that, the journalist echoed, adding: *Zumreta Alispahić was only thirteen years old when she died.*

Zoe and I read "Cries from the Korzo Motel" a million times. Until we knew almost every word by heart. It didn't take us long, on the basis of various hints M.N. had deftly scattered throughout the text, to figure out the identity of that mysterious "Neđo." It was a stroke of pure genius on Zoe's part that brought us to him after she whittled down a long list of suspects to the one and only name: Nenad Pavlović, alias Baboon. He was a well-known member of mainstream society, a successful businessman, a subject of numerous tabloid articles, and a regular guest on various talk shows airing on popular TV stations. We googled him immediately, clicked on the images tab, picked one of many photos, enlarged it, and stared deep into his eyes.

For a few seconds, the world stood still. And then Zoe closed our laptop. We didn't need any further proof.

Her father had looked back at us from the screen with Zoe's eyes. Identically green, with a hazel lining.

And that's that, as M.N. would say.

As for me, I've already said it, and I'll repeat it a hundred times: life with Zoe is not all sunshine and rainbows. Nobody knows this better than I do.

Sometimes Zoe'll sob in her sleep for nights on end. Or for days she'll break things in a rage that simply refuses to pass.

Occasionally she'll turn against herself. Scar after scar on her body, mirroring the ones in her heart.

Zoe can also be unbearably harsh and sarcastic toward me. Sometimes I know she can't help it. The pain Zoe carries in her heart, which has intensified through the course of her entire life, has finally neared the very limits of endurance. It is the kind of pain that nothing but pure exorcism can eliminate.

We had to do something about it as soon as possible.

"Stop here," Zoe speaks quietly through gritted teeth from the passenger seat. "Here," she says, "stop here."

Although she's a full twenty years younger than I am, it's crystal clear who's got the last word in our relationship.

So, I hit the brakes and pull up to the curb. I click on the hazard lights. I switch off the engine. I pull up the handbrake. Who am I, anyway, to object to Zoe's wishes and commands?

For some time we just sit in the dark and listen to the drumming from the trunk.

Zoe then removes a big hammer from the glove compartment. She squeezes it in one hand, placing the palm of the other over its black top.

I simultaneously pull out a large kitchen knife from underneath my seat. The sharp blade flashes in the darkness.

These are the weapons we chose together as a way to bring everything to an end. Quickly but brutally. Just as, we figured, it should be. For vengeance, of course, is best served cold. But on the other hand, it would be stupid for it not to hurt.

Zoe finally turns to me. "We goin'?" she asks. Only then does she, for the first time, actually look at me. From the side, with a questioning, observant glint in her eye.

"Yeah," I respond. And I laugh out loud, involuntarily.

Zoe laughs after me. It's always, I admit, nice to hear her laugh.

"Okay," she nods. "Then let's go."

We open our doors and step outside.

PART III

Once Upon a Time

NEON BLUES

BY DEJAN STOJILJKOVIĆ

The Manjež

Translated by Rachael Daum

I leaned over the terrace railing and puked into the hanging flowerpot. I wiped my mouth with my tie, called the waiter and ordered another double *vinjak*, Serbia's national treasure, created as the Communist version of cognac for the working class.

"Disgusting!" the woman at the next table spat at me. I turned to her with a polite nod and showed her that she could suck it.

My double *vinjak* arrived as my phone rang.

"Mr. Malavrazić?" came a hoarse voice. Hoarse from age, the bottle, or maybe throat cancer, I couldn't be sure.

"That's me," I said, sipping my drink.

"Could you spare a few minutes to discuss a case?"

"Depends on how much time you're asking for ..." Now *my* voice was hoarse. *Vinjak*, of course.

"I know you're busy, but you have to be interested in this."

"I don't *have* to do anything, sir."

"Ma'am."

"Ma'am?"

"Ljudmila Hajji Pešić." Ah. Her husband's family had completed their *hajj*, the Orthodox pilgrimage to the grave of Christ in Jerusalem.

"Your services were recommended to me."

"By whom?"

"Your grandfather."

"My grandfather?"

"You're the grandson of Arsenije Malavrazić, correct?"

"I am."

"Well . . ."

"Ma'am, my grandfather has been dead a long time. It would be difficult for you to get a recommendation from him. Unless you're St. Pete's secretary?"

"It'd be easiest if I explained everything in person."

"All right."

"The Manjež. Tonight at nine."

The line went dead and a mysterious rhythm pulsed from my phone's earpiece. Every beep was another question I asked myself: *Who is this woman? How does she know my grandfather? And how could a long-dead fart recommend . . . me?*

My head hurt from the mystery. I ordered another double *vinjak*.

I went to the Gusan for lunch. It was a good watering hole run by my friend Ernest. It was in the same area where a small, wild village had been founded long ago, where scum like me used to live.

That's where I found Uncle Ljuba, a native of the southern Serbian town Niš, who was solidly in his fifties.

"Malavrazić, I've had it up to here with you," he grumbled as he rolled his tobacco. "Didn't we agree that you'd finish that job for me?"

"What job?"

"The one you didn't finish."

"Didn't we say Wednesday?"

"Today *is* Wednesday."

We munched on *ćevapi* with cheese. The best in Belgrade. We washed them down with a few beers. I made sure not to overdo it since it wouldn't look good to be too drunk in front of a potential client. Just enough to warm me up.

Then a guy walked in and stomped up to our table. He had a big head covered in bad tattoos.

I looked at him, trying to remember where I knew him from. I thought I knew him from somewhere, but it goes like that sometimes—he could have been a taxi driver, a friend from my time in the army, someone I owed money . . .

"Did you touch my wife's ass?" he asked.

"Sure I did," I said. "What do you want? For me to do it again?"

The offended spouse came in. She didn't do anything for me. Black hair, middle-aged, small tits, and her ass was . . . well. I wouldn't have been able to miss it.

"Yes, that's him, that's the maniac!" she cried. "Fuck you!"

"Look at you," I said. "I wouldn't fuck you for a barrel of *vinjak*."

He grabbed me by the throat. "I'll fuck you up!"

I lifted my coat and showed him the weapon tucked into my belt. Without hesitation, he and his wife headed straight for the door.

"Still got jealous husbands on your tail?" Ljuba asked, like he actually cared.

"That one wasn't jealous, just stupid."

"Jealous, stupid . . . it's all the same. It was one of those guys who got you thrown off the police force."

"Ah, happy memories . . . Hey, Jelena!" I called to the waitress. "Get me and Ljuba another beer."

That's right. They threw me off the police force.

Not because I'd been an alcoholic, not because I'd been ir-
responsible or disrespectful . . . Not even because I'd spoken
out about the old government, or that I'd called the old head of
police a horse's ass. No, they booted me because I'd fucked the
deputy mayor's wife.

I'd have real problems if I'd banged the actual mayor's wife.
But the deputy mayor? Can you imagine what a loser he was if
I'd screwed his wife?

My old lady was no help. "If you're . . ." she said. "I knew
that your dick would fuck you over for good. Even when we
were married you couldn't keep it in your pants. I can only
imagine how it is now that you're fucking divorced."

"Come on, don't be like that . . ."

"Oh, now that you've smartened up so much? Been to your
dad's recently? What's he doing?"

"The fuck do you care?"

That's usually how our conversations ended.

Well, what more was there to say? My ex-wife was a minister of culture, and I was an inspector without a job. In Serbia.
In transitioning Belgrade. Basically, a bum. A loser. Or just another asshole drunk on the nonstop hunt for cash.

I paid my bill and headed to the Manjež.

In the *kafana* the waiters eyed me suspiciously. As though
I'd come to inspect their heating or steal their silverware. I po-
litely asked for Hajji Pešić, and a waiter pointed me to a table
in the corner.

A woman getting up there in years was seated, a proper lady,
with her hair done like Jackie Kennedy, a five-hundred-euro
manicure, and jewelry that could buy a building in the fanciest
part of town. Beside her was another woman, an old lady in a
wheelchair.

I cautiously made my way up to them and opened my mouth to introduce myself, but Hajji Pešić just tapped ash from her long cigarette into the ashtray and said, "Sit, Malavrazić."

I planted my ass on the chair across from her.

"Drink?" she asked.

"Sure."

As my double *vinjak* arrived, she decided to introduce the old woman: "This is my mother, Jefimija Dugalić."

"A pleasure, madam," I said.

She smiled cynically at that. Mean old hag.

"You look like him," said Hajji Pešić.

"Like who?"

"Your grandfather."

"You knew him?"

"No. But my mother did."

The old lady nodded.

"That's . . . nice." I didn't know what else to say.

Hajji Pešić pushed a folder across the table to me. It was old, battered, and on the front was written, *Police Administration Belgrade.*

I opened it. In it were some papers and black-and-white photographs of a handsome man in a three-piece suit, with a mustache like Clark Gable's. Taken a long time ago, before World War I. There was an obituary between the papers with the name *Aćim Dugalić.* The name didn't ring a bell.

"That's my grandfather," said Hajji Pešić, as though reading my thoughts. "My mother's father."

"Uh-huh . . ." I shook my head, not understanding.

"He died—well, actually, he was killed—almost a hundred years ago."

"I'm sorry to hear that."

The old lady nodded her head.

I closed the folder, sipped some *vinjak*. I still had no idea what was going on.

"You have the autopsy report there too," Hajji Pešić explained, waving away smoke. "The report from the head inspector who led the case . . ."

"Who cares about these reports after a hundred years?"

"I do, and so does my mother. The killer was never found."

"And you'd like me to find him?"

"If you can . . ."

"Maybe I could, if you could get me a time machine."

The old lady laughed.

"You can help us without that."

"Me? But why me?"

"Did you see the name of the inspector who led the investigation?"

I opened the folder again, glanced down at the piece of yellowed paper. At the bottom was clearly written: *Arsenije Malavrazić.* My grandfather.

"So . . . ?" said Hajji Pešić.

I looked at the old lady. Hey eyes shined with anticipation mixed with boundless sadness. I was suddenly reminded of the schnauzer that had died on me last year. Ah, what a dog . . .

"We'll pay you, of course. How much?"

"Fifty euros a day, plus expenses."

"Expenses meaning *vinjak*, cigarettes, and taxis, I suppose?"

"Tools of the trade."

She opened her expensive bag and handed me an envelope. Inside was more than was needed, but I didn't protest.

"Get yourself a new shirt," she said, and stood.

She pushed her mother to the door with the waiter's help. The old lady waved as they moved her down the ramp at the doors.

I ordered another *vinjak* and looked through the folder again. Aćim Dugalić in black-and-white photographs, smiling and long dead, the report from my grandfather that I'd study in detail later, the obit that didn't say much except that he'd died young, not even twenty-five years old . . .

Then I looked at the autopsy report. Poor Aćim had had a spectacular death: he had been beheaded. At the bottom was written the name of the doctor who had examined the body: *Dr. Edward Ryan*, an American.

My old man had been a cop, working in the criminal justice department with the Belgrade police. When he retired, he turned to one thing exclusively: making *rakija*. But strangely, he never drank it. He left that to me. I knew why: when you grow up watching your own dad destroyed by drink, you get to thinking that you'll never have a drop of the stuff yourself.

I found my father in the backyard, in front of the still. The house he rented was a few streets down from the Gusan.

My grandfather had also been an inspector. His mentor had been Tasa Milenković, the first school-trained Serbian policeman. He worked before and after the war in the Glavnjača.

It had been a happy spot. The Glavnjača was the nickname for the administrative building of the Belgrade police, but it was also the infamous prison where criminals and political prisoners were housed. Between the first and second world wars, it had been packed with Communists in particular. The police, like today, had been corrupt and in the pockets of criminals and politicians, so they served mainly as the cudgel of state authority and a good litmus test to show what condition the country was in. In the Glavnjača people were interrogated, tortured, and then killed. My grandfather himself had taken part in an incident where two inmates had barricaded themselves in a room with ammunition. They'd tried to negotiate with the city governor. Instead of negotiations, they got shot.

My old man kept away from all that and made an impressive career as an inspector in the criminal justice department. He nabbed scum and felons off the streets, rapists and killers, once he even caught a college professor who had raped a student. The guy got himself out thanks to his political buddies with a lot of pull. The girl withdrew her statement, and he walked out a free man. But he didn't know how we Malavrazićes are. My old man waited a few months and then got in touch with two crooks from the block who owed him a favor. They almost put our respected professor in a wheelchair. He wasn't raping anyone else after that. My old man called it "crime prevention," which was, obviously, more important than the risk of a suspension.

"Come to see if I'm still aboveground?" he asked as a greeting.

"Don't be like that . . ."

"Hand me the hydrometer."

While he tested the strength of the *rakija*, not looking at me, he asked a question: "What did Hajji Pešić want?"

"Is the waiter from the Manjež snitching on me?"

"No. The maître d'. I got his son out of jail ten, no, fifteen years ago. He drank a little too much and stole a car and wrecked it."

"Nice to see your old connections still paying off. How do you know Hajji Pešić?"

"She came to me as well. A few times. She offered money . . ."

"You refused, of course."

"Of course. How could I not?"

"But why?"

He stood, threw two logs into the fire under the still, wiped his hands on his blue work pants, and peered intensely at me. "Because it's better if no one finds out the truth."

"Why do you get to decide that?"

He smiled ironically. He went into the house, and I sipped some almost-done *rakija*. It had a mild sharpness and a strong aroma of grapes. My old man was a master.

He came back out when I was already on my third glass.

"Don't overdo it. It's got methyl in it. It's not fermented."

"I noticed," I said unsteadily, draining the glass.

He handed me a dusty, used notebook.

"What's this?"

"Your grandfather's journal."

"Journal? I didn't know this even existed."

"Now you do. Now you can find out about your . . . hmm . . . employer. Why she's hired you. Was the grape good at least?"

"The grape? Excellent."

I took the notebook feeling some sort of sacred respect. And some tingling glee. Maybe I wasn't a total loser after all. Something told me that I'd solve this case that even my grandfather hadn't been able to.

Serbs and Americans had once been friends.

Then came the nineties.

I remember that sometime at the beginning of '93 I saved a boy from a hanging whose only crime was that he'd worn a shirt with John Wayne on it, and so had insulted the pride and patriotic feelings of a few fans. I also remember that they'd had a good go at him before my colleague and I intervened. The legendary Duke on his chest had taken on blue and red hues, as though some hack artist had wanted to overlay his old black-and-white films.

And it had happened overnight. That hatred. Just like everything else in Serbia.

We grew up on John Houston, Frank Capra, and Don Siegel movies. All the girls were hot for Clint Eastwood. When you said "gentleman" you thought Gregory Peck. We all wanted to be Gary Cooper in *High Noon*. We wore Levi's. Drank Coca-Cola and Pepsi. Listened to Michael Jackson and Madonna. Yul Brynner played the part of a partisan in *Battle of Neretva*, the most expensive film made in the former Yugoslavia. Robert De Niro sat on the steps of the Sava Center while he watched flicks at the Belgrade Film Festival, FEST, the largest showcase of films on the Communist side of Europe during the Cold War. They say that before the festival he'd gotten lost in southern Serbia and was taken in by some nice folks in the village of Čokot, a stone's throw from Niš.

And then came the nineties. And everything changed.

Hate is the feeling most easy to manipulate. And there was a lot of hate in those years. It spilled out over the edges of our television screens, barked at us from our radios, leaked out like the black oil from *The X-Files* in freshly printed newspapers. It waited for us in places we least expected it. To beat and break us, like those who beat up the boy whose life my colleague and I may have saved.

Hate came from the other side too. The Americans gifted us a parcel of bombs in 1999.

But that didn't make Dr. Ryan any less significant, any less heroic.

I read my grandfather's description of him in his journal:

I met Dr. Edward Ryan, called Eddie, the head of the American Red Cross in Serbia, in the Belgrade army hospital. A solid, strong man, you didn't know if you were looking at a soldier or a doctor. He was a little of both. I'd seen him earlier, how he briskly walked down the Belgrade streets while the people cried out, "Viva, Ryan!" He was famous even before he came to the Serbian capital. Somehow the residents of Belgrade got wind of his heroism in Mexico, how when the Mexicans put him in front of a firing squad and accused him of being an American spy, he just smoked his pipe and waited for them to shoot, cool as a cucumber.

And now he was smoking that same pipe, looking at me as though he suspected something. Then he offered me some rakija. On the worktable lay an undetonated grenade.

"I like being around death," he told me. "So I'm always on the edge. Sharp as a bayonet. Ready for action."

And he really was.

With him, generally, there was no bullshitting. He knew he'd lock up his closest colleagues if they turned on him. He worked day and night. When he wasn't in the operating room he was roaming around Belgrade, picking up supplies, food, medicine, and training people amid the ruins.

He came to Belgrade on October 16, 1914, three months after the Austro-Hungarians attacked Serbia and started World War I. He stayed when they occupied it, the first time in autumn of 1914, and the second time in the autumn of 1915. The Germans wouldn't touch him since he was a citizen of a neutral country. Which he knew, and used to his advantage. He saved the hospital by ordering that an American flag be raised on the roof. The Austrians weren't allowed to shoot it.

I asked him about the headless body. He shrugged, and then said, rather cynically, "Well, we can rule out natural causes."

The headless body. Aćim Dugalić.

My grandfather wrote that the deceased had been in a special company responsible for creating diversions. It wasn't clear who was in charge. But one name did stand out.

Apis.

Dragutin Dimitrijević Apis, the leader of a secret society called the Black Hand—and also the conspirators who, in May 1903, killed King Aleksandar Obrenović and Queen Draga, and put King Petar from the rivaling Karađorđević dynasty on the throne. At the time he was something of a kingpin of all the Serbian secret services. A dangerous man.

My grandfather went on in his journal:

> That led me to believe that he was our main suspect. It could be that Aćim Dugalić had not been in Apis's good graces. And that he'd ordered his execution. In a conversation I had with an officer from Apis's innermost circle, a man from Niš named Vemić, I was informed that Dugalić had been known as someone who had "chosen the rival party."
>
> "Traitor . . ." a drunken Vemić told me, sitting at a table in the kafana Zlatna Moruna, the Golden Sturgeon.
>
> "And what does Apis do to traitors?" I asked him.
>
> "Nothing," he said, agreeing to another glass of rosé.
>
> He looked at me with glassy eyes and added, "He sends Nemanja."

So there we were. Major Nemanja Lukić. A suspect. Possibly a killer.

"What do you know about him?" I asked my father as he stoked the fire beneath the still.

"Arsenije never proved that Lukić killed Dugalić."

"That's not what I asked. Do you have any paperwork on him? Photographs? A dossier?"

"Lukić had been a doctor too. He trained in London. Since he spoke good English, our folks gave him to Ryan to help him out and assist in operations. Lukić had been a member of the Black Hand as well." He stood, broke a piece of dry wood, and tossed it aside, looking at me anxiously. "Grandpa left the case unsolved on purpose, which you probably know . . . ?"

"Yeah, I know. I just don't get why."

"Why? Because some secrets need to stay secret."

"Is that some kind of Black Hand motto?"

"No, son . . . Just, Grandpa figured it wasn't worth the trouble."

"He figured?"

"I suppose so. Murder during wartime? When so many people were already dying, who was counting one more body? But fuck it . . . Grandpa was a stubborn guy. Like you."

"Good to hear it's genetic."

"So's alcoholism. Just saying."

"Ah, what are you gonna do."

"I'll tell you something that isn't in the journal."

"I'm listening."

"One night, about a year before he died, he got drunk—you know how he got. He told me that in 1915, he got a visit from Lukić. Right in the Glavnjača. He'd never come so close to shitting his pants in his whole life."

I got to thinking, and my old man went back to stoking the fire under the still as though nothing had happened.

I didn't know a lot about my grandfather. Just what my father had told me and what I remembered through a haze. I was only nine when he died. But there was one thing I was sure of when it came to Arsenije Malavrezić: he didn't scare easy.

"If you really want to dig through it," my father piped up again, "there are some documents in the clinic archives."

The guy had to be nuts.

After all, how with-it could someone be who'd decided to spend their whole life surrounded by books and document registers that no one cared about?

The archivist in the clinic center, a tubby, middle-aged guy, collected vinyl fucking records. For half an hour he blathered on at me about how he didn't have enough room at home, so he'd brought some of his collection to the archives. He just droned on and on about it. But I had to put up with this idiot, at least until I got what the archive had on Lukić and Ryan. Then I'd tell him where he could stick his vinyl.

He pulled out a file and handed it to me. I started leafing through the documents.

"He's an interesting guy," said the archivist. "Dr. Lukić."

There were photos in the file too. Mostly from the war. Soldiers, officers, nurses, prisoners of war, the sick and wounded . . . everything to do with misery. War really is hell. That's why we keep doing it—we're a hellish people.

There was a photo of Dr. Ryan as well. He'd been the real deal. Dressed in his uniform, a face that radiated certainty, a close-cropped soldier's haircut, and large, piercing eyes.

"And what's this?" I asked, pointing to a photo of Serbian and British officers standing around a big cannon.

"British war mission. Members of the Royal Navy. They organized a blockade of the Danube and defended Belgrade in 1915 from the Austro-Hungarian flotilla that was bombing the city day and night. Admiral Ernest Troubridge was in command. That's this guy here. And next to him is his second-in-command, Lieutenant Charles Lester Kerr. This one right here."

The archivist wasn't as useless as he'd appeared at first glance. He seemed to know his way around a few things besides vinyl records.

"But who's this next to Kerr and Troubridge? This guy in the Serbian uniform?" I asked when my eye fell on a handsome, tall officer with a neatly trimmed beard and, strangely, for the time, long hair tied back in a ponytail.

"That's Major Nemanja Lukić, a Black Hand. One of Apis's close associates. Real fucked-up guy."

I stared at the face in disbelief, feeling a mixture of surprise and horror.

So, that was him. Aćim Dugalić's killer. Apis's friend. Real fucked-up guy.

"He was killed on the Danube quay when Major Dragutin Gavrilović led the famous attack telling the soldiers that their regiment was to be sacrificed for the defense of Belgrade, and that they didn't need to worry about their lives anymore, because they were about to end . . . Though there's some data about him that appears later, in World War II."

"Like what? After he was dead?"

"Ah, fuck it. Maybe there was an administrative error. Or maybe he'd just been injured and not killed?"

I picked up a photo to take a closer look. It was of Lukić again, in a more relaxed setting. He was sitting in the garden of a *kafana* with company; there was a sign that read, *Gostionica Atina*, the Athens Inn. On the back was written, *Niš. June 1944.*

"See anything interesting there?" asked the archivist.

"Oh, very much, my friend . . . Look—he hasn't aged a day."

My tubby friend put on his glasses and studied the photograph. "Maybe it isn't him," he said. "Maybe it's his son."

"Is there anything about him having kids?"

"From what I know . . . no."

"Then it's got to be him."

"But that's . . . not possible."

I paced the streets of gloomy Belgrade. As I walked three ambulances passed me. Their sirens were lost in the distance, dissolving into the cacophony of voices and sounds. The city was weeping and singing at the same time. The jackasses from city hall had already put up the Christmas lights even though it was only the start of November. Belgrade sparkled and trembled with unnatural colors, and there was that neon blues that appeared every fall. My hometown reminded me of an aging musician who pours out the rest of his talent into the bucket or the bottle.

The same as me. Except for what I'd been up to today.

I felt a huge emptiness in my chest. I was sorry for the old lady who I'd have to tell the truth about her father to. A new lie on a heap of old ones wouldn't be worth anything to her, or to me.

I stopped to light a cigarette. That was when someone whacked me in the head. I stumbled and got another whack. I fell face-first onto the sidewalk. Someone grabbed me from behind like a rabid dog.

"What's up, fucker?"

I raised my head, and saw the same chickenshit from the Gusan, the one with the big-assed wife, standing over me with a baseball bat in hand. The taxi driver, passerby, friend from the army . . . ah, fuck it. It didn't matter. I couldn't figure it out. The lights on the street gleamed faintly off his bald head. He'd jumped me good. He even knew where to do it. There wasn't a living soul around us. Just me and the moron with the rubber brain and the baseball bat.

"Now I'm gonna fuck you up so hard you'll remember me your whole life," he hissed.

"Can I smoke my cigarette first?" I asked.

"Sure, you can smoke, man . . ."

He turned, then stopped, staring off somewhere behind me.

From the darkness, fate emerged, a man in a long black coat who I only managed to see the back of.

He approached and grabbed the baseball bat my attacker was holding. It snapped like a dry branch.

The moron stared at the man, his mouth hanging open. He looked as if all the blood had rushed out of his head.

"All right," said the stranger. "March!"

The bald guy tossed aside what remained of the baseball bat and strategically withdrew without saying another word.

The stranger stopped, took out a silver case, and lit a cigarette. He looked into the darkness, waving away the smoke. Then he turned. I stared into the face I'd seen in the century-old photographs. My heart skipped several beats.

Nemanja Lukić just smiled and said, "Good evening, Mr. Malavrazić. I hear you've been looking for me?"

We sat in the Zlatna Moruna.

I wouldn't have been surprised if Lukić had told me that he'd been there a hundred years before, with the Black Hands, planning the assassination of Franz Ferdinand in Sarajevo that kicked off World War I. Not much would surprise me about this man. He was unusually animated, in great shape, his movements somehow fluid like a cat's, his eyes piercing like a vulture's. But his hands . . . well, maybe I'd overdone it the past few nights with the drinks, but they reminded me, strangely, of *claws*.

He ordered each of us a cognac. I didn't care much for that shit, but who's nuts enough to argue with a guy who could crush a baseball bat in his bare hand?

He smoked a cigarette, remaining silent.

"How did . . . How did you find out about me?" I asked cautiously.

"The maître d' at the Manjež."

"Oh, for fuck's sake."

"You went to Jefimija?"

"I did."

"What are you going to tell her?"

"The truth."

"And what's the truth, Mr. Malavrazić?"

"Well . . . that her father was killed on Apis's orders."

"That isn't true. Apis didn't order anything."

"So you didn't kill him?"

"No."

"So . . . he just showed up, headless, on the banks of the Sava?"

Lukić sipped a little cognac. He looked thoughtfully out the window for a second, then said, "A friend of mine, a British lieutenant named Charles Kerr, came one night with an order for us to create a distraction. He intended to sink an Austro-Hungarian ship. He was looking for volunteers . . . Seven reported."

"Including Dugalić?"

"Yes, including him. It was a very risky operation. We had to sail in the pitch black so the Germans wouldn't spot us. We managed to plant the explosives. Charlie was very adept at that, a true pyromaniac. And then . . ."

"What?"

"A steel wire that had bound two trucks snapped, and one solder was literally sliced in half . . ."

"And it beheaded Dugalić?"

"That's right. We never found the poor guy. But Dugalić's

headless body washed up the next day on the shores of the Sava. Some locals found him. Took him to the hospital. To Ryan."

"So that means we can name the Austro-Hungarian king Franz Josef as the killer?"

"You could also claim that it was an accident. Dr. Ryan did so after we told him what had happened."

So, that was the truth. The whole truth, intact, told from the mouth of a man who gave me the creeps. I could imagine how my grandfather reacted when this guy visited him in the Glavnjača and told him to keep quiet.

I sat in a salon in the old lady's home. The walls were decorated with antique wallpaper and a mass of framed photographs, watercolors, and oils on canvas. On the eastern wall was a painting of St. Nikola, and under it an officer's saber. I guessed that it had belonged to Aćim Dugalić.

Ms. Jefimija Dugalić sat across from me. Her fragile hands, covered in liver spots, rested on a prewar edition of Conrad's *Heart of Darkness* sitting in her lap. I had learned from her daughter, who was standing in front of the window like a guard dog, that she hadn't wanted to change her name when she'd married because she was the only offspring of the father she had loved so dearly.

She held a rosary in her hand. Her daughter, an absolute witch—I was sure of that now—stood beside her and glared at me. She stubbed out a cigarette in the massive crystal ashtray that sat on the table in front of me.

"Is this the truth, Mr. Malavrazić?" Jefimija asked me when I finished speaking.

"It is, madam."

"Are you sure?"

"I am, madam. Your father was not a traitor." I felt a lump in my throat. I sipped some water. Then added, "Your father was a hero."

Jefimija sighed, sipped a little *rakija* from her glass, a sort of toast to the soul of her unlucky father, and looked at me with eyes that had the same clarity as in the photos behind her, when she had been young and beautiful.

"My father was a good man. An honorable soldier. He served his homeland in three wars . . ." She lowered her head. "My father . . . my dear dad . . ."

She got up from her wheelchair with a lot of effort, and managed to stand. She gestured for me to come over to her. She leaned on me, indicating that she wanted me to walk her over to the wall with the St. Nikola painting.

Once there, she struck a match and lit a candle. She stroked the officer's saber that had belonged to her father, hero and martyr. A tear rolled down her face. She wiped it away with a shaking hand and said, "Now I can die."

I stood in front of a fresh mound in the Topčider Cemetery. Her name was written on the cross: *Jefimija Dugalić.* They told me she'd died in her sleep. She just fell asleep . . . and went.

Her daughter Ljudmila Hajji Pešić offered me payment, a thousand euros. I refused.

I didn't have the strength to go to the funeral, but here I was, ten days later, paying my respects to a wonderful, unlucky woman.

Nemanja Lukić offered me a cigarette. I took it, and he lit it with his antique Austrian soldier's lighter. I was freezing from the cold and the wind. He looked as though he felt none of it, his long hair just waving in the wind. His face expressionless, a little pale. The same as in the photographs from 1915.

"Death is . . . relative. Believe me, I know that better than anyone," he said.

He crossed himself and lit a candle.

He laid a hand on my shoulder. His hand still reminded me of a claw—the claw of a vampire.

THE CASE OF CLERK HINKO, A NOOSE, AND LUMINAL

BY MILJENKO JERGOVIĆ

Maršala Birjuzova Street

Translated by McKenna Marko

O ne could enter the hotel garage from Maršala Bir-juzova Street. Somewhat tucked away from the city, the street was murky, gray, and a bit damp, as if the sun never reached the ground or first floors of the buildings, most of them erected before World War II. The garage was tight, he could hardly maneuver in his Volkswagen Touareg rental. He was greeted by a short, older man whose modest attire made him look more like a beggar than a bellhop, garage guard, or receptionist. Murmuring pleasantries that he didn't pay attention to, the man led him into a cramped elevator that took him two floors up. He found himself in a hallway, where along the walls hung framed black-and-white photos of the hotel's illustrious past: a small, smiling black man in the role of an elevator operator, the architect and owner of the hotel with his family, the 1940 New Year's celebrations, Miroslav Krleža, one of the hotel's most famous guests . . . That same Krleža, a Croat, the best-known writer of the Yugoslav era, rushed head-long to Belgrade, to his Serbian friends, and he fought with gusto over national difference; his greatest pleasure was staying right here at the Hotel Majestic, the postwar gathering place of those the writer considered to be the most interesting of the epoch, but whom the outside world found most repugnant.

At the end of the hall there were stairs which descended to the reception desk. After checking in, the guest would climb back up these same stairs—there were five of them—to the elevator that went up to the rooms. It was a complicated system of ascents and descents, whether by foot or elevator, but the guest easily got the hang of it and quickly made himself at home in the hotel.

In the room, there were heavy curtains the color of ripe cherries and bed covers the exact same color and apparently cut from the same cloth. He detected an odor that reminded him of his very early childhood: kerosene. *Kerosene, from where?* He hadn't smelled it in thirty years.

He took the elevator, then went down the five stairs to reception, past the receptionists without even glancing at them, and exited through the main hotel entrance onto Obilićev Venac. The glare of the August sun caused a sharp pain, first in his eyes and then in his head. He stood there until it passed, and when he looked up again, he was surrounded on all sides by the colorful tables of the nearby cafés and restaurants. He could hear the humming of hundreds of people, mostly young women and men, who all seemed unbearably happy to him.

For the first time it occurred to him how strange it was that the street he had entered the hotel garage from was dominated by the gloom of the cloudy preautumnal afternoon, while on the opposite side, in front of the hotel's main entrance, it was a sunny summer's day. As if the Hotel Majestic stood on the border of two climate zones.

Ilija Soldo, chief of homicide investigations for the Zagreb police division, a still-attractive man of fifty-two years, was in Belgrade for the first time in his life. Just two months ago he'd believed—and repeated to himself a hundred times—that he'd never set foot in this city. The main reason for not coming was *not* that Ilija was a Croatian veteran who'd fought in the war beginning in the spring of 1991—first against the Serbs and the Yugoslav People's Army in Slavonia, then on the Dubrovnik front, only to fight against the Bosnian Muslims two years later; and then again against the Serbs in the spring and summer of 1995. He didn't hate those people he had looked at through the crosshairs; how could he hate those who were his only real company during the war and whose fate he shared, in both life and death? And he knew that they didn't have anything against him. He hadn't killed prisoners or civilians, nor had he set fire to villages or shot at random, and somehow it appeared to him that those he'd fought against hadn't done that either. Those sorts of things always happened wherever he wasn't, though often in his vicinity, only two or three kilometers away. And so, it always evaded him somehow. And why would he now hate his enemies, with whom he shared those years in winter, in snow, in rain, and in scorching heat? And why would he not go to Belgrade?

Something else tormented Ilija Soldo and warranted that he keep his distance from Serbs if he happened to come across them in the police force, and had kept him from going to Belgrade. Although he'd been born and raised in Zagreb, and despite sharing one of those characteristically Croatian surnames, Ilija was—through both his father and mother—a Serb. His father Marko, an old partisan, veteran of the struggle against Hitler and the German occupation, had spent his whole professional life in the police force and, of course, had not hidden the fact that he was a Serb, born in eastern Herzegovina where Soldos—although rare—also could be found among Serbs. But it didn't bother him if someone mistook him for a Croat. And so, little by little, as interethnic relations in Yugoslavia deteriorated and Marko grew closer to retiring, he tended to keep quiet about not being from the majority, but from the minority—that is to say, the Serbian Soldos.

At the end of the eighties, as the Communist system collapsed, and the first political parties were established, Joža Marunić, the former chief of the secret police and Marko Soldo's friend, invited him to be one of the founders of the HDZ, the radical Croatian nationalist party which was to be supported by the powerful and influential Catholic Church. What else could Marko do other than accept? Marunić knew, of course, that Soldo was a Serb, but most likely he'd thought that in having one of them on board, he'd keep those extremists under control.

His mother Jelica, a housewife from one of those Serbian villages in the Banija region, did not think too much about it and quickly agreed to the change in their family's identity. If you have luck with your first and last name, then it's easier to present yourself as a Croat to Croats, and a Serb to Serbs. But it'll burden you later on when you constantly have to think about who and what you really *are*, and who and what you certainly *are not*.

And this was the reason why Ilija Soldo promptly, even earlier than 1991, before the destruction of Yugoslavia and the establishment of the Croatian army, joined up with the volunteers and spent all those years at war with the Serbs. It would probably be going too far to say that he'd been fighting against himself and the latent Serb within him, but the fact was, he couldn't prove to himself that he was a Croat. He needed that war, after which no one was ever going to think that he was anything else.

And everything would have gone well, there wouldn't even

be this story and everything that'd follow, had Ilija's father not had a sister named Smiljana, and had Smiljana not been married to the doctor Miloš Stanojević, a renowned Yugoslav neurologist, who she had lived with in a villa in Senjak, the richest residential area of Belgrade. Marko Soldo had broken off all relations with his sister back in 1972, after quarreling bitterly with her husband about the political situation in the country. Dr. Stanojević had thrown Soldo out of his house when Soldo called him an American spy and a fascist scoundrel. They didn't speak again until the beginning of the war in 1991. Soldo didn't even contact his sister when, two years earlier, Dr. Stanojević had died unexpectedly. She, however, called him the very first autumn of the war when she heard on the radio that Yugoslav army planes were bombing Zagreb. She was afraid that they had killed her brother, and that was all that mattered.

After that they maintained their relations at a distance, staying in touch but not visiting each other. Aunt Smilja, as they called her endearingly, would have—had they ever invited her—gladly come to Zagreb, but they never did, lest their family's shame and fraud be uncovered, and their neighbors and all of Zagreb find out that they were not Croats, but Serbs.

Out of all this, Aunt Smilja had one great sorrow: she would never see Ilija again. He'd been six years old when she had last seen him. That was the day when her Miša—as she called her husband—threw Marko out of the house, and Jelica and the child left with him. Smiljana and Miloš could not have children, so her nephew had meant more to her than any son could have meant to his mother. Ilija represented all of her unborn children.

This was why she left him the villa in Senjak in her will.

To Ilija Soldo—who lived with his wife and their four children in a two-bedroom apartment in Zagreb, in one of those buildings from the seventies built during the time of the most vibrant socialist construction projects, producing what people called the "cans" because they were coated with waves of aluminum siding—Auntie's villa in Senjak felt like an unfathomable source of untapped wealth. It was worth well more than fifty times his own apartment.

He only needed to travel to Belgrade and attend the probate proceeding. Upon accepting the villa, and the incredible amount of cash that he would be left with after he sold it, he would, of course, have to accept the origin of his newfound wealth. And most likely everyone from whom he had been hiding his unfortunate identity would find out where the money had come from. Ilija Soldo might have been able to bear it somehow, if only it didn't seem that he was in the process of becoming a Serb—again.

He lied to his wife and said he was going on a business trip to Budapest.

And that's how we find him, confused and a little afraid, as he leaves the hotel and crosses sunny Obilićev Venac to a taxi stand.

The court hearing will begin on time and won't last longer than twenty-five minutes. On parting, the judge, a young and friendly woman, will ask him about Hvar, the Croatian island her family used to have a house on—the last time she was on Hvar was that summer before the war, when she was three years old, but she doesn't remember anything—and he will give her a friendly smile and, in order to not disappoint her, lie and say he loved Hvar too, even though he's never been to the island.

The decision regarding his inheritance was in a plastic envelope. He laid it on the bedside table, resolved to not leave the hotel again until morning, when he would return to Zagreb. He sat in the hotel bar, which had been one of the centers of

Belgrade social life after World War II, the place where the state and party heads, secret police agents and generals—some of whom Ilija had heard and read about, though it didn't interest him much—used to meet. It was important to him to pass the time and return to Zagreb as soon as possible. He felt like a good and faithful husband who had just cheated on his wife.

He returned to his room around nine, after sitting alone in the corner of the empty bar, where it seemed no one came anymore, drinking fifteen whiskeys, all in an effort to sedate himself and forget what had happened that day. He lay in bed and tried, unsuccessfully, to fall asleep. He got up and went to the window, struggling to unlock it. Barely succeeding, he leaned against the window ledge, breathing in the night air for a while and taking in the sounds that carried from Republic Square and Dorćol. Suddenly, he was struck by the thought of what it would have been like if he had gone to the other side in 1991, if he had—instead of joining the Croatian volunteers— left for Aunt Smilja's in Belgrade, and that thought made him afraid and ashamed and he tried to think of something else, of raspberries, which he had heard grew very well in Serbia, of plums, which somehow, he supposed, Serbia had more of than Croatia, and in the end, though he tried to avoid it, he began to think intensely about Serbia and what kind of a country it really was. What did it mean to him after he, one way or another, had spent the best years of his life fighting against it? It meant nothing to him. Like all other countries that meant nothing to him, including the one he lived in. A country is there so a person has something to lose and something to compromise himself for. He thought about that, closed the window, lay down, and finally fell asleep.

He was climbing up the stairs. With difficulty, one foot in front of the other. He was heavier in his dream than in reality.

He barely managed to reach the fifth floor, already more out of breath than he'd ever been in his life. He knocked on the door of the apartment where the clerk Hinko Ajzler lived. He was investigating the circumstances surrounding a street incident in which Ajzler had shoved a Mrs. Petronijević, because, he said, her poodle sneered at him. The old woman had fallen and broken her hip, and three days later her son-in-law, also a senior clerk in the Ministry of Internal Affairs, filed a complaint. And now they had sent him, a known softie, to investigate Ajzler. They knew that Inspector Joso Rakita never said no. In his dream, Ilija Soldo was Inspector Joso Rakita, the year was 1941, the day Friday, April 4, but it didn't surprise him at all that in his dream he could simultaneously be Ilija Soldo, chief of homicide investigations for the Zagreb police in 2019.

No one, however, opened the door. And just as he was starting to wonder what to do and to pity his unfortunate fate, someone tapped Joso Rakita or Ilija Soldo on the shoulder.

"Sorry, sir!" Mento Josef Konforti, the postman, no taller than a seven-year-old and equally timid, introduced himself. "It's been days since Mr. Ajzler has opened the door. Everyone thinks that something has happened to him."

In the dream he didn't have to go down the stairs and climb again to the fifth floor with the notary Dušan Marković, an ill-tempered, fat, middle-aged man who was the spitting image of the minister of foreign affairs, Cincar Marković (who Ilija Soldo only knew about in his dream), along with two more colleagues from the police, the aids and witnesses for his investigation of Hinko Ajzler's apartment. The repeated ascending and descending of stairs in dreams, as in a good story or novel, is an unnecessary detail that the consciousness censures. This fact provided Joso Rakita with a sense of relief.

He pulled the pick out of his pocket and easily opened

the shoddy lock. He was hit with the stench of urine, gravy, and some sort of chemical. The stench was more real than anything he'd ever experienced in real life. Inspector Joso Rakita was seized with terror, as was the chief of homicide investigations for the Zagreb police, Ilija Soldo. He approached the bed on which, gray as the wall behind him, lay a balding man with a clothesline tied in a sloppy noose around his neck. On the nightstand by the bed there were two empty bottles of the phenobarbital Luminal, a sedative once made famous in Hollywood movies, which is still used today as an antiepileptic. But Joso Rakita hardly noticed the bottles of Luminal, because more interesting to him, as to Ilija Soldo in whose head he resided, was the amateurly-tied noose. *He couldn't have hung himself like that*, he thought, and then it seemed to him that the man was alive, staring bug-eyed at the low ceiling.

Along Ajzler's right eye, below the yellowish iris, crawled a small black ant, sliding across it as if on ice.

Rakita moved to pluck the ant from Ajzler's eye with his fingers.

And then something happened which could hardly be translated from dream to reality. Suddenly the person lying there was no longer Hinko Ajzler, and the fingers did not belong to Joso Rakita; instead the ant was crawling across Joso's wide-open eye and Hinko's fingers went for it. He could feel the ant moving but he couldn't blink or move his eyeballs.

At this point, he awoke with a scream. He grasped his neck, but there was no noose. Underneath him, his halfway-expelled shit was smeared across the hotel bedsheets.

This should have been the greatest fright in the life of the Croatian war veteran and esteemed policeman Ilija Soldo, the inheritor of the most beautiful villa in Senjak.

But this was just the beginning.

For the next ten nights upon returning to Zagreb, Ilija Soldo couldn't sleep. He lay in bed staring at the ceiling, devoid of any thoughts. He said nothing to his wife, nothing of his trip to Belgrade instead of Budapest, nothing of the considerable wealth he had inherited, nor of the dream he'd had the last time he'd fallen asleep. Over time, his silences and lies multiplied.

On the eleventh morning he got on a bus to Belgrade. He called in sick to work and told his wife that he was traveling to Vinkovci, out toward Serbia, where a few days earlier a thirty-year-old railroad worker had smothered his two children and then disappeared. He'd left a short note for the mother of his children, who in the police report was listed as his "domestic partner," where he wrote that he had smothered the children because she had been cheating on him with a waiter from the railroad station café. He was suspected to have escaped across the border to Serbia.

As awake as Ilija had been over the past days and nights, he rode east on the empty highway. When they crossed the border and entered Serbia, he closed his eyes, thinking he'd be able to sleep now. But no. The world was just as clear, real, and awake as on the other side of the border. What doesn't sleep in Croatia will not sleep in Serbia either!

Those words, as if regimented, were drilled into his head: What doesn't sleep in Croatia will not sleep in Serbia either.

He quickly glanced across the endless flat land in the direction of Sremska Mitrovica and Ruma, following the perfect geometrical shapes of the black, freshly plowed earth, and he tried to think about something far away from what his life was mutating into, away from the villa in Senjak and Aunt Smilja's inheritance, away from the lies which he was guarding himself from the world or from himself with, away from insomnia which, he was sure, was caused by that strange, terrible dream in the Hotel Majestic. And that's how he came to the case of the crazy switchman from Vinkovci, who had smothered his nine-month-old daughter and a three-year-old son with a pillow, and then wrote to his wife that this was how he was punishing her and promised that if she mended her ways, he would give her new children. He was crazy, but really, should police be the ones dealing with crazy people? How could he conduct an investigation against a disturbed mind? He thought about it, and then by association, through those mysterious and inexplicable trips that a person takes as they transition from one thought to the next, from thinking about the world to thinking about themselves, it occurred to him that what he was currently going through was also a criminal case in need of further investigation. The fact that the crime had happened in his dream, or perhaps it wasn't a crime but a suicide, didn't change anything. Or it changed only the fact that now he couldn't go to the police, neither in Belgrade nor in Zagreb, and report his suspicions of murder; now he had to investigate the case himself.

All kinds of nonsense occur to you while riding the bus from Zagreb to Belgrade. Especially if you're a police detective who hasn't slept in ten days.

It was late afternoon, almost evening, but the main hotel entrance on Obilićev Venac was still bathed in light. The other side, the entrance on Maršala Birjuzova, was surely dark. Was it Ilija Soldo who thought that? Later he'll be sure it was. And maybe it really was.

Luckily, there were rooms, as there would be in ten, twenty, thirty days, whenever Soldo came back on his regular future trips to Belgrade, when he would depart every eleventh day, after not having slept for the past ten nights. This will go on for six months, and each time it'll happen according to that fatal identical scenario, which would probably make a good twelve-hour experimental film that wouldn't be shown in regular theaters, but maybe in the Museum of Modern Art in New York. But the story about a case, which Ilija Soldo, the chief of homicide investigations for the Zagreb police, finds himself in the middle of, requires that all those nights at the hotel be told in the same breath, and that the reader or listener bears in mind the unbearable and frightening repetition, the monotony of terror that our unfortunate Ilija endures.

The receptionists get to know him. He lies, saying that he is a traveling salesman; he isn't going to tell them that he's a police officer. They look for the best room for him, he'll even sleep in the presidential suite, where Marshall Tito and his minister of police in Communist times allegedly held meetings with the many heads of their secret police—regular citizens had no idea how many there had been; he agrees to all this only to avoid appearing suspicious to the receptionists. Then he enters the elevator, and once in his room, he gets undressed, lies on the bed, and five or six hours later wakes up to his own scream. The same dream repeats itself without any variation, only each time he finds out more and more about himself, about Inspector Joso Rakita, a Croat from Lika, serving in the Belgrade police at the beginning of April 1941. He already knows as much about him as he knows about the other one, supposedly his actual self, Ilija Soldo, who in his dream exists alongside Rakita. He is, however, unable to change anything in his dream, like not breaking into Hinko Ajzler's apartment, or not attempting to pluck the dead ant from Hinko's dead eye, or not turning into the dead Hinko, who he still knows nothing about.

The logic of dreams differs from the logic of reality. This logic ought to be investigated so that one knows how to behave in their dreams, or so that a good police investigator can investigate his own dream.

During these six months he didn't say a word to his wife. She, of course, noticed that Ilija wasn't sleeping. At first, she urged him to see a doctor, but he didn't want to, so she got him sleeping pills, which he took, though they didn't do a thing to help him sleep. Finally she started to suspect that her Ilija was having an affair. This suspicion generated domestic hell, which, besides the two of them and their four children, involved the neighbors, her parents, her brother and sister-in-law. He derived a strange pleasure from this since it distracted him from his dream and the futile investigation he was leading, becoming ever more convinced of the difficulty of carrying out an investigation from afar. Is there a greater distance than the separation of dreams from reality in the very same head?

After six months, the investigation led him to the following conclusion: the only place where he could fall asleep was the Hotel Majestic; everything around that hotel, Belgrade, Zagreb, the whole world, was the space where his insomnia dwelled. At night, as soon as his head hit the hotel pillow, after a few hours of deep and empty sleep, similar to being in a coma, he had the same dream; in the middle of that dream was the police case from the beginning of April 1941, most likely from Friday, April 4.

He went to the Croatian State Archives, then to the Zagreb national and university libraries, digging through newspaper documents, searching in vain for the name Hinko Ajzler. He also asked about him in Belgrade; through his police connections he requested that Serbian colleagues look into the name, but they likewise found nothing. Finally, by complete accident—most great discoveries are made by accident—he discovered on the Internet that the Archives of Serbia had digitized their entire collection of the daily newspaper *Politika*, from the very first issue, printed on January 12, 1904, to the very last, printed on April 6, 1941, a few hours before the German bombing of Belgrade. It took him ten minutes to find an unsigned article with the headline "Mentally Disturbed Clerk Poisons and Hangs Himself," appearing on the tenth page of the issue from April 5, 1941. The text described his dream word for word, while the accompanying photograph showed Hinko Ajzler looking just as he had in the dreams, perhaps slightly younger.

Ilija Soldo was tremendously relieved. So, the case had existed in reality, although that reality was imprisoned in the depths of the past, in the year 1941. This completely freed him of the fear that had tormented him from the start, so unspeakable that it couldn't even be mentioned in this story—that he had gone insane and that his dream and the persistence of his insomnia were only symptoms of a serious and irreversible psychological disorder. If everything was as real as in this article from *Politika*, then he couldn't be crazy. Especially since there was no way he could have known about this article before he'd first had his dream.

He came upon a detail in the article that would, it seemed, lead to the unraveling of this case. The murder, or suicide—as it had already been suggested in *Politika*'s headline—took place on April 4, 1941, on the fifth floor of a building located at 30 Kosmajska Street. Easily, without anyone's help, and using only the Internet, he found out that in 1941 Maršala Birjuzova was called Kosmajska. On the virtual map of the city, intended for tourists and those who easily get lost in Belgrade, he was pointed to the gray and damp street that he'd taken to the Hotel Majestic's garage on his first visit. That perpetually quiet, empty, and gray street, that clouded-over street, while Obilićev Venac, which the main hotel entrance opened out onto, was always bright and sunny.

Although he only arrived at this great discovery on the third day without sleep, by early morning the next day he was already on the bus to Belgrade. As he approached the border between Croatia and Serbia, at one time two warring countries whose mutual intolerance was turning into some sort of cultural tradition, his wife, whose name has been omitted here to avoid putting her in an awkward position, was packing up herself and the children, firm in her decision to get a divorce. But in Ilija's crazed euphoria he didn't care about anything anymore, because it seemed he was on the verge of cracking the greatest case of his police career.

Before he went to the hotel, Ilija Soldo walked up and down the short street called Maršala Birjuzova—named after the Soviet general and one of the liberators of the city, who was killed in a plane crash on his way to celebrate the twentieth anniversary of the city's liberation—and recognized that the building in which Hinko Ajzler had lived no longer exists. It was most likely destroyed during the bombing during World War II, perhaps even by April 6, 1941. He peeked over a tall wall which surrounded a synagogue and peered furtively at a police officer, who had come out from the little glass house to monitor the man who kept crossing back and forth in front of him. But he let him pass, which is how the young Belgrade police officer by the name of Perica Utješanović—the son of Jova Utješanović and Stoja Utješanović, née Ćopić, who came to Serbia in August 1995 in a long line of Serbs expelled from Croatia during Operation Storm, the last major Croatian war operation, settling in Borča, the poorest suburb of Belgrade, now married, a father of two-year-old twins, a little girl and boy—would never find out that he had failed to identify a senior Croatian police officer, who in the subsequent days and months would be in the headlines of all of Belgrade's tabloids.

Ilija Soldo suffered a serious brain hemorrhage that night and fell into a coma from which he has not awoken to this very day. For the next seven days he lay at the Military Medical Academy Hospital in Belgrade and was then secretly airlifted back to one of Zagreb's hospitals. The Zagreb media have not reported this event, nor have they said what happened to the chief of homicide investigations in the largest Croatian police department, and what kind of a secret mission led one of the most recognized Croatian officers to Belgrade. In Zagreb, the revelations published in the Belgrade tabloids were taken as yet another, though this time quite bizarre, expression of Serbian hostility toward Croatia.

PHANTOM OF THE NATIONAL THEATER

BY ALEKSANDAR GATALICA

Republic Square

Translated by Nada Petković

My name is Dr. Erich Hetzel. I am a theater director. I am German, an evangelical Christian, but
because I married a Jewish woman, I found myself
on the Nazis' list of seven artists at the National Theater to be
eliminated in 1941. I remember it was a hot day, shortly after
the German bombing of Belgrade on April 6, when our interim
director Veljković summoned me to his half-destroyed office
above Republic Square and said: "My dear Dr. Hetzel, you, a
pure-blooded Aryan, why did you need this affair with a Jewish
woman ... ? Well, what should I do now? You, so to speak, 'dug
your own grave.' Here, look at Articles 18 to 20 in the decree of
General Förster, the military governor of the German-occupied
territory of Serbia. In Article 18 it reads clearly: *A Jew is considered any person descended from at least three Jewish ancestors (this
assumes the parents of both one's father and mother)."*

Veljković looked at me with a weasel-like gaze and continued: "Rather, in your case, whether or not your dad's dad is Jewish, you fall under Article 19. Look—look what it says: *In the
same way, a Jew is a Jewish mutt married to a Jewess.* And there
we are! What am I to do? You are married to a Jewish woman.

No, no, I have to oust you from the National Theater. You'll put on one more performance, and that will be the end. Let your Old Testament god save you, my esteemed Dr. Hetzel."

Barbara, my dear wife, what a strong and murderous rage I felt in that moment. I thought I would become a killer that very day, as soon as I clenched my hands around the neck of that Veljković. Instead, I didn't join the trade until 1942.

That same year, Miodrag Mika Golubjev was the detective on the job. He wore a pinstriped suit with an always starched shirt collar. He gnawed on a toothpick and had an unfilled cavity in his upper molar, which didn't smell too bad. He was careful not to show his stubborn dandruff on the shoulders of his dark suit, which could ruin his reputation. With his mediocre education, Miodrag Mika had been known as a clever policeman even before the war. He turned down an offer from his cousin Sergei Golubjev—the Belgrade police chief Dragomir Jovanović's right-hand man—to transfer to the Special Police Department and become "Mr. Officer who chases Communists." Instead, he chose to stay with the Criminal Investigation Bureau, affirming: "Never will the time come when people are killed for their Communist ideas; rather, crimes of passion will rule in the new social order."

The track record of Detective Miodrag Mika Golubjev in 1941 was as follows. He solved two murders-for-hire at the open market, one particularly cruel family homicide in the home of a former upper-class Belgrade family in the Dedinje quarter, and the murder of an old lady on Krunska Street, committed by an insane provincial student on the basis of some philosophical ideas. His feats during the first year of the German occupation included catching two arsonists, a woman who'd committed infanticide, one pedophile, and one pillager.

"He was lucky," his colleagues gossiped when he was promoted and assigned the most difficult case in 1942. "It will rain on his parade," jabbered less successful detectives from the crime division, and it appears that—at least at first—they were right.

The following article that ran in the local paper *Opštinske Novine* attests to this:

> *The Criminal Investigation Bureau, every day throughout all of Belgrade, prevents violence, arson, and vile homicides that many believe could be committed today and go unpunished, under the veil of war, poverty, and limited access. Nothing can surprise the well-prepared detectives from all seven of the Belgrade quarters. They've seen all sorts of riffraff and vagabonds, even before the Germans seized control of Belgrade. And yet, one brutal and ferocious murder before the eyes of hundreds of spectators surprised even the most seasoned police officer of the First Belgrade Precinct.*
>
> *The drama* Elga *by Gerhart Hauptmann was staged at the newly reopened National Theater. In one scene, a confirmed bachelor, played by the actor Miodrag Marinković Baća, alias Dude, is waiting for his sweetheart, but there is no sign of her. The bachelor twiddles his thumbs, smooths the lapels of his frock coat, and, in the end, dozes off. The bride is due to appear, trailed by a flood of audience laughter, and poses many daunting questions to which the snoring bachelor has no answers. This is how it happened, except that the bachelor did not snore as written in the script, rather he fell "dead asleep." One after the other, her questions went unanswered. Silence. According to the script the bachelor is supposed to startle and jump—but he didn't move. The prompters were puzzled, the stage manager didn't know*

what to do; the actors started improvising, until suddenly, Dude fell from the chair, blood running from his lips, completely soiling his coat.

As a result, the National Theater audience certainly witnessed the most vile murder of 1942. As we have been informed, the case was assigned to the best detective in the First Belgrade Precinct, Miodrag Mika Golubjev, who arrived at the crime scene in no time and forbade spectators from leaving the grand hall of the recently reopened theater. Word has it that throughout the night he questioned the audience—member by member—and only in the wee hours did he begin interrogating the actors.

The set designer Vladimir Žedrinski, a refugee from Russia, muttered something in Russian and the composer Mihovil Logar, a refugee from Slovenia, said something in Slovenian. The others rattled on in some unknown language. Out of those potentially involved in the crime, only the director, Dr. Erich Hetzel, was missing from the scene. Thus, this experienced policeman immediately had a suspect; he tossed away his toothpick, called it a day, and went home to get a few hours of sleep.

We will inform our loyal readers as to how the event unfolds.

I, Erich Hetzel, killed Dude. What a moron—he is not guilty of anything. I have a plan to kill—one by one—all the actors in the National Theater. I'll do it because of my wife Barbara, who has drawn me into Judaism. I am banned from further work at the theater. *Elga,* by Gerhart Hauptmann, was my last performance. They believe that I've fled to a village like a protagonist in some Russian drama, but I am still hiding in the theater building. I descend floor by floor. I am now closest to the bloody stone of the Turkish gallows upon which the National Theater was built. In old times, the Turkish Stambol Gate stood here—the starting point of the road to Istanbul—but it was also the place where criminals and rebels were hung as a warning to travelers entering and leaving the city.

No one knows as well as I do the passageways and doors of the National Theater. One of the doors is quite peculiar . . .

It is now 2019. The actors have just ended a big strike and replaced one director with another, who is just as disliked as the previous one, so they wonder what to do: should they go through directors like Kleenex or take charge of the situation? But how? From that deep and fruitful thought, a forgotten event (although recorded in the nation's theatrical history) stirs them. Someone was murdered onstage.

In 2019, the role of Nikolai Ivanov, a long-standing member of the Council of Peasant Affairs, in the Chekhov drama *Ivanov*, was played by Svetolik Beložanski, also known as Dude. Toward the end of the play, the Dude from 2019 spoke his lines:

IVANOV: What do you mean, come on? I'll put an end to all this here and now. I feel like a young man again, it's my old self that's speaking. [Takes out his revolver.]
SASHA: [Screams] I know what he wants to do. Nikolai, for God's sake!
IVANOV: I've rolled downhill long enough, it's time to call a halt. I've outstayed my welcome. Go away. Thank you, Sasha.
SASHA: [Shouts] Nikolai, for God's sake! Stop him!
IVANOV: Leave me alone! [Runs to one side and shoots himself.]

At that moment Nikolai Ivanov, i.e. the actor Dude, pulled out the prop pistol, placed it against his temple, and fired. A stream of real blood rushed down from his head like a fountain. A body, which at that very instant died, convincingly collapsed on stage. The audience was impressed by this realistic theater of what appeared to be a daring stage direction. The applause did not fade. Next to the dead Dude the other actors, always craving praise, kept returning to the stage. Seven curtain calls—is that not enough? Only when the curtain finally fell did someone scream. Soon word got out that an unknown individual had planted an old trophy pistol on Dude, loaded with real bullets.

The detective in 2019 was Slobodan Jovićević—he was without a nickname; a worker, a purist, quiet, assiduous, precise in accommodating his supervisors, yet talented in solving difficult cases.

As soon as he heard about the shooting, Jovićević rushed from the Majke Jevrosime Street police station, which is responsible for the National Theater district. Ivanov did shoot himself onstage, but the detective had suspicions, and immediately classified the case as premeditated murder. The question was: who killed him? Again, this time, none present were allowed to leave the theater before being interrogated. When he was done with the audience, Jovićević addressed his questions to the actors. Everyone had a good alibi. They were all gathered backstage; only the actress playing Sasha was with Dude before the audience. She had the best alibi.

Jovićević returned to the police station to think, having ordered the actors not to leave Belgrade, which some of them accepted only begrudgingly because it disrupted their plans for guest appearances in the Romanian town of Cluj. As he was leaving the theater, the detective failed to notice a shadow which quietly slipped backstage, descending underground with silent footsteps, and continuing one level farther down via metal stairs. The phantom opened a rusty door, slammed it behind him, and disappeared from this era.

Seventy-seven years earlier, in September 1942, on this very stage, another murder occurred. The victim was the actress Jovanka Dvorniković. According to the press—not only *Opštinske Novine*, but also *Novo Vreme*—this time the authorities were far more prepared. Here is what the reporter from *Novo Vreme* observed:

> *Led by the great German Reich, Serbia becomes the safest country of the new Europe. The wisdom of our keepers of public order is completely by the book. Do you recall, respected readers, the murderer at the National Theater? He escaped the authorities by a hair, and why, I beg your pardon? Because a killer is always at an advantage. By the time the crime is uncovered, people are alerted, and the detective arrives at the scene of the crime, the killer has had enough time not only to flee but to commit another murder. After realizing that he was dealing with a crafty beast, Detective Miodrag Mika Golubjev, with a toothpick in his mouth, returned to the National Theater night after night. Not that our guardian of the law had begun to like our theater, nor did he care in the least for the actors themselves, but he knew that only by working at the crime scene would he be able to act quickly.*
>
> *He was right. As soon as Jovanka Dvorniković paused midsentence and stopped center stage, the detective, sitting in the dark in the third row, clearly saw the actress foaming at the mouth (typical for cyanide poisoning). He jumped*

up immediately, threw away his toothpick, ripped off his hat, sprang over the two rows in front of him, and ran after the phantom shadow. He almost caught it backstage, but the shadow disappeared behind a large prop. Chasing the suspect, the detective descended one floor, then another. When, according to Golubjev himself, both the persecuted and persecutor were close to the bloody stone of the Turkish gallows lodged in the foundations of the National Theater, the detective saw the hunted man shut a rusty door behind him. Golubjev ran to the door, opened it, and found a small and empty boiler room. One detail puzzled him: the suspect could not have escaped because the room had only one door. Golubjev searched, but he found no one behind the boilers.

When I killed the Dude of 1942, I ran through that rusty door, but when I slammed it shut, there was no boiler room in front of me; rather, there was a door which led directly to the street. I was immersed in a strange futuristic era. I glanced at a newspaper and saw that the date was June 11, 2019. Some oddly shaped cars sped down the street behind the theater, which had been extended all the way to Braće Jugovića Street; one of the vehicles almost hit me when I, like a sleepwalker, stepped into the street despite the red light. I asked an old woman where the Germans were, and whether the curfew still existed; she looked at me in astonishment and said, "Have you escaped from a movie set or the psychiatric hospital?"

I realized that I needed to calm down and that I shouldn't reveal who I was. I needed money—and to be honest, I stole some. I returned to the rear of the theater, and got a haircut at the barbershop, Sweeney Todd. I couldn't place the name of the shop, so I asked. "Don't you know?" replied the young barber. "It's a famous film. Sweeney Todd shaved his customers and, in the end, slit their throats, turned their chairs upside down, and threw them in a pit. Ha-ha! Maybe we'll do the same to you."

They shaved me and didn't slit my throat. I knew, however, that I could slit throats, poison, and kill whomever I wanted, passing back and forth through an ordinary rusty door. On the future side, the first murder I committed occurred during the twenty-sixth run of Chekhov's drama *Ivanov*. I returned to 1942 and killed Jovanka Dvorniković, then again escaped to 2019. At that moment, I felt powerful, unbelievably grand. I, Dr. Erich Hetzel, assassinate people with impunity, sowing fear at the National Theater. I am not sure if I still do it because of my wife Barbara, or whether my power has become like a scar which suits my face nicely . . .

Whom to kill next? wondered Dr. Erich Hetzel in 1942. Should he assault the lives of the most famous actors: Olga Spiridonović, Pavle Bogatinčević, Ljubinka Bobić, Žanka Stokić, Nevenka Urbanova, Milivoje Živanović?

Or should he first check what they had achieved and what legacy they had left behind in the future? Once again, he passed through the time door, now without running away from the sound of the steps of justice at his heels. He realized that Spiridonović, Bogatinčević, Bobić, Stokić, Urbanova, and Živanović had laid the foundations for our theatrical life after the German defeat and the creation of a new Yugoslavia. What did the scar on his face tell him? To begin eliminating the most famous and, by doing so, not only avenge the National Theater but also its entire history.

Luckily for the history of theater, he stopped, mulled it over, and decided to kill those who, owing to their talents, had not deserved any recognition, including those in the audience. In 2019, he was the perpetrator of one more spectacular murder onstage; in 1942, two more, by which point the final tally of this serial killer reached six.

Confident after his sixth victim, puffed up like a bird, Dr. Hetzel believed he was God. He had no guilt; he eliminated bad actors one after the other and spared the future greats. In both time frames, he practically expected doormen to kiss his hand when he walked into the building; however, in such a state of mind, he underestimated the skill of those two detectives: Slobodan Jovićević from 2019 and Mika Golubjev from 1942.

Just like Mika the Toothpick, Jovićević also bumped into the boiler room door, only to realize that the suspect was nowhere to be found in the room where there was no way of escaping.

Jovićević thought to himself.

Mika the Toothpick thought to himself.

Unexpectedly, Mika Golubjev arrived at a genius idea.

He was unsure how it occurred to him that there had to be a time portal through which the killer escaped by the skin of his teeth. He continued this train of thought: In that future time, the killer certainly could not be content with a quiet life, as he had shown himself a person who persists to the end without fear or hesitation. That meant he killed both here and there. The detective of the future could not be aware of him, but Mika Golubjev, from the past, would somehow figure out how to warn his colleague of the future so that each of them could trap the killer on either side.

It immediately occurred to him how to do this. Today's newspapers turn yellow after seventy-seven years, but with a little luck, they are still available. Hence, our detective of the First Belgrade Precinct placed an ad in *Opštinske Novine*. It read:

I have an unusual tomcat. This cat has proven to have seven lives. In his first life, while with me, he caught four mice. He butchered all four and threw them at my feet to show off. Then he died. I kindly ask the owner in a distant future, with whom my cat now lives his seventh life, to take good care of him, and closely watch his movements. In his first life, my cat had his own little house. In his seventh life, he certainly also has one. I propose that I, the cat's owner from his first life, and the unknown owner from his seventh life, sneak into his little house and ambush him.

Initially, the night editor didn't want to accept the ad. He dismissed the text as gibberish. Had he not been a well-known detective, moreover a relative of the frightening Sergei Golubjev of the Special Police, the night editor would surely not have run the ad. But he had to. The typesetters were laughing while piling the letters into their short rows.

"A cat who has a little house."

"Owners to move into the house and ambush the cat."

"Ha-ha."

But Miodrag Mika Golubjev knew what he was doing. He pictured his colleague of the distant future reading the ad. By then, Germany would have certainly won on all fronts. The new Europe would have emerged. Hitler would have died long ago and his successors would have since taken turns as führer, serving a monarchy called "Hitler." Berlin, now called Germania, would have become the city of all cities—a megalopolis covering larger portions of Germany and Austria, boasting uninterrupted boulevards along which hundreds of kilometers of impressive structures would stand. Gazillions of people would wait their turn for years to see Germania; the luckiest would win it through a lottery.

Certainly, all of this was not apparent in 2019, but a paper yellows with time.

It took three weeks for detective Jovićević at the Majke Jevrosime Street police station to stumble upon the ad in *Opštinske Novine* from 1942. Actually, this was the work of a clerk at the National Library who reprinted this unusual ad in the September 11, 2019, issue of the daily paper *Politika*.

It didn't take Slobodan Jovićević long to figure out that this was like a message in a bottle, floating for three-quarters of a century until he had discovered it. He had to hurry though.

In 2019, he already had evidence: *seven mice caught*. The theater canceled performances of *The Lower Depths*, *Electra*, and *The Balkan Spy*, stating that the cancellations were due to "actors' illnesses" (incurable, one should say). As a result, the number of people murdered by Dr. Hetzel, alias Sweeney Todd, rose to eleven, including the four corpses of 1942.

What could Detective Jovićević do? He rushed to the boiler room, stocked up on food and water, and settled in. He didn't bathe, so what? Policemen do not like water, anyway. He also had rotten teeth. A cavity in his upper molar bothered him, so what? It didn't smell too bad. The stench of fuel dominated the boiler room, anyway.

Detective Jovićević waited for more than a week. In darkness. In silence. Alone. Eating the last remnants of food prepared by the loyal officer's wife.

On the ninth day, he heard echoes of footsteps. At first from afar, but then ever closer.

I don't understand. I can't believe my eyes. I am opening the door to the boiler room on the 1942 side, but, instead of the street, in front of me is the boiler room of 2019, with a detective tapping a stick against the metal pipes and pulling out a gun. I turn around—breathless and distraught—again I pass through the door of 2019 and back again, yet there in 1942 stands another detective, the Toothpick, clanking some chains. Both men want to see me finished, without judge and jury— me, the god of the National Theater, who has selectively killed only talentless actors. In desperation, I turn and run to the wall. I think: better to bust my own head than allow them to catch me in either 1942 or 2019. And what ensues: instead of shattering my skull, I fall into the wall—simply fall through it. I smell mortar in my nostrils, brick dust in my lungs. I realize that I'll remain a part of that wall forever and no justice will ever reach me, yet there is no exit.

I'm still here. Over time, I have crawled up from the lower levels to the wall dividing the box seats of the first gallery. From there, I watch performances through the seasons. Sometimes I scare the actors during rehearsals with my mysterious sigh or roaring laughter, the source of which they are confused about.

But in spite of it all, I'm bored . . .

THE MAN WHO WASN'T MARS
BY VULE ŽURIĆ
Pioneer Park

Translated by Jennifer Zoble, Mirza Purić

A new and powerful revival of the grotesque took place in the twentieth century, although the word revival is not exactly suited to the most recent forms.
—Mikhail Bakhtin (translated by Hélène Iswolsky)

A tall, portly officer in a tight and tattered overcoat stood smoking beneath the bare branches of a tree at the edge of the large park. As the two Red Army soldiers in front of him dug a hole that increasingly resembled a grave, there was not a trace of tension to be seen on his round face.

The equanimity with which he released the smoke from his Soviet lungs confirmed that this was a man who was well acquainted with the world on the other side of certainty. And for him, that world could be found, on this late October afternoon in 1944, on the other side of the fence surrounding the Old Royal Palace Garden, right in the center of the capital of Yugoslavia.

Just twenty minutes before, at the park's entrance, there'd been an enemy fire position. The German Schwarzlose machine gun had relentlessly barked from the watchtower that, in the words of the Partisan lieutenant, had been transported stone by stone from Kaimakchalan after World War I.

"Kai . . . Ka . . ." the Soviet officer tried unsuccessfully to repeat the strange name of the mountain on the border of Macedonia and Greece, whose conquering by the Serbian army had perhaps decided the outcome of World War I.

"That's where my father and uncle died," added the lieutenant, who sometime after noon had received special orders from Partisan Supreme Headquarters to have his platoon "take the Red Army operational group along the shortest and safest route to the Old Royal Palace Garden and be at their disposal until they've completed their special assignment."

"A good combat position is always a good combat position," said the Russian at last, having once more surveyed the space between the Old Palace and the new Parliament building.

He would have liked to formulate a theory on how these two structures were separated not by a park, but rather by a historical period during which the seeds of poverty had sprouted another offshoot of the world revolution, but the Partisan lieutenant clearly had no feel for the rhythms of such discourse.

"With your brotherly assistance, we have once again liberated our capital," the Partisan declared like an actor in a bad propaganda film, so for a few moments the whole scene continued to flicker in black and white, accompanied by the sounds of one of those revolutionary marches.

"The Germans are fleeing from Belgrade again, and the stone watchtower will, from this day forward, serve as a monument to yet another great victory for our side. I've heard it's already been decided that this park will be renamed Pioneer Park. Young Pioneers from all corners of Yugoslavia and the entire free world will come to this place to experience the glory of our people's revolutionary liberation war."

The Soviet officer knew that the lieutenant expected him to offer an even more pathetic reply, in which he'd invoke Joseph Vissarionovich Stalin, the great leader of the even greater world revolution, and summarize the vision of a just, classless society, but the crack of single shots and machine-gun bursts again resounded in a nearby street, while muffled detonations continued to come from the direction of the setting sun, which for some time had been hiding behind the battalion of large gray clouds sprawled across the remaining roofs.

Everything returned to Technicolor, replacing the ceremonial military music with the sound of gunfire, and the air endeavored to conceal its scent of blood and death.

A mere thirty minutes earlier the sun had warmed the battle for the city, but now the only stars that shone were those on the caps of its liberators. *Darkness falls at the dawn of freedom*, the Soviet officer would have mused, but clambering up his cordovan boots was the sound of a trench spade hitting human bone.

"*Konačno*," the Partisan lieutenant said in Serbian from across the dug-out grave, gesturing toward a nearby fence, where his soldiers kept their guns trained on the assembly building, the main post office, and the central square known as Terazije, where, it seemed, the fighting raged on.

The Soviet officer considered how the Serbian word *konačno* could very easily be taken to mean "of course" instead of "finally," given its similarity to the Russian word for "of course," конечно. So he briefly nodded, stamped out his cigarette butt, and said to the young man that, as far as he was concerned, the assignment had been completed.

"You're free to go."

"Yes, Comrade Makhin," said the lieutenant, and took off with his platoon toward the buildings at whose doors freedom had not yet knocked. The colonel approached the hole where a pair of soldiers had carefully placed the ivory bones in an empty ammunition crate.

Only he and that skeleton knew that the outcome could very easily have been (he searched a moment for the phrase that would most precisely describe such a set of circumstances) the exact opposite: that those bones, first and foremost, could have been his own, and perhaps they would have been discovered by the very man whose remains he was under special, top secret orders to find "at all costs, unearth, and send posthaste to Moscow!"

"Comrade Makhin, it seems Fritz broke every bone in this guy before they finished him off," said the first Red Army soldier.

They may have broken the bones, Makhin ruminated, but they hadn't broken the man.

For even if one of the comrades dared to think that their fellow soldier had betrayed them at the blows of some unbearable bludgeon, a portion of the notes from his interrogation that they'd obtained the previous winter had said unequivocally that in that grave lay not only the remains of perhaps the greatest hero of the world revolution, but all its darkest secrets too.

And one of these secrets most directly concerned Makhin, who in the spring of '41 had stayed in Belgrade illegally on assignment. The Germans had just crushed Yugoslavia and much of the rubble in the bombarded capital had yet to be cleared.

It was agreed that he would meet, in this park, the man whose bones the soldiers were now transferring into an empty ammunition crate.

The treetops were in full leaf that day, the sky clear, but the two of them were, like all experienced intelligence officers, as relaxed in the shadows as they were tense and alert.

They exchanged a few of those meaningless opening words

that expressed recognition and served to establish communication. Then they set off on a leisurely stroll, during which they exchanged but a few brief glances and almost no long, ambiguous words.

Makhin was tasked with conveying an important directive from Moscow to this man before traveling back to Thessaloniki later that afternoon. From there he'd proceed to Istanbul, where they'd failed previously to destroy the man who was known in Moscow as Walter, and who in the meantime had become the marshal and supreme commander of the Partisan army, the new ruler of the even newer Yugoslavia for whom the liberated people of Belgrade would enthusiastically cheer, "Ti-to, Ti-to!"

The message he'd brought to that park in the spring of '41 had pertained to the new plan of the Central Committee in Moscow to remove this man from the leadership of the Yugoslav Communists.

The plan had been canceled for the time being.

The order from Moscow was indeed a little unusual, but crystal clear.

"*Uncle* wants you to leave the *swallow* in her nest for now." Makhin rattled off this nonsense as if he were Hamlet and then lit a cigarette like Bogart in *Casablanca*.

The man on whose grave Makhin now stood didn't say a word. He knew very well that nothing would've been different had he been the one who bore the important orders from the Central Committee and Makhin, the fellow he was meeting in the park, the one to carry them out.

They had both been taught to accept all orders without question. They were both accustomed to the fact that it didn't matter who delivered the orders and who received them. The only thing that did and ever would matter was who issued them. The two men, just like the tens, hundreds, thousands of secret agents scattered across the globe, served in their roles so that life for the planet's inhabitants would change forever.

Therefore the man didn't nod, nor did he blink, but rather turned toward a woman who'd just passed by. She'd left behind the scent of French perfume, and her gait was all about everything but getting from point A to point B.

Yet, as Makhin had heard from many others who knew the man whose bones lay in the place where they'd met that one and only time, the world of romance was pure mathematics for him. The number of women he'd been with was considerable, and one might say the way he'd recruited them was right out of a textbook.

One could clearly see from the interrogation notes that the Germans, thanks to the information obtained from a detective in the local Serbian police, knew about the meeting in the park, but it was even more clear that they in fact had no clue whom they'd nabbed. Gestapo chief Helm had thoroughly interrogated the captive about his false documents and connections to the black market and viewed his confiscated weapon as the basic tool of most common criminals. But he'd insisted most emphatically on knowing the name of his prisoner. He kept asking the suspect the same question, like a kind of refrain: "Are you Mars?"

Police agents had most likely found out about their meeting through some petty informant who worked for both the Germans and the Communists, and who was convinced that the man he'd betrayed deserved even worse because he was a party defector and traitor, and that his downfall would only strengthen the revolutionary movement.

Still, Makhin was bothered by the fact that the Germans had learned his code name.

"I can understand how they know the two of us have met

because Tito's people have been tailing the man who posed the biggest possible threat to them," he said to Stalin after reviewing the notes from the interrogation. "But, Joseph Vissarionovich, where did my name come from?"

Stalin fixed him with that foxish gaze he had that led his interlocutor first to believe he'd been personally responsible for the suffering of Jesus, and then to sign a statement accusing Christ of collaborating with the Romans himself.

"Fyodor Yevdokimovich," Stalin began softly, "neither you nor I are new to this game."

"No, we're not," affirmed Makhin, completely aware that, as usual, he was not expected to say anything else.

"The two of us have worn more code names than coats."

"We have."

"Your name simply . . ."

"Came up?"

"Exactly, came up," said Stalin almost cheerfully, even though Makhin could never tell what the generalissimo was really thinking. "Came up like an empty shell in which they found nothing."

The notes from the interrogation proved this.

The Germans had simultaneously captured a man and overheard a name. And so they wanted to somehow connect them. For that reason they couldn't grasp that one of the top Soviet secret agents had fallen into their hands, one who, among other things, had laid the groundwork for Trotsky's liquidation.

"And you, Fyodor Yevdokimovich, know for sure that he was a hero?" Another soldier hopped into the grave, startling Makhin, picked up a large skull, and looked the martyr of the world revolution deep in the eye, while the muffled strains of Katyusha rockets drifted in from the edge of town.

"Certainly. And Comrade Stalin knows it too," said Makhin.

The two Red Army soldiers stood at attention, and it was as if the whole front had suddenly fallen silent.

A silence much more complex reigned over the Kremlin the following day, when the leader of the world revolution laid that same skull on his desk and read carefully to himself Makhin's message written in a steady hand on a frozen piece of paper.

Dear Comrade Stalin,
Acting on your personal orders, I send you the remains of the hero Mustafa Golubić from liberated Belgrade.
Mars

The contents of the message had so thoroughly absorbed Stalin's attention that its baroque style went right over his head.

Even the best intelligence officers suffer from the desire to say much in as few words as possible, he thought. He struck a match, lit the piece of paper, and then his pipe with it, taking a few short, apprehensive puffs. Trying quickly to conjure a thought about silence as the only appropriate means of expression for comrades who, in the darkest basements of the Party, had been exterminating traitors hell-bent on subverting the foundations of world revolution (though it could just as well be the reverse: the basements of the revolution, and the foundations of the Party), Stalin went to the window where the vista of the war's last winter unfurled.

Oh, my dear . . . he wanted to say to his fallen comrade, but suddenly he couldn't remember a single one of the ten or so code names this one had used, so he returned to his desk, sat back down, and lowered his gaze to the dead man's skull. Although there was no mustache on it, nor those oddly sagging sallow cheeks, it was the head of the only one who'd fearlessly dared to tell him what he really thought, and who wouldn't have hesitated to liquidate even Karl Marx himself had the Party ordered it.

"There," murmured Stalin, satisfied. "Now I can finally look you right in the eye, unafraid!"

The same couldn't be said, however, by the German soldiers from the firing squad that stood, in late August 1941, facing the stout, mangled man, who was tied to a chair under the green treetops in a corner of the large park.

They stood while he sat and stared at them.

They were healthy and whole, while he was battered and broken; they would leave that park alive, while he would stay dead and buried.

Nevertheless, the man looked at them as if all of this were an ordinary lie. Some of them were ready to admit that it wouldn't have surprised them if, at the command "Aim!" he had pulled out a weapon and carefully aimed it at them.

But when the command to shoot finally came down and they fired, everything seemed to move in slow motion.

The German officer who commanded the firing squad thought for a moment that time would snap like a strip of film, then darkness would descend and the convict would manage to escape into some quiet Belgrade street, after which they'd lose the war.

At that same moment, apart from thinking as well that the Germans would surely lose the war, Mustafa Golubić noticed how the Russian equivalent for the Serbian word for "finally," *konačno* (в конце концов), could very easily be heard in Serbian as *na kraju krajeva*, or "after all."

But before that, as if to fulfill his own last wish, he recalled many men, women, and cities, and among them Comrade Mars, from whom he'd received, in this very same park, the directive that until further orders from Moscow he was to do nothing against those who'd prompted his return to Belgrade the year before.

In those penultimate moments, his life lost nothing of its purpose and meaning. He was a committed Communist who'd been given the opportunity to die honorably for his ideas, and he accepted this opportunity without hesitation, not wanting to guess who might've been the one to betray him.

For he didn't see his capture as his downfall.

Sitting on the chair beneath the vast leafy branches, he didn't just feel strongly, but knew with certainty, that this park was not the site of his death, but the place where the full potential of world revolution would slowly be achieved.

"Any last words?" asked the German commander of the firing squad.

"I wish I could stand."

The German officer knew how to conduct such conversations, and offered a cigarette to the man tied to the chair.

"Very kind of you, but my ribs are broken. It would hurt to inhale, and there's no need to suffer anymore."

Helm had declared something very similar at the end of the final interrogation.

"You need not suffer anymore," the Gestapo chief, in a spotless uniform, had told him, while his crushed, broken body had tried to arrange itself around the searing stabs of pain that day by day had transformed into a new expression of his undying faith.

I began with hope in anger and physical strength, I continued with great faith and even greater doubt in the spoken word, and I will meet my end believing only in pain. He'd drawn an invisible line under his secret life before fainting as they'd tried to lift him from the floor of his solitary-confinement cell and carry him out into the street.

It was as if the Germans had only then realized that a man in his condition wouldn't be able to walk to the gallows.

First, they'd wanted to carry him to the park in a blanket, and then someone had suggested tying him to a chair because they could then shoot him like that.

He'd come to halfway between the prison and the park. He'd watched the sidewalk passing under him and first thought that it was all over, that he was already flying; but then he'd felt the ropes.

There was still more suffering to endure.

"Well, you're going to your death like a king," said Helm with just a hint of sarcasm, and he smiled back, refraining from saying that he, truth be told, had ceased to exist a long time before, and being invisible was an even greater threat to those he was still preying on.

He considered saying something witty about the king remark, but he bottled those words up forever and waited for Helm to ask him once again if he was Mars, at which he quickly shook his head, looking the gestapo chief right in the tiny metal buttons of his eyes.

And who knows what he would've told them had they not beaten him?! Who knows what would've bobbed up from the bottom of him in that icy ocean of endless silence in which he'd been floating for one whole day, between the first and second interrogations?

While he sat in his cell and ate the lunch that the waiter, Mladen, had brought from the Ero Gurman *kafana* along with a message from his best friend Čedo to hang on, he felt for the first time in all those years of uncertainty and conspiracy something that could have been a hint of real fear. But he wasn't shaken by the fact that his friend had done a stupid thing, as friends do, and ultimately paid with his head for wanting his buddy to "stuff himself with the finest *ćevapi* even under the Krauts." While he swallowed the last bite, he was barely able to keep from shaking at the discovery that all the torture devices had been forged for nothing.

A man should simply be left to himself and the flow of time.

What if they abandoned him to oblivion? What if they left him in peace? What if no one ever gave him a second thought? What if his terrible secrets were covered in spiderwebs and became worthless?

Fortunately, the very next day they took him from the prison and brought him once again to Helm's office on the first floor of the police precinct across the street, right by Terazije Square.

"Are you Mars?" Helm asked him, and he told him the truth.

And as soon as they beat him in the same way he'd beaten his own victims so many times, he knew he was safe.

Instead of time killing him, he would kill time—he would have enough of it to remember, at his leisure, what was most important. Alongside Helm's investigation, he would finally have the opportunity to investigate himself, but not in order to discover where he'd erred (because he'd made no errors), but in order to revel for the last time in everything he'd accomplished.

"I'll ask you again," Helm said resolutely. "Are you Mars?"

"No." He gave the truthful answer intending, while he received all those professionally inflicted punches, to remind himself of the events in his life that had made him worthy of such an end.

That everyone must die doesn't necessarily mean that everyone has lived. But he had lived, and always at least two lives at the same time.

For while the Germans were convinced that the man

they'd beaten was a black-marketeer and supplier of counter-feit passports who was stubbornly refusing to admit that he was Mars—he recalled his only meeting with the man who, under this pseudonym, had come to Belgrade in the late spring of '41 carrying a message from Moscow about the postponement of Walter's liquidation.

The Germans had, with the help of local scoundrels, al-ready established their rule, but his life hadn't changed at all. The shadows he lurked in were even deeper now, the secrets safer, but the goal remained the same.

What had changed was the world aboveground, the scen-ery in which he constantly moved, changing roles and clothes. For most people, losing one's life was indeed easier than living it, but this could only help the world revolution.

The old world had literally crumbled and shown people its diabolical underside, but because of this, there were more women who experienced a completely different kind of change.

They revealed their slender necks in a novel way; they took slower sidelong glances; and their short, almost inaudible breath said more than a dozen of the most common impertinent words.

Such was the woman he'd followed home right after he'd said goodbye to Mars. Such were all the woman he'd been with, and he tried keeping the number of women he kissed higher than the number of men he killed.

"And how do you do that?" asked one of the Kamarić sisters, whose house had been his first refuge upon arrival in Belgrade.

All three of them were young, pretty, and cheerful; all three knew that Gojko Tamindžić surely wasn't his real name and he surely wasn't a locksmith. But they felt that this tall, powerful man who'd been brought to the house by their father's acquain-tance, a prominent Belgrade attorney, had in no time unlocked hearts in which he could leave whatever he wanted.

The lawyer told their father that he was a war buddy from Kaimakchalan, that he had a nervous disorder he was seeking treatment for in Belgrade. But it was instantly clear to everyone in the house that if someone was crazy, it was the rest of the world, and if there was someone who could heal, it was their new tenant, whom they soon stopped charging rent because his stories about Moscow, Mexico, Spain, Turkey, and Herzegovina were more valuable.

He told them about the Russian winter, the Mexican sun, the Spanish bullfights, and the Herzegovinian *stećak* tombstones.

And about women.

"So how many have you had?" asked Vera, and he replied that he'd left a piece of his heart with each one.

"Do we know any of them?" Nada asked, snickering, and he asked whether they'd heard of Greta Garbo or Marlene Dietrich.

"And how do you do that?" asked Ljubica, but their father entered the kitchen and said that an unfamiliar man had inquired as to whether they perhaps had a tenant.

Five months later they arrested them all.

It wasn't the first time the police had surrounded a house where he'd been hiding.

He could've snuck out through the basement, quietly overpowered the two agents standing guard there, and found another safe haven by evening.

"Why did you surrender?" Helm asked him near the end of the final interrogation, knowing that a beaten man in his condition couldn't answer him even if he wanted to.

"Why did he surrender?" Makhin asked Stalin as soon as he read the last page of the interrogation notes.

Stalin stood at the window and Makhin saw in the glass the reflection of his motionless face.

"He didn't surrender," Stalin said under his breath, and then, generously permitting the readers to imagine a newborn silence, pulled on his pipe and exhaled a fragrant cloud that soon vanished into the shadows of the chamber's high ceiling.

"He di . . . didn't?" Makhin stuttered, lacking the courage to put a simpler question behind these simple words.

"Didn't," repeated Stalin, looking his reflection right in the eye. "He merely carried out an order."

"I understand," said Makhin, though to him, as to most of us, it wasn't at all clear what the hell that was supposed to mean.

My editor even flew into a fit.

"Man, you can't ruin a good story like that!" He was almost screaming when I decided to respond to his call.

"You really think it's good?" I asked after a few moments of silence.

"Excellent. But it will be mediocre rubbish if you don't change the end," he said in a calmer tone, justifiably afraid that I'd hang up, remove the SIM from my cell phone, delete the file, and never write another sentence.

"Listen, man . . ." He waited to see if I was still there.

"I'm listening."

"Let's meet somewhere and figure it out."

So here I am in Pioneer Park, where I arrived ten minutes prior to our agreed-upon time. It's a sunny day; children are playing; pensioners are sitting on the benches, reading the paper. Cars and buses speed along the boulevard, behind which sits the National Assembly building, and at the curb on the park's edge stands an open double-decker bus that will soon take visitors on a sightseeing tour of the city.

I'll take my editor sightseeing in the park.

I'll show him where the Germans shot one of the most enigmatic and dedicated of Stalin's secret agents. Then I'll show him his grave. Later on, we'll walk the same path that he and Mars took, and then we'll head toward Terazije, where he'll have to imagine buildings that no longer exist, where they interrogated the agent, and where he lay in his wounds, beaten and broken.

"That's all well and good," I know he'll say, after taking his first sip of beer in the garden of some nearby café. "But, man, that part where Stalin is standing at the window saying Mustafa Golubić hasn't surrendered but rather carried out an order—what does he mean by that?!"

I'll look him right in the eye for quite a while, and then helplessly shrug. My editor will stub out his cigarette, stand up, put his hand on my shoulder, and leave, and as soon as I get home, I'll write two more scenes for the ending.

The first will take place in the Kremlin, in the same room where Stalin stood by the window and stared at his reflection in the Soviet glass. This time, behind his back will stand one of his most enigmatic and dedicated secret agents, just returned from Mexico, where he'd laid the groundwork for the assassination of Leon Davidovich Trotsky, the greatest enemy of the world revolution.

The other final scene will take place in a house on the outskirts of Belgrade, which was surrounded by the German police early one morning in June 1941.

Mustafa Golubić will have shaving soap on his chin, but instead of holding a razor, he'll be holding his revolver.

Weighing his options for escape, he'll remember the conversation he had with Stalin after returning from Mexico.

"Joseph Vissarionovich, what are my orders?" he asked, interrupting the silence that, in his presence, was more cautious than a wild cat poised to sneak off into darkness.

"There's only one more," said Stalin, not daring to turn and look him in the eye.

"Yes?"

"Recognize the opportunity to go out as a hero."

Here is that opportunity, Golubić will think brightly, already aiming for the body of the first German policeman he can see through the small bathroom window, but then he'll realize that he's been given the opportunity not only to die at the enemy's hand but to be executed and buried in the very heart of the great city.

So I will never be forgotten, he thought as he rinsed the shaving soap from his face and looked in the mirror for the last time.

One could even say he was happy.

PART IV

KISS ME DEADLY

THE TOUCH OF EVIL

BY VERICA VINCENT COLE

Lekino Brdo

November 1, 2018

Viktor Marković *is a dead man.*
Why? The world will be a better place without him, that's why. Or maybe there are other reasons.

I know that there is a bit of evil in all of us. Hidden behind the masks we agree to wear for the sake of civilization, it is balanced by goodness, controlled by the societal conventions. Yet at times, evil turns into Evil, a fairy-tale monster that eats children alive. And with this comes the sign. Most people fail to see it, although the sensitive ones often feel a need to avert their gaze from the faces of those in whom Evil lives. I call it the sign of the beast and I saw it on the face of Viktor Marković the moment I met him.

But I needed time to convince myself of the truth. I was scared, persuading myself for months that I must be wrong. And forgetting, at that, the futility of such exertion: for Evil refuses to forgive weakness. Evil grants no favors. And Evil is contagious.

Am I not the perfect example? To liberate the world from Evil, I have to let it inside of me. That's the modus operandi of Evil, whether we are talking NATO's "humanitarian intervention" or me, Neda Adamović. So it is not really a surprise that it is "other reasons" that guide our actions, is it? There's no place for noblesse in the story of Evil.

Yet, I can't help but wonder—what would some other people do in my position? Could they really kill another human being? Pull

*the trigger and put a bullet into someone's forehead—bang bang,
you're dead! Probably not: most noble, gentle people living in pain
would rather kill themselves.*

Until yesterday, I considered myself one of them.

*Today I decided that "Neda Adamović, Everyone's Favorite
Victim" will not be my epitaph. That it is time for a bang in my life.*

April 30, 1999

Whether it's Jack the Ripper or the armed forces, the pathology
is the same: the killer first objectifies the victims to obliterate
their humanity, so they are not human beings anymore, just collateral damage, Neda thought to herself, walking through the
strangely quiet streets of Lekino Brdo, so innocent and quaint
under the April sun as if totally unaware of what could happen to it at any moment. She was still seething at what she'd
just seen from her friend Mariana's thirteenth-floor balcony:
Avala—the hill which, with its meager 1,700 feet, qualified as
a mountain—without its TV tower! During the night, the precisely guided NATO missile had wiped the tower out, and the
resulting scenery belonged in a parallel reality. Like everything
else these days, for that matter: how could Serbia, the country which had always been on the right side of history, always
the good guy, be bombed by the allies? Maybe because, as the
saying went, it was in a habit of winning in war and losing in
peace? But who could win over NATO? Martians?

"Making war to get peace is the same as fucking to get virginity," Mariana had said as they drank coffee made from tepid
water from the water heater, since this part of town was once
again without electricity.

Neda couldn't agree more.

Air-raid sirens began their shrill scream while she was entering "the little woods"—a wooded area that covered the block

below her old high school—which usually had a calming effect on her nerves. Feeling like she was about to explode without any help from a NATO missile, Neda started singing from the top of her lungs: a song Belgrade Gypsies had sung during World War II, while German Stukas bombed the unfortunate town, which seemed to be everybody's favorite target.

NATO intervention was the last straw for Neda. A private language school where she was teaching German collapsed under Western sanctions, leaving her without an income. So once again, she was depending on her parents. Upon retiring, her parents had moved to a village in the northern Serbian province of Vojvodina, and once in a while they would send her some cash and homemade goods. Making her feel worthless, if not suicidal.

Neda decided there was no reason to hurry home, to the little house on Todora Dukina Street, where she expected at any moment to turn into collateral damage under its old bricks. After all, it was in these woods where she had had her first kiss. A first kiss, perhaps the last day of life—wasn't she a proper heroine from some Remarque novel?

The woods seemed empty, save an old man who sat on a bench by the path, staring at nothing as he ignored the sirens. Either deaf, thought Neda, or just didn't give a shit. Perhaps he found it better to be killed by a bomb than to fade away in some poorly supplied hospital, living on bread with margarine.

The sirens stopped as suddenly as they had started. Knowing what was coming, Neda chose a bench for herself and sat to wait for the hard rock delivered by NATO to overpower the Gypsy lament.

June 15, 1999

In Dača's *kafana*, time had stopped somewhere in the seventies:

plaid tablecloths, glassware with a little line marking volume, a menu limited to barbeque and the daily course of cooked meals. And guests who asked for *kilo-kilo*—a liter of white wine and a liter of sparkling water.

"Bread, circuses, and cigarettes," said Goran, taking a carton of Winstons from his bag, making a face as the exhaust fumes from the number 26 bus, passing down the street, prevailed for a moment over the scent of linden in the air of the *kafana*'s terrace. "That's how the saying should go."

"If only they'd had cigarettes in ancient Rome," said Neda. "Thank you. You know I—"

Goran made a gesture to stop her. Knowing that she was completely broke, he didn't expect money for the cigarettes. They had known each other for quite some time and he helped her when he could. It was all part of their friendship, which endured despite their differences in life philosophy. Goran was practical. He always knew what he wanted from life and would find a way to get it. Neda was a seeker. The only thing she knew for sure was what she didn't want, or that what she wanted was rather more complex than the university-marriage-children recipe. Although in her late thirties and despite all her problems, she still hoped to tumble into the right path eventually, one that her "own blood whispers to her," as her favorite writer put it.

"Now buy me a drink and I'll forget about the fact that you brought me here to exploit my feminine charms," she said, lighting a cigarette and inhaling with unconcealed pleasure.

"Who else if not you?" said Goran, smirking. "You are the only Swede I know, and I have no better ideas, even if this one's kinda wicked. Besides, you have better chances than me. I could only hope to worm my way in."

Neda smiled, thinking of the nickname "Swede" someone had given her a long time ago, on account of her being a natural blonde. In her experience, most men reacted to strong statements, so in addition to her main allure—her long blond hair—tonight she wore a short red dress, an *Olé!* for the rich bull.

"So where is this friend of yours?" she asked.

"An acquaintance of an acquaintance," Goran quickly corrected her, slightly offended.

Said "acquaintance of an acquaintance" was their last hope at finding a job. The weekly newspaper Goran used to work for had been forcefully shut down by the regime and now he generated his income by selling smuggled gasoline and cigarettes on the black market. But those days were quickly coming to an end, partly because of the bombings, partly because a monopoly on smuggling seemed to be changing hands.

"Whatever, as long as he'll pay for a round."

"I think he's coming," said Goran, looking over the terrace's metal fence at the silver BMW pulling into a parking spot. "Charm him from the start and we could get ourselves a nice dinner. For him, it'd be pocket change."

"How did he get his money?" Neda inquired, taking a long look at the corpulent man in black jeans and a red polo shirt approaching their table.

"These days you don't ask questions like that," whispered Goran.

"A criminal?"

"Quiet. It's all relative, isn't it? As long as he doesn't ask me to smuggle drugs or people or be a professional assassin, it's okay with me."

Neda shook hands with Viktor Marković. He was in his early forties, bearing the wide-set, dark eyes of a shark. Eyes that didn't reflect his thin-lipped smile, yet in a second had likely rated her and categorized her somewhere in his mind. He could be called handsome—or at least interesting, with that air of self-confidence and his velvet baritone. Yet, something about his face looked wrong, as if someone had disassembled it and then reassembled it, but made some sort of a mistake along the way. She couldn't describe the fault, but it was definitely there. A fault that made Neda want to avert her eyes.

August 30, 1999

I understand that in a way, I betrayed myself. I guess it was the result of weariness. Fatigue and struggle without rewards quickly exhaust one's mind. But my situation needed a solution, and it came down to an attempt to balance my needs and the price I'd have to pay.

In all honesty, it's not like you'd have had to bend my arm for me to sleep with him. He's one of those men who radiate power like body odor and, as much as it confuses me, his power pleases me in some primal way. I let the woman in me out—nota bene: a rather lonely woman—and let him take the lead. I let myself enjoy it: being just a woman, "the weaker sex."

Speaking practically: besides giving me a job and a more-than-decent salary, through his connections he acquired the medicine my father needed, making my parents' lives easier. Instead of taking from them, I'm finally able to help them. God, how good it is not to feel guilty anymore.

Yes, I am perfectly aware that he is not somebody I can talk to about the universe and freedom. But isn't that something people like me contemplate in solitude anyway?

No, I'm not lost, I am still me. This arrangement is a temporary solution, just one little bump obstructing the right path of my life.

September 30, 1999

At Vimark Consulting, where she officially worked as one of the secretaries—though it was clear that her more significant role was serving as a hostess at the business lunches and dinners Marković often organized—Neda got wind of the existence of his children. But she never asked him, not about children nor his marital status; not even during their intimate meetings in the small private hotel owned by one of his friends.

Actually, the answer wasn't important: what was happening between them was not a relationship but a trade, a transaction in which, for the first time in her life, she used her looks and her body as currency.

Marković was a skilled but uninspired lover and it suited Neda. At first, she had expected something different. She often had a feeling that "different" was there—some small move, the way he grasped her, the expression in his eyes would almost reveal . . . what? Neda couldn't finish the thought, or maybe she was afraid to do so. Making her curious and excited at the beginning, "different" was starting to scare her.

Then things happened and she didn't know what to do.

"I have a problem which I have to solve fast if . . ." said Marković, standing naked by the window of the hotel room with a glass of cognac in his hand. He was relaxed in his nudity, as a man who knew very well that power is a substitute for most flaws. "Actually, that part is none of your business. What's important is that our friend from the Ministry of the Interior can help me. You've met him. I think you are aware of what he wants in return."

He took a small sip of his cognac, and looked at her, tilting his head as if to better focus on her reply. "I've heard he has a somewhat specific taste, but you are an experienced woman, aren't you?"

At first, Neda was not sure if she had heard him properly. Then she realized she wasn't *that* surprised. No matter how much she wanted to believe she was special to him, not just one of many, she was actually prepared for something like this.

He came closer, slid to the edge of the bed, firmly took her ankle in his hand, and looked her in the eyes. Behind the darkness of his gaze, there was no room for discussion.

"Life is an expensive adventure, Neda. We all pay a price. What we get depends on what we pay. Simple economics. Do we understand each other?"

Neda swallowed hard and averted her gaze from his wrongly assembled face.

October 30, 1999

What did I expect? To be honest—I have no idea. I jumped into the water and waited to see if I was going to float.

The first time I said I simply couldn't do something like that, a nightmare descended on me, something horrendous and yet unreal, like a monster in a child's dreams. Loose teeth, cuts inside my mouth, and a wide range of bruises unequivocally confirmed the reality of it.

Thinking of all this now, I realize it wasn't the physical abuse that frightened me the most. It was the silence in which it happened. Can such a methodic manifestation of rage be categorized as rage at all? I don't think so. I believe the wrath of Viktor Marković is a much more complicated animal, something that draws its black energy from a deep source older than time. Sometimes I wonder what would've happened if I hadn't escaped, if I hadn't, without a coat or any of my belongings, hawked a cab and given the driver Goran's address.

Goran was fired the very next day. He wasn't upset—he was already sick of driving around drunken idiots and taking care of the vomit and other nasty stains from the company's Mercedes.

So, calling it all an unenviable situation is a euphemism for the deep shit I'm in. But I didn't have a choice, right? I tried my best, but when it comes to sex, we all have our boundaries. And once the precedent was set, who can say what the other creatures from Marković's powerful circle would ask me to do?

But at this moment, I am only concerned with whether or not I want to keep the child growing in my womb. One part of me still obstinately desires the life I promised myself, a life with much more freedom and space for seeking than single motherhood can offer. Yet I feel instinct overcoming me. It is a frightening but powerful force, more powerful than any obstacle, be it of philosophical or practical nature.

Yes, I know that my freedom has just been incarcerated by the solid walls of impending day-to-day duty. But I am an almost-middle-aged woman living in Serbia, not a Greek philosopher strolling through the groves of Aristotle's Lyceum.

What do I live on? Mainly on a creative mix of hormones and dreams of revenge.

October 21, 2007

Occasionally, usually when she had to borrow money to buy Milena something "all the other kids have," Neda wished she had Marković's private phone number so she could send him a picture of his daughter. Maybe the snapshot from her first day of school, with her famous broad toothless smile. Milena thought she looked scary when she smiled that way, and she absolutely loved it.

School was a new expense, which Neda's underpaid jobs in boutiques and corner stores, or the occasional instruction of German, couldn't cover. Employers were afraid of single mothers, and the school was full of children with parents who thought that jealousy-inducing clothes and gadgets were important enough to sacrifice a good part of a family's budget for them. Neda's little house stood like a relic from an ancient time among the modern buildings springing up around Lekino Brdo like mushrooms in the forest. Selling it would resolve some of her financial problems, but her father, who grew more senile by the day, refused to do so, passionately talking about his intention to plant an apricot tree, the one he had actually planted forty years ago. Neda didn't argue with him. She didn't want to point out that her father was incapable of proper reasoning. Besides, it was the last house on the street with climbing roses hanging over the fence—living proof that, in spite of everything, she and her world were something separate, something special.

Last year, Marković had founded the Vimark TV station and he became a media personality. Thanks to his new public face, Neda developed extensive knowledge about his family—the photogenic TV hostess who was not the first Mrs. Marković, the daughter who studied design in Italy, and the son who owned his own business of an undefined nature.

"Mommy, my friend Sara says that in Greece—they *always* go on holiday in Greece, you know—there was a stone statue of a naked woman." Milena put her little hand over her toothless mouth and giggled. "That is one of the goddesses, you know. Sara stood in front of her and made a wish and it came true."

The girl stirred her cornflakes around in the bowl, while they waited for the arrival of their neighbor, who took Milena to school every day along with her son. She was late, so Neda was late for work. She hoped her boss wouldn't threaten to fire her again. She desperately needed money to pay the bills, which were piling up quickly.

"Did you put on new panties?" Neda asked, looking at her watch. She still couldn't forget the shame she had felt when

Milena went to an unexpected annual physical at school wearing old, faded underpants.

"Yes, but I wish you would buy me the ones with little frills like Sara has. Do you know what I would wish for if I visited the stone woman?"

Neda hoped Milena wouldn't wish for knowledge of her father. For her, Daddy was someone who lived far away and, *No, he won't come see them soon.* Neda further embellished the story in accordance with Milena's age. Whenever she considered telling her the truth, she always concluded that she didn't want to traumatize her daughter with a very certain turndown from her father.

"What would you wish for?"

"A pot of gold," Milena said.

Neda wasn't sure she liked this answer any better.

"So what would you do with all that gold?"

"I would buy . . ." Milena paused, considering her options.

"What?"

There was a sly look in the girl's eyes—the very same black, opaque eyes of her father.

"Everything!"

Neda felt guilt overwhelming her. Milena wore cheap clothes bought in thrift stores. She couldn't afford fancy sneakers or other luxurious objects important to the children of the new age. Neda always wanted to explain to her daughter that having material possessions was not the most important aspect of life, that it was sometimes better to be different from everybody else, to be unique and special, but she warned herself that it was too early to introduce that kind of thinking.

January 21, 2018

Milena's tattoo was not a butterfly, a heart, or the name of a boy she was in love with. No. Above her shoulder blades spread a pair of midnight-black wings.

Neda put her hand over her mouth to stop herself from gasping. Ever since Milena had become a teenager, Neda had made sure to never enter her room without knocking. But for some time now, the girl had been refusing every attempt at communication and Neda was worried that her daughter was turning into one of those problematic adolescents who easily lose their way. What she wanted most was to build a different world for her child. Yes, she was aware that instead of Neda's need to "understand Buddha," Milena had taken after her father and his materialistic spirit. But she was still a child. There was still time for Neda to change her spiritual viewpoint, and give her a chance to look at life from a different angle.

"Stop staring," said the girl. "I know what you're thinking, but I don't care. Besides, you didn't pay for it."

For the first time in her life, Neda wanted to hit her child. To let the Evil in, and beat her senseless. Instead, she burst into tears.

"What do you want, Milena? What is it that you want?" she asked when she was finally able to stop sobbing.

As Milena tilted her head and carefully dissected her mother with those dark eyes, Neda realized the strength of Marković's genes.

"What do I want? Everything I don't have, Mother. Everything. I. Don't. Have. Isn't it logical? Don't all people want that? Not you, of course. Oh, no. You have to be special, even if you are starving. Go read your books and give me a break!"

October 30, 2018

Neda had never watched reality TV. Her brain simply couldn't understand the purpose. She asked people who couldn't miss an episode what attracted them to these shows. She didn't ask what was on the tip of her tongue: how could they watch uninteresting people talk about uninteresting things, peppering it with all sorts of equally boring exhibitionism? She had never gotten a satisfying answer. Either those she asked didn't have the inclination or capability to dive into their inner self, or maybe they intuitively knew they wouldn't like what they'd find there.

So she ignored the whole phenomenon, that plastic, toxic package of basic instincts and vulgarities that made headlines in the media.

So the information that her daughter, who was legally a minor, had become the youngest participant of Vimark TV's *Commune*—the newest and, according to newspapers, most expensive reality show in a sea of humiliating circuses aimed to make people forget about more important things—was something she couldn't believe at first. And once she was forced to believe it, she couldn't really feel it. It was just like all those tsunamis and massacres in distant parts of the world that make you sad but are too far away to break your heart the way one crippled beggar child in the street you see with your own eyes can.

Milena used the name "Millie Wow" on the show. She was reportedly seen fucking one of the male participants in front of the cameras.

So for the first time, Neda sat down to watch *Commune*. She poured vodka into a highball glass and watched Milena showing off her thong while kissing some simpleton with a strange haircut who used vulgar language. Neda couldn't help remembering her daughter's faded underpants from the annual physical at school. Was that the event that led her to where she was now?

As she refilled the glass, Neda wondered how Millie Wow would feel if she knew that her bare butt funded the jet-set lifestyle of the TV station owner's recognized children. While sadness replaced every other feeling in her, a single spark of rage began to burn within her broken heart.

Maybe it was finally time to reset things. Maybe it was finally time for a bang in her life, something that would completely rearrange it, even if, along the way, it first broke it into a thousand pieces.

November 15, 2018

After some time, Neda's plan was in place, complete with logistical support: Goran could certainly get her a weapon. Swearing like a sailor whenever he heard Marković's name, he clearly felt quite good about it.

As Marković was a man who loved control, Neda knew that he would be there early, just in time for Vimark TV's morning show. So it was still dark outside when she resolutely entered the main building of the television studio just after him, passed by his still-smiling secretary, and opened the padded doors of his office.

The room was full of tasteful pieces of art and books—a declaration that the father of carnal entertainment was a spiritual person who was above the audience paying for all of it.

Looking at her with his impenetrable eyes, he slowly put his cell phone down on his antique writing desk.

As always, Neda had the urge to avert her eyes from his face. But she knew she couldn't do that. Not this time. Her hand slowly reached into her bag. She saw Marković gripping the edge of the desk. She almost chuckled, but she just smiled instead and pulled from the bag the newest edition of *Flash*, a tabloid with the largest circulation in the country, where Goran had made his living for several years. In a few minutes, readers who wanted to know who was screwing whom, literally or metaphorically, would be able to buy it themselves on their way to work.

"Frame this cover page and put it by that Dürer print," she said, before turning and leaving the office.

November 16, 2018

Well, like a true representative of those without imagination or courage for actual drastic changes in their lives, to which, gladly or not, I now belong, I chose a "fart" instead of a "bang."

The Fart, directed by Neda Adamović, looks like this: tabloid headlines, bold with avarice, scream that the illegitimate daughter of Vimark TV's owner takes part in his reality show! I am sure that for a man who at a certain point in his life started to believe that money could transform a ravenous cannibal into a Renaissance man, those headlines were more painful than a bullet through his head. Yes, a bullet was my original plan. But I abandoned it when I realized that the anger in me was more complex than simple rage directed at Viktor Marković.

Mind you—he was certainly a very suitable devil for the exorcism I needed to perform.

New headlines kept coming as I'd predicted. Divorce! Rumor has it that Mr. Marković "has very specific tastes in sex." Namely, it seemed that Mrs. Marković had received photographs of an unidentified long-haired blonde doing something nasty with Mr. Marković. I could just imagine horny readers making faces of disgust, wondering at the same time if they should try something like that. Marković can insist the images are photoshopped until he's blue in the face, but who would believe a man who let his own daughter fuck in front of a camera?

And just like NATO—thanks to Goran and his permanently

geared-up journalistic instinct—I have an infinite wealth of weapons. Such as the many images of certain high-ranking men with "specific tastes" enjoying the company of Marković's merry "secretaries." To stop these photos from leaking to the press, I had a price. Goran and I were laughing while we split the money. Truth be told, it was quite therapeutic.

As for Milena, she is an adult now and ready for her fate. I won't give up on her, of course. Even with the set of genes she inherited, I hope she will eventually realize the difference between the real starry sky and the one where the shine of the stars is measured by their nudity and vulgarity.

And if I share a few things with her, she might like the fact that her mother can be a badass bitch too.

You see, I can avert my gaze as much as I want, but I must accept that Evil is ultimately appreciated these days. To people made insensitive by all the loud distractions of modern times, it is exciting and exotic. How else would all those snakes, parasites, and leeches, all those stains on the face of humanity, become media darlings?

There's one thing consoling me in this newly found cynicism: I am not a killer. Of people, countries, or culture.

ALTER EGO INC.

BY GORAN SKROBONJA

Učiteljsko Naselje

Translated by Nataša Milas

After many years, she visited Učiteljsko Naselje again. She'd grown up in this neighborhood, but since she'd moved away she'd had no reason to come back. She remembered the place—located between Konjarnik, Šumice, and Zvezdara—as unpleasant, shabby, and depressing.

What she saw from the taxi—a small, inexpensive, autonomous, and noiseless electric Asian vehicle—Marija didn't recognize, nor did she associate it with any of her childhood memories. The neighborhood that she remembered consisted of several narrow streets and residential buildings erected around two large factories built back in the 1960s when the area was still at the edge of urban Belgrade. At the time when Marija left Učiteljsko Naselje, huge concrete buildings with broken windows were turned into furniture warehouses, yoga and pilates studios, and squats for struggling artists. The same streets were now covered with solar panels, placed on every corner, looking like phantasmagoric, dazzling sculptures.

Marija got out of the car in front of a restaurant—quite a popular one, judging by the various web ratings. When she turned around she found the entrance to the business she was looking for in a four-story building. Next to the large aluminum and glass doors, there was a brass plaque with *AE Inc.* engraved on it. It was abbreviated from *Alter Ego Inc.*, the full name of Isak's start-up.

She wondered again why Isak had placed such a promising company in this part of the city, assuming that the reason could only be the cheap rent. Everything else in the neighborhood was far from being prestigious and appealing to ambitious investors and international firms. She shrugged, turned back again, looked over at the indifferent facades of the buildings and the indifferent faces of the passersby, and approached the intercom. A split second later—as if somebody had been watching her the entire time—a soft buzz sounded and the door opened before her.

The director was excited. He spoke very quickly: "Mr. Lero explained everything to me. Trust me, you'll be delighted when you see what we've achieved so far. The technology our start-up has developed is quite revolutionary and I'm excited that we'll be taking the key step in its testing thanks to you—"

"Excuse me," she interrupted. "How long will this all take? I have a lot of errands today." This was true: she'd taken the day off but had a waxing appointment at one. She had lunch with Isak after that, and then another appointment at the beauty parlor.

"Don't worry," he replied, "we'll do it as fast as we can. Do you want to start right away?"

"Of course." She looked over empty walls and modest office furniture. "Here?"

"Oh, no ma'am, absolutely not." He got up and theatrically opened the door. "This way, please."

The director hurried to the elevator and smiled again nervously. When they entered the elevator, she watched as he pressed -2.

The door closed and Marija felt the elevator sliding below street level.

She had met Isak Lero at a reception at the Swiss ambassador's residence.

Her husband had received an invitation because he had been placed on the list of some of the major NGOs that followed the work of the most promising coders and openly recruited their services for foreign technology giants. Aleksandar Vranješ had previously programmed several interesting apps for mobile platforms. The most popular among them was the Trailblazers platform intended for drivers navigating Belgrade's chaotic traffic. Trailblazers' algorithms had enabled autonomous vehicles to *monitor the situation* and constantly report to each other where they were going in order to optimize traffic flow, and had significantly reduced traffic congestion. As he liked to say, these algorithms had definitely *put him on the map*—which the invitation to the residence of His Excellency proved. This had happened at a time when the two of them would go for days without uttering a single word: he was buried in work and programmed at night and slept during the day; she went to work, moving through the day like a zombie, sleeping at night. A depressing time. The time after Mina.

The only thing she remembered from this reception—which she'd attended unwillingly—was Isak. Amid the throng of officials and the waiters who were clumsily dragging themselves through the crowd carrying trays with canapés and cocktails, she tried to find her way to the nearest chair, where she planned to stay until Aleksandar had had enough of chatting with the IT team and took her home. At some point she snuck out to a room on the ground floor of the residence. As she looked around, slightly perplexed, she became aware of someone's presence.

"Would you like to get out of here too?" asked large man in an elegant jacket and a light-colored shirt without a tie. She looked up at his face—he was much taller than her—and saw a mild frown creasing his forehead.

A man who knows that you don't say "Wanna," but "Would you like," she thought to herself.

"Are you okay?" he asked, looking sincerely concerned.

How terrible I must look, if he only took one glance at me and figured out that I wasn't feeling very well, she thought. *I like his voice.*

"I can't stand the crowds," she said, shaking her head. "It's stifling in here."

"We'll take care of that." He smiled and Marija realized that it was hard for her to look away from his warm eyes. *How old is he,* she wondered, *in his fifties?*

He gently took her by the arm and led her through the corridor. He opened the door, which allowed in a refreshing breeze and the scent of late spring. "Here, this way," he said, and they continued to an illuminated garden.

"Sit down. I'll get you something to drink." He paused as she obediently sat on a wooden bench near a white gravel path. He noticed the expression on her face. "Maybe some water . . ."

She put her fingers on his hand and smiled, now more naturally. "Campari and juice, please. If they have it."

He nodded. As he went back into the house to find an open bar and bring her a drink, she felt that something had irreversibly changed. She accepted the change as a life-saving exit.

More than three years had passed since that evening. More than three years of their secret relationship, and almost as long since Aleksandar became a leading developer in Lero Technologies, the main investor in the Alter Ego Inc. start-up.

* * *

"I won't bother you with details," said the director as he walked next to her. "I'm sure you are familiar with the basic principles of the procedure."

They walked between glass boxes in which men and women in white coats stood by unusual machines, hospital beds on wheels, computer workstations, and chairs that reminded Marija of well-equipped dentist offices. In some boxes, these machines—3-D printers she now recognized—were painfully, slowly forming something that, she realized, feeling the hair on the back of her next stand up, looked like different parts of human bodies.

The director stopped and pointed to a long glass wall and motionless figures behind him. She gasped. There were a few dozen of them. They stood motionless. They were naked like old classical statues, but were made of a material that was so convincing that she couldn't help thinking that someone was detaining these men and women, making them stand so stiffly with no hope of ever being allowed to move.

"We've run into a lot of problems," the director muttered, moving to a section in the corner of a large, well-lit underground room that reminded Marija of the automatic photo booths she had seen in old movies. "Mainly legal in nature: in this sphere, things develop rapidly, but bureaucracy decides on the rules and lags behind hopelessly. EU directives covering artificial intelligence and robotics have become obsolete ever since the first computer passed the Captcha test. They can't understand, they just can't understand . . . But, somehow, we will get to the bottom of it. Mr. Lero has a good legal team."

"Do I . . . need to come in here?" she asked.

The thin man smiled and nodded. "This won't take long," he said. "We've perfected the scanning so well that what used to take hours may now be accomplished in just under fifteen

236 // Belgrade Noir

minutes. But this is not the key—your DNA is the basis for the print, while the scanning results are actually used for the finishing touches. The main thing is to capture the personality of the subject—*your* personality: the inner rainbow of the mind, your special light, whatever you want to call it. Recording and storing it in the mainframes that occupy the whole underground floor beneath us. Yottabytes and yottabytes of data—all that makes *you*, one, unique. And now, thanks to the algorithm for which this will be the final test, one more—doubled."

Yes, she thought, entering a small room, the door slamming closed behind her, *this algorithm wouldn't exist without my husband.*

She examined the memory foam mattress lifted upright at an angle on a shining hydraulic stand. She sighed and began to undress. At one point, as she neatly folded the black blouse and the tight pencil skirt Isak loved so much, she thought that the director was probably watching her on the screen out there. She shrugged her shoulders and went to the mattress. The time for shyness had long passed. Soon all employees in this company would have access not only to the image of her naked body but also to all her memories and thoughts. Isak explained to her that she shouldn't worry, that this database—the data that made her *her*—would not be accessed by anyone without the appropriate password, a password that only the director of Alter Ego and Isak would have. She knew that for the commercial realization of this process one of the key conditions was the protection, safety, and inviolability of client data, but then again . . . how many people would be willing to risk exposing themselves to such an extent?

"We can start now," she heard the director's voice through the speaker. "Buckle up, please."

She did. The hydraulics hissed, the color of the lights

changed, the bed began to shift its incline, and Marija closed her eyes.

"Do you even know *why* you are doing this?"

Marija sat on the terrace of a restaurant overlooking the promenade near the Sava River with Tamara, her best friend.

"You know," she said thoughtfully, "a few weeks ago we had a bad fight."

"You and Isak?"

"Of course. I wish I could have a fight with Aleksandar."

"Let me guess: you've been thinking about where your relationship is going?"

"Well, yes," Marija answered. "I complained that he's so closed off, that whenever I bring up my divorce from Aleksandar and our happy future life together, he just shuts down. I told him how much this was tearing me apart—how much it hurts me—that I completely give myself to him, that I sacrifice myself . . ."

"And?"

"Imagine what he said! Wait, I'll try to remember exactly how he put it . . ." She frowned slightly after taking a sip of her cocktail. "Something like this: *What are you actually sacrificing? Your relationship with your husband? As far as I know, it was ruined before we met . . . Would—if the situation were different—you sacrifice your relationship with your child for us?* He went straight for the jugular."

"That's awful," said Tamara with a smile. "But he's *your* awful guy."

Marija finished the last of her cocktail and lit up another cigarette. "You know, I shouldn't have told you all this. About the experiment. I mean, it's all still very top secret, a big project for Isak's company, but you're the only one I can really trust—"

"Don't worry," her friend cut in, and waved the waitress over to order another round. "I *always* keep our secrets. What are your plans? How are you spending these fifteen days while waiting for . . . your replacement?"

Marija leaned back in her chair while Tamara ordered two more cocktails, and waited for the waitress to walk away. "Isak organized a trip. The first eight days—Madrid, Barcelona, and Lisbon. Then a week in the Côte d'Azur."

Marija sat back and put out her half-smoked cigarette in the ashtray. After a minute or so, she sighed and said: "I would love it if Aleksandar found someone . . . if he cheated on me. To *find out.* I think it would change everything."

"Let's call her . . . Marija 2.0. All right?"

The director was smiling so broadly that Marija felt nauseous. Or was the cause of that nausea deeper? She felt uncomfortable as she watched her copy sitting silently on a chair in a laboratory glass box.

She was dressed in a simple white nightgown. Bare ankles and feet with nails painted in her favorite color, arms folded in her lap. The eyes of Marija 2.0 were closed, the face completely devoid of expression.

She felt her mouth drying. Somewhere in the back of her head, a hard-core panic was setting in. This was not like standing in front of a mirror. This was something completely different. Marija gulped and moistened her lips with her tongue.

"Her memory now includes your experiences from the last few days to avoid unwanted holes in memory," the director continued breezily. "Everything we recorded this morning has been smoothly transferred to her personality."

"Please . . . please," Marija said, "I want to . . . I want to see *it* . . . without clothes."

The director looked at her, raising his eyebrows. He nodded his head and typed something on the tablet. Marija 2.0 opened her eyes, slowly stood up, and pulled the nightgown over her head.

Marija didn't pay attention to the fact that her body—even if it was just a copy—was exposed to the view of the director and other lab technicians. An irresistible curiosity now prompted her to walk around the naked woman standing in front of her, to carefully see her body from all sides. Suddenly she wanted to see herself as Isak saw her. She was both excited and filled with anxiety.

She remembered yesterday's conversation in bed, after having sex, when, half-jokingly, she said, *You've done all this just so you can have a threesome—with two of me.* He'd wanted to answer her, to dissuade her, but he'd only dropped a kiss on her lips that were still hot from his gentle bites and said: *You know, I didn't even think about it, but now that you mention it . . . well—I think it would be hot to see you make love to yourself. Would you do that for me?*

Would she?

As she watched her replica, she felt a flurry of almost pleasurable anxiety. She used to fantasize about lesbian sex—she assumed that all women did—but usually in her threesome fantasies, where she and another woman (sometimes Tamara, sometimes another friend, or someone she didn't know at all) shared the same lover, there would inevitably be those exciting, forbidden touches. But if the other woman was her, *herself?* She looked down the upright back of Marija 2.0, to her firm buttocks, sculpted muscles, golden skin with a few tiny spots, and thought about making love to herself—she knows exactly what turns her on, she feels it under her toes and under her tongue, the juices and the warmth that Isak feels every time they sleep together.

She snapped out of it and cleared her throat. "May I . . . hear *its* . . . voice?" she asked.

"Of course." The director's face lit up and again he typed something on the tablet. "Tell us your name."

The creature before them looked at him for the first time and responded calmly: "Marija. Marija Vranješ."

She couldn't detect any difference in tone or inflection. It was creepy.

"Please . . . let it get dressed again."

"Of course, ma'am."

After her double got dressed and sat down again following the director's instructions he entered into the tablet, Marija asked: "So, how are we going to do this?"

He nervously smiled and nodded to the device he held in his hand. "We have already entered the bulk of the instructions, including your usual schedule—going to yoga, pilates, massage and cosmetic treatments . . ."

"And suntanning. Suntanning is essential—I travel where there is a lot of sun; I'll be tan, at least on my face, neck, and shoulders, I mustn't forget that."

"Yes, yes, certainly, you've already mentioned this to us. You have scheduled the appointments already, right? No worries, Marija 2.0 will not miss a single one."

"I have to ask you—I read a little about . . . singularity. It seems to me that no one has figured out whether it's possible if—"

"If artificial intelligence becomes real? Equal to a human's?" He spread his arms and shrugged. "I think we are very, very far from it. Anyway, you don't have to worry about that."

"How can you be sure?"

"It's never happened before, and we've experimented a lot. Marija 2.0 will perfectly fulfill her role: she will live for you in your home, while you are where you really want to be. No one will notice the difference. When I turn on the autonomous mode, your specific wave front will enter the scene—what makes you unique—and she will react to every situation as you would. Did you bring things for her?"

Marija lifted a large paper bag containing her purse, wallet, makeup, car and house keys, clothes, socks, shoes, bracelet, necklace, and wristwatch—identical to those she had on her. The director took the bag from her, approached the chair with the silent Marija 2.0, and lowered her to the floor.

"Nevertheless . . ."

"Yes?" Marija asked.

"In order to be completely safe—in the event that something unforeseen happens—we will also program a safe word. Say something that you would remember in an instant, so it can serve as a kind of switch . . ."

"Mombasa," she said without thinking. It was the name of a luxurious perfume, the first gift she'd received from Isak. The perfume that she had not stopped using since then.

"*Mombasa!* Excellent." The director typed the word on the tablet with pleasure. "Let's try it?"

He swiped his fingers across the touch screen, and Marija 2.0 stood up, turned to her, looked her straight in the eyes, and stepped forward.

Marija felt a sudden shudder along her spine and gave him a look. The director nodded.

"Mombasa!" she exclaimed.

Marija 2.0 immediately stopped.

"Perfect," he said, and the duplicate, after the newly typed instructions, returned to her place. "We still need to agree on the logistics. Do you want her to go back to your apartment right now?"

"Yes."

"Then I suggest putting her into autopilot mode when she gets in your car. And when you return . . ."

"You programmed her to come back here in fifteen days at this exact time?"

"Of course. It's easiest that way. However, if for some reason her independent return is not possible, it may be best to replace her at your place. You have the safe word, so you can invite me to come, and I will arrange for her to be returned to the lab."

Marija looked at her calm face on the woman who stood nearly a foot from her. "Then what will happen to her?" she asked.

"We'll put her back," he said indifferently.

"Into her previous state?"

"Yes. We will dissolve her into proteins, water, minerals, everything that makes a human organism."

Marija gulped. "And what about the . . . software?"

He looked a little surprised. "You mean what will happen to the scanned person who is now in our server? Mr. Lero ordered that we delete this information as soon as this fifteen-day trial is over. Except, of course, if you want to preserve it for some future opportunity."

"All right," Marija said. "I'll tell you when I've made a decision about that. This is all too new and strange for me."

"And for us too, Mrs. Vranješ," the director said. "For us too."

As Marija entered the elevator, her perfect copy slowly took out clothes from the bag and started to get dressed.

What is your name?
Marija. Marija Vranješ.

She frowned, leaning on the sink as the phantom words

passed through her head again. She washed her cup and ashtray and lay both on the drying rack.

She couldn't explain the feeling of duplication that had followed her the past few days. It was there while she was driving to work, letting the autonomous system operate the vehicle through the central city streets. It was there while she worked in the office surrounded by colleagues she had known for more than ten years. It was there while she presented a concept for the next museum exhibition to her boss who always only half listened to her proposals and usually accepted them without objections. There was this feeling of duplication while she was spending time with her friends, during beauty treatments, at the hairdresser's, yoga classes, in tanning booths . . . For some reason she couldn't understand this artificial tanning in the least bit—she had never, as far as she recalled, resorted to that dangerous method of tanning.

It was as if she were in her own body and somewhere else, where she watched herself behave naturally, easily, spontaneously, in all these everyday situations. The situation at home wasn't helping, either.

When did she and Aleksandar actually start drinking coffee separately, in separate rooms, in their own worlds? She was reluctant to think about it in more detail: she would always stop herself as if sitting in front of a closed door that she didn't want to open out of fear of what was behind it. She saw him at home in the evenings, when he returned from work and continued to program until late into the night. She was reserved with him because she felt she *should* behave this way, not because she could remember the right reason. She looked at the apartment and the things they owned as though she was seeing them for the first time, even though she knew when they had bought most of the things—decorations, paintings, or pieces of clothing and furniture—together or on their own. And the mirrors were another story: every time she looked at her reflection in her bedroom, bathroom, hallway, even in the corner of a windowpane, it was as if a shadow was present at the very edge, *her* shadow where it couldn't possibly be. Soon, she began to avoid mirrors altogether and used them only when she absolutely needed to.

Then one night she opened the lower drawer in her bureau in the bedroom—a bedroom with a queen bed that she slept in by herself—and pulled out a box.

It was made of wood, decorated with abstract patterns, lacquered, rather heavy. She set it close to her feet. She felt an irresistible desire to open it; she also felt fear. She stood there indecisively for a long time, aware that the sense of division—duplication—would continue to bite at her more and more mercilessly, all the more insatiable if she didn't do anything about it.

She lifted the lid.

Mina.

She closed her eyes and felt dizzy, thinking that she'd lose her balance.

The door opened. And behind it was a wave that swept across her whole being, filled up all the voids she had felt, uncovered everything buried deep under the mud of nonsense.

Mina.

A pink rabbit with a ripped left ear, where the old yellowish filling was spilling out. Zeka-Peka, funny bunny, the one she slept with, the one who still smelled like her, Mina the baby. A green woolen vest that Marija's mother knitted when Mina was six months old and a pair of socks of the same color, from the same wool. Photographs—from the hospital, after childbirth; also from the hospital, four years later. A lock of hair in a decorative ring with a label and a date. She remembered when she'd cut off that lock—Mina was almost two years old and just getting used to sleeping without a pacifier.

Eighteen months later, Mina had no hair. And she got used to sleeping with a plastic tube in her esophagus.

The pain was enormous, unbearable. Marija thought at one point that she wouldn't be able to breathe again. The pain was gray, tough, and impenetrable, the pain was a wall that grew from tragedy, from the meaningless death, for them the greatest tragedy in the world. The wall grew, forcing her and her husband, the parents who had done nothing wrong—their child had been genetically cursed—dividing them forever and bringing silence to them heavier than any cry, sharper than any scream.

As she lowered the cover of the box it seemed to her that the duplication was real—the one that she felt in the shadows of the mirror—stronger than ever before, like Warhol's pictures of runners on skates with discordant colors and contours. She rose and moved away from the box. She placed a fist in her mouth to swallow up the mute scream that leaped from her stomach: she'd realized that it had been years since she'd visited Mina's grave. That she had found a solution to pretend that all of this had never happened. That she had cut her ties, as much as she could, with her own parents, with her father-in-law who lived outside the city and whom she hadn't seen even once since the funeral.

With Aleksandar.

She found him in his study in front of an open laptop.

She approached him silently, walking barefoot on the thick carpet, so that he didn't have the chance to close the computer screen, to not let her see the photo of a skinny child with a bare scalp covered with blue veins, with big chestnut eyes and an absurdly happy smile, with a beloved pink bunny pressed against her cheek.

When he felt her presence behind him, he quickly reached his hand toward the laptop, as if he was ashamed of looking at that photograph himself, but his hand halted in the air halfway and loosely dropped. When he turned his face toward her, she saw that it was covered with tears. Just like hers.

Without a word, he embraced her and pressed his head into her waist. When his shoulders stopped shaking, she lowered her hand to his forehead, and gently touched him.

How much time has passed since our last embrace? she wondered. *How long since we last made love?*

She took him by the hand and pulled him slightly toward her. For a moment it seemed that he'd resist, refuse, and return to the solitude of the photograph to which he had condemned himself, but no—he got up, accepted the grip of her hand, and followed her.

When the orgasm came, he seemed at once like a good old friend and someone completely new. And Warhol's contours and colors seemed as if they had finally merged, made a complete, coherent image.

Now, after so much silence, it was time to talk.

"It all started with the three-dimensional printing of transplant organs," Aleksandar said. She was silent, pressing her body against his.

"Top-level bioengineering. Saving lives. Help for people sentenced to death from kidney, liver, pancreas failure . . . Technology is evolving so fast and the results are here. And now this—the quantum leap forward, artificial intelligence and bio reconstruction merging—is fascinating and frightening. Do you know why?"

She shook her head, embracing him tightly.

"Because now we can—without any obstacles—save someone who is close to us, someone we love, as we save images or sounds, to create it again if we lose it, if . . ." He went silent. It was too hard for him to continue.

She took a sharp breath and whispered, "All you've been doing for years—everything you've put into the codes and programs . . . it was all because of *her?* Because of our little girl?"

For several moments he tried unsuccessfully to find his voice, and then managed to utter without tears, clearly, slowly, quietly, "Yes. But too late. Too late for her. For us."

She was silent for a while, playing with the hairs on his chest, listening to his heartbeat. "You know," she finally said, "we could try again."

He held his breath and turned toward her, looked her in the eye. "Again?"

She leaned on her elbow. Their faces were only an inch apart. "Yes. With a new child. A new baby. It's not too late." She smiled briefly, nervously, as he observed her.

"Where did that come from?"

She shrugged. "I think that's what we need if we want to stay together at all."

"Would you be willing to go through everything again, everything we went through with Mina?"

She sighed. "It's different now. Of course, our genetics are the same, and there's still the risk. But things have changed. *You* changed them."

Aleksandar rubbed his eyes and straightened himself against the pillow. He now had a glint in his eyes that she had not seen for years. "Yes . . . Now it would certainly be different. Lero deserves recognition for this—even though he only wants money, he's done something revolutionary, something that will change the game from the get-go. Something that'll make humankind redefine itself."

She barely heard his last sentence. She felt as if he had punched her in her stomach. The name he'd uttered suddenly opened a new door, a door she hadn't even known existed.

Lero. Isak. Her husband's employer. A polite and attentive lover. The man she'd been seeing for three years.

Učiteljsko Naselje.

Let's call her . . . Marija 2.0.

I read a little about singularity. It seems to me that no one has figured out whether it's possible if . . .

I think we are very, very far from it.

The stream of words. Conversation fragments. Someone heard it, some just reproduced it from her own/others' memory.

We'll put her back . . . We will dissolve her into proteins, water, minerals, everything that makes a human organism.

Mombasa.

Was it just a moment or an eternity? She wasn't sure how long this blinding white light lasted after the last piece of the puzzle fell into place. She became aware that Aleksandar was squeezing her hands hard, that he was trying to get her attention—to bring her back to reality—his face distorted from care and fear.

"*Marija!* Marija, what's going on with you? You turned so pale, like you saw a ghost! Say something! Are you okay? Should I call an ambulance?"

Her eyes regained focus. He saw that she really saw him again and the spasm was passing, though despite her tan she was still white as a ghost. He relaxed the grip on her hands and gently lowered her back to the bed.

"Are you okay?" Aleksandar repeated.

She answered him with a smile that looked more like another spasm as she licked her dry lips. She cleared her throat and peered deeply into his warm, worried eyes. "I have to . . . I need to tell you something."

* * *

She felt like she was walking on clouds.

She had just spent the most beautiful and happiest fifteen days of her life. The future looked bright and perfect.

They had enjoyed each other, absorbed the scents and tastes of Spain and Portugal, visited museums, indulged in culinary delights, enjoyed the luxury of expensive hotels, and made love—often, relaxed, free of sorrow and guilt. Then, two days before their return, while having a dinner in Nice, Isak told her that he was ready if she wanted to do it.

Marija was enthusiastic. She didn't say anything to anyone. She only messaged Tamara, hinting that she had *great news*. When they headed back, Isak flew to Frankfurt for a three-day artificial intelligence conference, and she returned on a direct flight to Belgrade to a new, completely altered reality.

As she drove home from the airport, her telephone rang. When she answered, she saw on the small screen the little rat face of that tiny man in the white coat—the director.

"Mrs. Vranješ?"

"Yes?"

"There have been ... ah ... some changes."

"What changes? I don't understand."

The director avoided looking her in the eye. "Marija 2.0 didn't return to the location. We assume there has been some kind of coding error."

She felt a sudden rage, accompanied by fear. "And now what? Where is she?"

The little man shrugged. "We are not sure. We think she's in the apartment. In *your* apartment. The GPS signal from the mobile device that you left for her indicates that she is there. But, of course, she could have left the phone and gone out without it."

Marija tried to calm down. Where was Aleksandar now? The day before yesterday, Isak had told her offhandedly, as if it were something irrelevant, Aleksandar had asked for—and received—several days off work so he could go visit his sick father. This worked in her favor—he wouldn't be home when she faced her replacement.

"What are you suggesting?" she asked coldly, and saw from the expression on the director's face that his whole career was at risk.

"Hmm . . ." He coughed. "I . . . I hired an ambulance that belongs to a clinic that is part of Mr. Lero's holdings. The vehicle will wait with the team discreetly in the side street near your building. If you find Marija 2.0 in the apartment, use the safe word and let me know. The team will get her here right away."

"And if it's not there?"

He shrugged again, an apologetic expression on his face. "We'll wait till she's back. And in the meantime, we'll try to locate her some other way."

Marija hung up without saying goodbye.

Ten minutes later, she unlocked the front door with a spare set of keys, entered the apartment, and put her suitcase down. It was getting dark outside, and the only light in the apartment came from the spacious living room. She paused at the door, looked inside, and saw the floor lamp turned on. And there, on the sofa, was a human form.

When she got up the courage, Marija entered the room and turned on the overhead light. Marija 2.0 turned her face toward her, smiled, and stood up.

"You got a nice tan," she said. "Much nicer than mine. I suppose everything went well? Was Isak a chivalrous lover, a man who will take care of you?"

Marija gulped, then panicked. This was totally wrong. This

shouldn't be happening. If the programmed return of her artificial copy went wrong—what *else* could have gone wrong?

"You know," continued the woman in front of her who was—and was not—her, "Aleksandar and I had a long, long talk." She smiled, staring into Marija's eyes. "And we agree on what is to be done." Marija 2.0 took a step toward her.

"Mom . . . Mombasa!" she shouted. "*Mombasa!*"

"You were interested in singularity. I have something to tell you about singularity. But we don't have time for that." Marija 2.0's smile was now wider but didn't reach the woman's eyes.

"Mombasa, motherfucker!" Marija yelled. "*Momb—*" She backed up against something and turned around. Her husband stood right in front of her and smiled, just like the creature she was trying to retreat from.

She felt a sting in her neck and looked at Aleksandar's hand. She saw a plastic syringe full of clear liquid and a long glittering needle. She lifted her hand toward the spot where he'd injected her and stared at him with disbelief. Then she crashed onto the parquet floor.

The worst of it was that she was aware of everything.

Her eyes were open, she could see, she could hear what was going on, but she couldn't move or feel anything while they removed her clothes and redressed her. She heard her phone ringing, how Marija 2.0 answered it. "Yes," she confirmed to the director. "She is here. I used the safe word. You can come for her."

Aleksandar looked at her for the last time before he left so the members of the director's team wouldn't notice him as they were coming out of the apartment. He peered at her with complete indifference, like she was an object, before he disappeared forever from her sight.

She didn't feel someone else's hands lifting her onto the

hospital bed, but she heard voices that mumbled an apology and greeted her copy. She watched the concrete ceiling of the hallway as they pushed her toward the elevator, then a clear night sky with the reflection of the ambulance's rotating lights, before the view was replaced by the inside roof of the ambulance. The door closed. Her companions were silent while the vehicle moved with the sound of the siren. She tried to estimate how long it would take until they reached Učiteljsko Naselje, and then she gave up. She wondered how this new her, Marija 2.0, would explain to Isak why she had changed her mind. And what would she tell Tamara and her other friends?

I will disappear and nobody will notice. Because, of course, I will still be here.

At some point, her pupils narrowed in the presence of the glaring light of the laboratory. The director's face appeared before her.

"Perfectly faithful to the original," he said with undisguised admiration. Marija heard his words, saw the bright light and his face, but she still couldn't feel her own body, she couldn't move, blink, speak.

"Are we following the plan?" someone asked outside of her field of vision, probably one of the technicians.

"Yes," the director replied. "The object is to be recycled. We'll look for an error in the software. There is certainly a trace somewhere, something that will indicate the moment when there was a deviation from the programmed behavior."

"Look," said a technician, his finger touching her right eye, then immediately removing it, shining with moisture.

"Tears," the director said. "Unusual."

While the technician pushed her on the stretcher toward a small room, he closed her eyelids. Now she had only hearing left—the crunch of rubber wheels on the floor, the distant buzzing of the appliances, and the quiet hum of the air conditioners—and smell: a sweaty technician tilted over her, traces of the cigarette she had smoked on the way from the airport, and hints of the heavy, sweet smell of the expensive perfume that she had used that day, spraying it on her neck, behind her ears, on the insides of her wrists. If she could move her facial muscles, she would have smiled ironically to herself.

It was the perfume she hadn't parted with in more than three years.

Mombasa.

THE RAT

BY MISHA GLENNY

Dorćol

Miloš calculated that on average, during a six-day week, he was completely bored roughly 61 percent of the time. Eighteen percent of the time, he was able to distract himself by playing Xenonauts 2. He was impressed by the transition from the original Xenonauts which featured 2-D sprites. Although he loved these sprites, like most Xenonauts devotees, he was surprised and genuinely impressed by the transition to 3-D graphics in the updated version.

As long as his boss wasn't around, he could play. The assistant manager, Jovana, didn't care, while Bane was so in awe of Miloš that he wouldn't dare snitch.

The remaining 21 percent of his time was taken up dealing with customers. This being Knez Mihailova, a notable proportion of the customers were well off. Miloš had quickly noticed that there was no apparent correlation between wealth and intelligence. The richer the client, the more they struggled with their smartphones. Almost all had mastered turning the device off and on. Beyond that, most could usually manage phone calls, WhatsApp messages, SMS, and playing music. But even these simple functions still baffled some.

Miloš pondered long and hard as to why people were so stupid, but he struggled to come up with any answer. It didn't really bother him. Quite the contrary—their incompetence provided him with endless entertainment. Whether selling a new phone or just swapping a SIM card, he had ample time to install the custom malware that he had written which acted as a Remote Access Tool (RAT). The customers, of course, had absolutely no idea what Miloš was up to. Nor did the service providers, nor did Google or Apple, who had created the environment in which Miloš liked to play.

Instead, the customers squealed with delight when Miloš got their shiny new phones up and running and demonstrated how to play Flappy Bird which, again to his surprise, they considered to be some form of achievement (here I differ from Miloš as I believe that Flappy Bird is irritatingly difficult and that Miloš underestimates his facility with this game—of course, by his standards the Flappy Bird trick is indeed unremarkable).

Having safely built his RAT a new lair on the customer's device, he would stroll back home across Studentski Trg and down Dositijeva before he arrived at his father's large, ghostly apartment.

Here he would start remotely scanning the contents of his latest victim's phone. His favorite sport was going through WhatsApp. He had noticed early on that people were invariably less discreet and less inhibited on WhatsApp than they were on their normal messaging apps.

He calculated that 73 percent of users talked with disarming frankness about sex in their exchanges. Roughly 18 percent would regularly send explicit photographs or videos of themselves. These were not always what one might expect. One middle-aged man sent short videos of himself eating breakfast naked. Miloš concluded that the recipient was another man. The morning fare consisted of a bowl of fruit. After the recipient had viewed the video, he would send back one word—the name of a new fruit. And the next morning, the sender would once again sit at his breakfast table, but with the new fruit.

Miloš watched this ritual for about a week before getting witlessly bored. But it did give him a few days of contemplation. Whichever way he considered it, intellectually or emotionally, he simply couldn't grasp *why* anyone would derive the least pleasure from this activity, although, he noted, the fruits were ever more exotic, and it had inspired him to track down and sample a passion fruit. Not as easy in Belgrade as you might think, even these days.

Blackmail, threats, and passive aggression were almost ubiquitous on the WhatsApp exchanges. Again, this perplexed Miloš. Why were people so unpleasant to each other? What satisfaction did they derive from this? And did his relative calm mean that he was too ordinary?

In truth, he knew he was far from ordinary, but the vicious and cruel emotional habits of so many humans were still something he could not fathom.

Leaving aside the monstrous intrusion into others' privacy, his examination of the phones was vital to sustaining Miloš's good humor. Ever since his mother died when he was fourteen, his emotional life had all but atrophied. His father, whom he suspected of having had a role in his mother's death, showed no interest in Miloš whatsoever. Recently, Miloš had been researching his father's past to discover that his rise to wealth and notoriety had coincided with the eleven years of Miloševic's turbulent reign.

The more he understood his father, the less he liked him. Yet he was entirely dependent on him financially. His father barely exchanged any words with Miloš. But he was generous and did not use money as a tool to blackmail or control his son. There was always food in the house, and on those rare occasions when Miloš asked for something extra, his father gave it to him without hesitation. But in exchange, his father made it clear that he wished to have no relationship with his son beyond this. Miloš was alone.

Miloš sometimes came home to find his father entertaining his rather crude, unpleasant colleagues. There was business in the air, but Miloš didn't know what, nor did he inquire. Sometimes, instead of a business colleague, the visitor would be an impressionable young woman draping herself around his father. Just as he couldn't quite understand the stupidity of wealthy people, he was dumbfounded that any woman who was more or less his own age would want to engage in any kind of sexual interaction with his father.

One spring morning, Miloš was at work alone. No colleagues, no customers. He smiled and settled into his chair to explore the Farm in the American Midwest. He had received intelligence that aliens had recently landed. He suspected they may have been preparing for an all-out attack. Again, he was called upon to save the earth from executors of the dreaded Supreme Intergalactic Court.

In the distance, he spotted one and began to creep toward the target with exactly the requisite stealth to ensure that the alien wouldn't be alerted to his presence. His finger was on the trigger of his laser grenade launcher—the alien perfectly in his sights. Hit this guy and Miloš will have delivered perhaps a fatal blow to the aliens' tactics of establishing their forward base in North America. But accuracy was everything . . .

"Good morning." The interruption caused him to lose his balance. The alien's head turned. Miloš had no choice but to cut, run, and lose most of the data from the session.

Inside he was seething.

Then he saw the customer. Never had anger dissipated with such rapidity and such sincerity. *If this is a dream*, Miloš thought, *then let me never wake up*. Unlike so many young women Miloš had observed, there was nothing artificial about her. No hair dye, no spray-on tan, only the merest hint of makeup, the most discreet jewelry, deep green eyes set in features symmetrical enough to launch a thousand Xenonauts.

Miloš had to close his half-open mouth consciously. It had momentarily suffered an unexpected attack of lockjaw. Pulling himself together, he inquired how he could help her.

As effortless as she was in her appearance, so was she in verbal exchanges. "Why, thank you. I do hope you can sort this out. My iPhone appears to run out of power in less than an hour. Is it time to ask for an upgrade?"

"Normally, madame," said Miloš before clearing his throat, "I would suggest that you invest in an expensive upgrade. Under pressure from my superiors, you understand. But, in all honesty, you probably only need to replace the battery. It'll take an hour or so, but once I've done it, it should be as good as new."

"That is so very kind of you," the woman replied.

"You're most welcome," said Miloš with exaggerated politeness.

She pulled the iPhone out of her back pocket, placed it on the desk, and then with those green eyes seizing Miloš's gaze, she gently waved goodbye. "See you in an hour . . ."

As he examined her iPhone, unrestrained desire surged through Miloš's body. The phone requested a code. He tapped in *0000* and the lock screen dissolved to reveal the woman's secrets. Notwithstanding his sudden infatuation, he muttered his familiar rhetorical question, "Why do they make it so easy?"

That evening, his usual saunter turned into a breathless sprint down Dositijeva. Once home, he kicked off his shoes and walked quickly through the large, empty apartment until he

reached his bedroom. He switched on his computer and immediately accessed the phone remotely.

She was twenty-five years old. Along with Serbian, she
spoke English, Italian, and German. She traveled *a lot* but he
could find nothing about her employment. He realized that
this was her personal phone and she must have used another
one for work. Her friends were not just Serbian but from across
Europe and the US.

He hesitated before entering WhatsApp but eventually
got up enough courage. He knew that this would reveal much
about her intimate life. He was torn between his vision of her
purity and his barely controllable desire to soak in the imagined
reality of her sexual being.

Just as he decided to finally click on the app, an alert flashed
on his screen. The remote phone had been attached to another
device. Miloš rushed to his laptop and flipped it open before
feverishly typing in various commands. Within a minute, he
had access to her desktop. Using the RAT, he activated her
camera.

Her bedroom was predictably elegant. Minimalist but not
austere. Above a luxurious but tasteful sofa, there was a poster
of a giant cat smirking and holding a gun. Below this, a small
table upon which sat a large metal statuette—a man in a great
coat smoking a cigar. Miloš zoomed in. Underneath the bust on
a little plinth was the inscription: *Comrade Tito*. To the left was
what looked like a walk-in closet and to the right side of the
computer, Miloš assumed there was a door leading out of the
room. Against the wall, a large double bed.

Katarina started playing something on her iTunes. Miloš
had never heard the song although he identified it as German.
So he looked on her computer—Udo Lindenberg, "Unterm
Säufermond." She was lying on her sofa, and as the melancholic

sounds floated over her, he focused on those green eyes and realized that she had begun to cry.

He was frozen with a sympathy that he couldn't articulate. Least of all to her. As the song came to an end, she left the room, returning with a large glass of red wine. Miloš longed to be there to offer her comfort. But, real as this was, it was mediated by virtual deception.

At this point, Katarina started to remove her top. This was too much for Miloš to process and he slammed his computer shut.

Try as he might, Miloš could not keep away from her computer. Each time he watched her undress, he would wait a little longer before slamming down the top of his computer, overcome with guilt and anger at himself. At the same time, he felt betrayed because her WhatsApp messages indicated that she was having an affair. Her lover had yet to pay a visit to her apartment, but Miloš suspected it was only a matter of time.

Xenonauts 2 still provided a healthy distraction. The latest version was proving to be a magnificent challenge. He would play with intense concentration for two hours and then he would return to Katarina. By now, he knew every contour of what he considered her celestial body. Deep inside, his conscience was telling him that what he was doing was infernally immoral. Unfortunately, burning desire could outmaneuver his conscience. When at work, he distracted himself by thinking of ways in which he might approach her, how he might declare his resolute, adamantine, and eternal love. Should he casually bump into her as she was leaving her apartment? But what would he say? *Hey, miss, you remember me? I fixed your iPhone. Fancy a drink?* Preposterous.

Perhaps he could research fine red wines and present a rare

bottle to her as a gift. There was something about this idea that appealed to him. He could get the necessary cash from his father.

But he couldn't quite complete the plan in his head. How would he actually fashion a situation whereby giving her the bottle of wine would not appear, well, weird? Would he suggest that they drink it together? Or simply walk away with a euphoric smile on his face? These were details he had yet to finalize. But he felt that he had at least a seed of an idea.

Newly inspired, Miloš flipped open the lid of his computer. It was six thirty p.m., around the time that Katarina usually arrived home. He was in luck. The RAT told him her computer was already on. He switched on the camera. Early on, he had programmed the little green light at the top of her Mac only to turn on if she used it. So, as he was watching her, she would be ignorant of his presence.

As soon as the familiar room came up on his screen, he noted that something was odd. Something was distorting the image of the room which was by now seared into the screen of his mind. Then he spotted it. There were two glasses by the now familiar bottle of French wine. Not one.

Miloš's insides began to churn. He'd known that this moment would come at some point. He'd known he would have to watch his beloved Katarina have sex with somebody else. In his mind, he didn't reproach her for it. How could she carry any blame? She was unaware of the depth, the sincerity, not to mention the existence of his passion for her. He believed that once their friendship and companionship were established, then the cursory carnal pleasures that her other male friends delivered would disappear into the woods.

Suddenly, Katarina returned, switching off the main bedroom light as she entered before flicking another switch. Her bedside lamp threw but a modest dull circle of light across the left side of her bed. The lamp was beyond Miloš's field of vision and so it was only the dark shapes of Katarina and her friend that he observed in a state of controlled frenzy as they impatiently removed each other's clothes. Miloš was close to tears as he watched her being defiled and dishonored. But he could no longer restrain himself and less than a minute into the event, his reluctant excitement was seeping stickily into the keyboard.

He felt transformed into a bottom feeder in an ocean of shame. He had never felt so miserable. He was desperate to slam shut his laptop in order to end the tortured on-screen show and its associated sighs and grunts. But he knew well that this would soak his motherboard with the viscous liquid and render it unusable. All the data of his Xenonauts conquests lay there. So he did the only thing he could: he started to cry before finding some tissues with which he could clean up the mess and turn the machine off.

Over the next few days, Miloš refused to even open his computer. Not only did he stop spying on Katarina, he actually stopped playing Xenonauts. At work, he retreated into his own thoughts. Bane and Jovana tiptoed around him—aware that something was very wrong, but apprehensive about doing anything that might trigger what they suspected was an emotional volcano.

Five days later, Miloš could no longer resist the lure of Xenonauts and so he lifted the lid on his laptop. He stared at the keyboard, the focus of his recent embarrassment. He thought he detected a couple of small stains which he carefully removed with a dab of water on a tissue. Before long, he was back—this time in a new environment that the aliens were seeking to establish as their base in the Middle East.

It was soon after he had stumbled across an oasis south of

Mosul that the alert sounded. It was six thirty-five p.m. Katarina had returned home. He froze the Iraqi action and flipped over to her webcam, his heart pounding. Deploying those hawk eyes which had been the downfall of so many aliens, he clocked the two glasses next to the wine.

Jealousy, anger, prurience, desire, tristesse, curiosity. Which impulse would take over? As they vied for his attention, something most unexpected occurred, recalibrating all his emotions into a wave of astonishment. A dinner plate came flying through the door and sailed right across the bedroom before exiting into the bathroom, followed by a loud crash which was efficiently picked up by the microphone on Katarina's Mac.

Worse followed. Much worse. Miloš heard Katarina scream as she fell back into the room before the man with a swift, expert sleight of hand immobilized her. It reminded him of the Vulcan nerve grip that Mr. Spock was able to deploy so fatally in his close-combat encounters aboard the USS *Enterprise*. The man squatted over her with his back to Miloš. Having kicked her to ensure she remained on the floor, the man turned to grab Comrade Tito before raising the statuette above his head in preparation to strike.

Miloš was suddenly confronted with a truth that he had always suspected somewhere deep down. The man inflicting the harm, reponsible for the violence, was his father. He looked as indifferent as he did at the breakfast table. A man without humanity who could take a life as nonchalantly as he might sip a whiskey.

Years of Xenonautical strategic thinking kicked in. Miloš called up a GIF of talking lips on a white background and lit up the screen with them. He also filtered his voice through an alien distorter. *"Gvero! Your actions are being monitored in real time. Desist now! Failure to do so will result in the Supreme In-*

tergalactic Court ordering your immediate liquidation. The court is already considering its verdict in the case of the death of Dragana Gvero."

Miloš's father gaped at the screen—baffled, terrified. He dropped the Comrade Tito statue, which hit the floor with a thud, narrowly missing Katarina, who had also turned her eyes to the screen, as bewildered as her attacker. Without even glancing down at her, Gvero ran out of the room and a moment later Miloš heard what he assumed was the front door open.

The lips continued, *"Thank you, Katarina, for your courageous role in ensnaring the defendant."* The lips morphed into a big eye. It winked.

Miloš walked into the kitchen to brew a cup of tea. As he sat back down at his laptop, he thought, *How on earth can I follow that?* Within three hours, he had cleared the entire Middle East of aliens.

Mission complete.

ABOUT THE CONTRIBUTORS

VLADIMIR ARSENIJEVIĆ was born in 1965 in Pula, Croatia. His first book—*In the Hold*, an antiwar novel—won the 1994 NIN Award and was translated into twenty languages. Since then, Arsenijević has published numerous novels, graphic novels, and essay collections. He is the founder and president of Association KROKODIL that runs one of the most distinguished literary festivals in the former Yugoslavia. He lives and works in Belgrade.

MUHAREM BAZDULJ was born in Travnik, Bosnia, in 1977. His novels, essays, and short stories have appeared in twenty languages. Three of his books have been translated into English and published in the UK and US: *The Second Book, Byron and the Beauty*, and *Transit, Comet, Eclipse*. He lives in Belgrade.

JAMIE CLEGG is a PhD student of comparative literature at the University of Michigan. She is interested in contemporary Diné (Navajo) poetry and histories, and modern Palestinian literature. She translates from Arabic and Bosnian/Croatian/Serbian.

VERICA VINCENT COLE is a crime writer whose novels introduced to readers Belgrade's first fictional private detective. Cole was born in Belgrade, where, prior to moving to Malta in 1999, she had her own practice as an attorney. After obtaining her degree in international maritime law at the IMO International Maritime Law Institute, she stayed to work at the Institute. She lives in the old city of Rabat, Malta, with her husband Kenneth and their two dogs.

RACHAEL DAUM received her BA in creative writing from the University of Rochester and MA in Slavic Studies from Indiana University; she also received certificates in literary translation from both institutions. Her original work and translations have appeared in *Tupelo Quarterly, Two Lines, EuropeNow, Queen Mob's Teahouse,* and elsewhere. Daum is the communications and awards manager at the American Literary Translators Association and lives in Cologne, Germany.

MIRJANA ĐURĐEVIĆ was born in Belgrade in 1956. She has published seventeen novels, as well as several short stories and essays. Her novel *Deda Rankove riblje teorije (Grandpa Ranko's Fish Theories)* won the Female Pen Award in 2004. For her novel *Kaya, Belgrade and the Good American,* she received the prestigious Meša Selimović Award for the best book in the region in 2009. Her works have been translated into English and Slovenian.

Edi Matić

SIBELAN FORRESTER is a professor of Russian language and literature at Swarthmore College in Pennsylvania. Her translations include Irena Vrkljan's lyrical autobiography *The Silk, the Shears and Marina,* Milica Mićić Dimovska's novel *The Cataract,* and a book of selected poetry by Marija Knežević, *Tehnika Disanja (Breathing Technique).*

Raian Forrester-Herndon

ALEKSANDAR GATALICA was born in 1964 in Belgrade. He graduated with a world literature degree in Ancient Greek from the University of Belgrade's Faculty of Philology. He is a writer, critic, and translator, best known for his novel *The Great War,* winner of the NIN Award for Best Serbian Novel of the year. His works have been translated into more than ten languages.

MISHA GLENNY is an award-winning writer and broadcaster. His best-selling nonfiction book *McMafia* was translated into thirty-two languages and was broadcast as a BBC and AMC fictional TV drama series. A former BBC Central Europe correspondent, Glenny won the Sony Gold Award for Outstanding Contribution to Broadcasting for his work during the wars in the former Yugoslavia. His books include *The Balkans: Nationalism, War, and the Great Powers, 1804-2011* and *The Fall of Yugoslavia.*

Teresa Walton

VESNA GOLDSWORTHY was born in Belgrade in 1961 and has lived in England since 1986. She is a best-selling writer, academic, and broadcaster. Her books have been translated into twenty-three languages. Her novel *Gorsky,* serialized on the BBC, was a Waterstones's Book of the Year and a *New York Times* Editors' Choice in 2015. *Monsieur Ka,* which imagines the life of Anna Karenina's son, was a London *Times* Summer Reads for 2019.

Martin Figura

Aki Roukala

KATI HIEKKAPELTO was born in 1970 in Oulu, Finland, and has lived in Kanjiža, Serbia. She is a crime writer, punk singer, and performance artist. The protagonist of her novels is Detective Anna Fekete, a Hungarian born in Serbia who fled to Finland as a child during the Yugoslav Wars. Her novels have been translated into fifteen languages, and in 2015 she won the Clew of the Year Award, presented by the Finnish Whodunnit Society for the best Finnish crime novel of the year.

MILORAD IVANOVIĆ is a Serbian investigative reporter and editor. He was editor in chief of the Serbian edition of *Newsweek*, and executive editor of the daily paper *Blic* and the weekly publication *Novi Magazin*. Presently he is an editor at BIRN Serbia in Belgrade. He has a special interest in cross-border journalism and is a member of the International Consortium of Investigative Journalists. His investigations have included work on human trafficking, Balkan mercenaries in Iraq, and clinical trials.

Ivan Posavec

MILJENKO JERGOVIĆ was born in 1966 in Sarajevo, Bosnia. He published his first article in 1983, and his first book of poetry, *Warsaw Observatory,* in 1988. He has written several collections of short stories and a dozen novels. In 2012, he received the Angelus Central European Literature Award and in 2018 he won the Georg Dehio Book Prize. His stories and novels have been translated into more than twenty languages. Jergović currently lives and works in Zagreb, Croatia.

Joyce Nicholls

ALEKSI KOPONEN is an opera singer and translator who has previously worked as a script reader and literary editor. He lives in London.

MCKENNA MARKO is a graduate student of Slavic languages and literatures at the University of Michigan currently residing in Budapest, Hungary. Her research interests include Hungarian and Yugoslav literature, film, and culture. She translates from Hungarian and Bosnian/Serbian/Croatian.

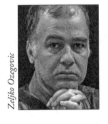

Željko Ozegovic

VLADAN MATIJEVIĆ was born in 1962 in Čačak, in central Serbia. He served in the Yugoslav People's Army in the territory of present-day Northern Macedonia. He has published twelve books, has received various awards, and has been translated into several languages. His novels *Very Little Light* and *The Adventures of Mace Aksentijević* were both especially successful in France. He lives in Serbia, on the outskirts of a small, gloomy town, and does not like guests.

NATAŠA MILAS was born in 1976 in Sarajevo. She is a scholar of Russian and South Slavic literature and film, and a translator from Bosnian/Croatian/Serbian. Milas edited a special issue of the literary journal *Absinthe 20: New European Writing*, focusing on Bosnian prose. Her translation of Muharem Bazdulj's novel *Transit, Comet, Eclipse* was published by Dalkey Archive Press in 2018. Milas lives in New York City and teaches at New York University.

Zerlina Chiu

GENTA NISHKU is a PhD candidate in the Comparative Literature Department at the University of Michigan and holds a graduate certificate in critical translation studies from the same department. Her research focuses on modern and contemporary Balkan literatures, as well as activism and resistance. She translates from Albanian, Bosnian/Croatian/Serbian, and Italian.

OTO OLTVANJI was born in 1971 in Subotica, in northern Serbia. He is the author of the novels *Black Shoes*, *The Backbone of the Night*, and *Splinter*. Some of his fifty crime, horror, and science fiction short stories were published in his collection *The Tales of Mystery and Magic*. He has translated, into Serbian, numerous Jonathan Lethem books. His latest book is a children's mystery, *How I Became a Detective*. He lives in Belgrade with his wife and daughter.

NADA PETKOVIĆ is an instructional professor at the University of Chicago. A native of Belgrade, she joined the Slavic Department in the late eighties and prefers to refer to herself as Yugoslav. Her projects include the book *Balkan Epic: Song, History, Modernity*, coedited with Philip V. Bohlman, and the reader *Po naški through Fiction*. She is the recipient of honors and awards from the Fulbright Program, the Mellon Foundation, and the Consortium for Language Teaching and Learning.

MIRZA PURIĆ is a literary translator, a contributing editor at *EuropeNow*, and a former editor at large at *Asymptote*. His book-length translations include works by Nathan Englander, Michael Köhlmeier, and Rabih Alameddine. In 2019, Istros Books published his translation of Faruk Šehić's novel *Under Pressure*. His cotranslation, with Ellen Elias-Bursać, of Miljenko Jergović's *Inshallah, Madonna, Inshallah* will be published by Archipelago Books.

ENA SELIMOVIĆ, born in Belgrade, spent much of her childhood in Turkey before migrating to the US in 1998. She is completing her PhD in comparative literature at Washington University in St. Louis. Her research brings a comparative approach to the study of twentieth- and twenty-first-century US and Balkan literatures, with an interest in establishing their interimperial, racialized, and multilingual network in the historical *longue durée*.

GORAN SKROBONJA is one of the leading genre authors in Serbia. He was born in Belgrade in 1962. His publishing and translation work introduced modern horror literature to Serbian readers in the 1990s—books by Stephen King, Clive Barker, and James Herbert. His first horror novel, *The Brood*, was published in 1993, and he went on to publish several story collections and novels, including his best-selling title, *The Man Who Killed Tesla*.

DEJAN STOJILJKOVIĆ was born in 1976 in Niš, in southern Serbia. His book *Constantine's Crossing* was a hugely successful, riveting, multigenre novel. That was just the first in a long line of releases that have won prestigious literary awards and critical accolades. Stojiljković has also written several comic scripts and a collection of essays on comics. His writing style spills from fantasy to horror and everywhere in between.

JENNIFER ZOBLE translates literature from Bosnian/Croatian/Serbian and Spanish. Her translation of the short story collection *Mars* by Asja Bakić was published by Feminist Press in 2019. She received a 2018 NYSCA grant for her translation of *Zovite me Esteban* by Lejla Kalamujić. She's an assistant clinical professor in the Liberal Studies program at NYU, coeditor of InTranslation at the *Brooklyn Rail*, and coproducer of the international audio drama podcast *Play for Voices*.

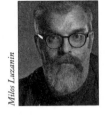

Milos Luzanin

VULE ŽURIĆ is a Serbian writer who was born in 1969 in Sarajevo. He is the author of eleven novels, seven short story collections, and also writes for screen and radio. He has won several major Serbian literature prizes, including the Ivo Andrić Award for Best Book of Short Stories in 2015. He lives in Pančevo, near Belgrade.